XIPHOS

ALEX ARTHUR

Published in Australia in 2016 by Alex Arthur

Email: brucearthur01@outlook.com
Website: www.alexarthur.net

**National Library of Australia Cataloguing-in-Publication
entry:**

Creator:	Arthur, Bruce A., author.
Title:	Xiphos /Alex Arthur.
ISBN:	9780994634009 (paperback)
Subjects:	Bronze age – Fiction
	Mythology, Greek – Fiction
Dewey No:	A823.4

Edited by Judy Fredriksen
Cover design and line illustrations by Rachel Arthur
Typesetting by Epiphany Editing & Publishing
Printed in Australia by SOS Media + Print

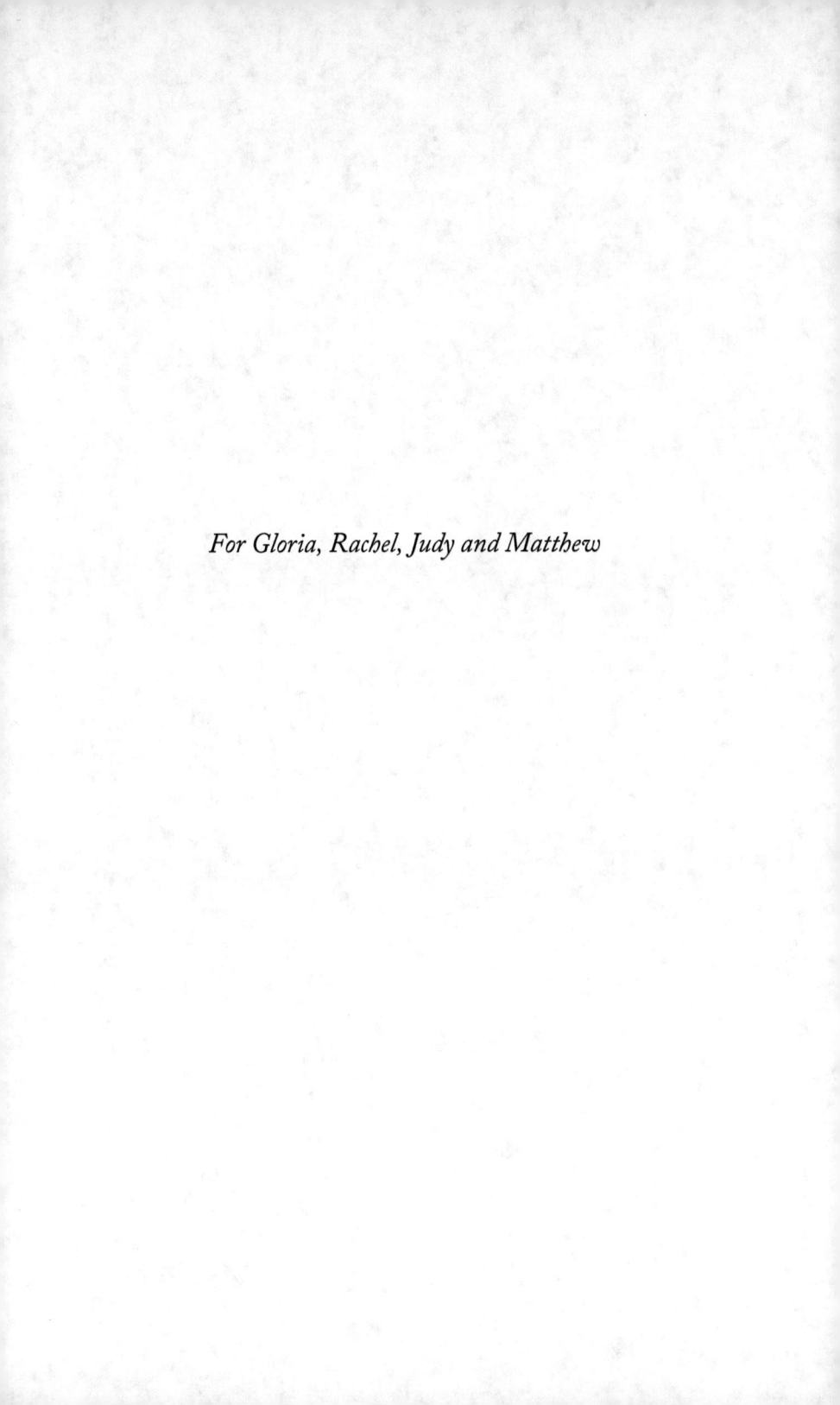

For Gloria, Rachel, Judy and Matthew

For Gloria, Rachel, Judy and Matthew

Acknowledgements

In 2007, my wife and I visited the Land of the Ancient Heroes: Agamemnon, Menelaus, Achilles, Odysseus, Hector and Helen. I thank the Greek people for their endless hospitality and fine Mediterranean cuisine throughout our journey. Many Greek tour guides and hosts are also amateur archaeologists and ancient historians, and I thank them for much of the information used in the novel.

My wife Gloria, and my daughter Rachel, have been instrumental in encouraging me to write this novel, and without their support, I don't think there would have been a *Xiphos*.

I thank the endless array of people who have assisted in some way with parts of the novel, including my GP, for information on congenital human deformities (the Minotaur), numerous proofreaders who have given me some feedback on different chapters, University Third Age Rainbow Writer's Group, metallurgists, people of the sea (boaties), Queensland Writer's Centre, Historical Novel Writer's Assn., UNE Creative Writing tutors, my editor and publisher, and many more.

The tutors and lecturers in the Humanities Faculty at the University of New England (UNE), Armidale, NSW, have taken me on a fascinating journey through the ancient world over the past ten years. It is to the lecturers in Archaeology, Ancient History and the Classics that I owe the knowledge and setting for this book.

efcharisto

PROLOGUE

Greek Dark Ages

Christian Jurgensen Thomsen (1788–1865) was a Danish antiquarian who first proposed the three age system for classifying archaeological time periods. The three ages were the Stone Age, Bronze Age and Iron Age. The dating of these ages varies depending on the spread of technology in various parts of the world. In Europe, the Bronze Age encompassed a wide time period in world history, from 3200 BC to 600 BC. The first archaeological evidence of serious iron smelters comes from Anatolia in 1200 BC. This technology spread to the Near East, the Aegean and the Levant from 1200 BC to 600 BC. The novel is set in the transition period – the late Bronze Age Aegean and the early Iron Age in Asia Minor. These early metalworkers must have wondered why they had turned to this useless new metal (iron), which I have called aforinium. Julius Caesar's *de bello Gallico* (58–50 BC) records some poor-quality early iron swords which bent in battle with the Gauls. These low-fired, soft alloys contained low percentages of carbon. On the other hand, excessive carbon ratios made very brittle iron and Medieval knights record stories of their blades breaking when struck by better quality weapons.

The collapse of the Bronze Age has been discussed at length by many historians and scientists and, as science progresses, more theories are expounded. The end of the Bronze Age in the Mediterranean led to a historical black hole from 1100 BC to the age of Homer in 800–700 BC. This period has been labelled the *Greek Dark Ages*. Scientists working in this area have shown that several factors led to the collapse. These include severe climate change, earthquakes, tsunamis and volcanic eruptions and the shortage of tin to make bronze.

In addition, roving bands of warriors, called the Sea People, devastated most established civilizations in the Mediterranean, searching for fertile soil, food and a better life. These are the antagonists in my story and they knew nothing but pillage and destruction. They overthrew nearly fifty major cities of the late Bronze Age, throwing law and order (such as it was) into chaos. Their principal targets were the Hittites, the Minoans, Mycenaean Greeks and the Egyptians. The Sea People only had eyes for their ultimate prize – the Nile Delta. They could not read or write and left no record of their conquests. A stroke of good fortune for historians and archaeologists was that the New Kingdom pharaohs of Merneptah, Ramesses II and Ramesses III recorded great victories over these tribes on mortuary stele at Medinet Habu. Without these inscriptions at Thebes, we may never have known of the Sea People.

Homer knew of these ancient oral traditions. He used some of this knowledge when writing *The Iliad* and *The Odyssey*. He uses words from the Egyptian stele, words like *Dorians* and *Achaeans*. Some researchers think that the Trojan War may even be Homer's version of an attack on the Hittites (Trojans) at Troy by a combined force of Sea People which he calls *Achaeans*.

From as early as 1625 BC, the Minoans used writing very like Egyptian hieroglyphs – a system called Cretan hiero-glyphs – which is still not understood. Over the next four hundred years, this developed into their own system called linear A. When the Mycenaeans invaded Keftui (Crete) circa 1400 BC, they modified linear A into linear B. The code behind linear B was broken by Alice Kober, Michael Ventris and John Chadwick in 1952. This gave archaeologists a unique insight into life in late Bronze Age Greece. Those early scribes used their writing system to mainly record palace inventories. All inscriptions used in the novel are actual linear B symbols translated into English by Ventris and Chadwick.

The heroic Greek figures of Prince Theseus of Athens and his half-brother, Prince Callias of Attica, learn to grow up in a hurry when they have to battle the Minotaur. All major events in the novel are based on historical and archaeo-logical facts. This novel is not an empirical record of events in Ancient Greece. Rather, it is the story of a minor Greek Prince's journey from boyhood to manhood in the late Bronze Age.

Alex Arthur 2016

EPOCH I

'But in fact, Daedalus himself, having pitied the great love of the queen, unravelled the traps and windings of the building, directing blind footsteps, with a thread.'

Virgil's Aeneid 6.14–33 (70 BC–19 BC)

CHAPTER I

'Callias, put those scrolls away and find your brother. I want you both in my chambers as soon as possible, I have a mission for you,' Aegeus called out.

King Aegeus, my stepfather, had always been kind to me, but I knew I was forever in his debt. Had he not taken me in, my mother would have been forced to abandon me, leaving me in danger of becoming a slave. I had come to Athens as an adolescent youth from Attica, with my mother, seven sun years ago. My mother, Meta, was Aegeus's second wife. The mighty king already had a son, Theseus, who was one year older than I. Although we had endured the pain and pleasure of learning, loving and fighting together all these years, I was always in awe of his privileged position.

His own mother, Aethra, died of the fever when he was in his second year. The leeches could not cure her and all the sacrifices to Asclepius only made her worse. He didn't talk about her much, probably because he was so young when she died. My own mother was given to Aegeus by our king in Attica, to form a tribal alliance.

My own father was mortally wounded in the never-ending struggle with Thebes. Attica and Thebes were almost

13

neighbours, but the Thebans' appetite for more land was insatiable. The new king of Attica had grabbed the opportunity to align us with Athens by pledging my mother to the king of Athens. I didn't understand the constant jockeying of politics. Most of it was above my head.

I heard my father's call, but as usual, the slaves had no idea where Theseus was.

He was much taller than I and girls were naturally attracted to him because of his outgoing personality and good looks. It annoyed me that his misdemeanours constantly went unnoticed by our father and that he hadn't bothered to learn to read or write.

Most of my childhood had been spent with the Mycenaean scribes, while my brother was trying to win a heart somewhere.

A moth landed on the mosaic floor and flapped its wings in its death throws. It would make a valuable addition to my collection.

'Callias, did you hear me?' my father called out again.

I remembered. Theseus had winked at me one sun ago as he pulled Imira, one of the ladies-in-waiting, into his bedchamber. *Would I just barge in and catch them in the act?* He had embarrassed me so many times – belittling my manhood – that I felt no guilt at repaying his trickery.

At the last feast of Demeter, he organised a lovely princess from Etrusca for me. She was a beautiful looking girl, dressed in delicate robes and spoke with a silken voice. But the delight of my first sweet encounter with a woman was devastating. When she took her clothes off in my chambers, I realised I had been completely fooled. She turned out to be a boy.

It amused Theseus immensely; he liked both boys and girls. I was the palace laughing stock for many moons.

A Persian slave, carrying an empty tray, scurried down the passageway from Theseus's room. Imira's groans of pleasure could be heard through the door.

Seizing the opportunity, I remembered the sign for "fire" which the Pylos scribes had taught me and drew it on a small piece of parchment.

Theseus couldn't read it, but it would add to my revenge. Ignoring their sounds of passion, I fired the arrow carrying the message through the window. It whistled over their heads and sunk into the tall timber bedhead.

'What in the name of Hade …?' Theseus exclaimed.

'Fire!' I yelled. 'Read the sign!' My brother scrambled to wrap his loin cloth around his rapidly deflating manhood. Imira tried to cover herself with a linen sheet. They both raced for the door, clutching at clothes and dragging bedclothes onto the tiles.

'False alarm,' I laughed. 'Father wants to see us urgently.'

'Vlaka!' Theseus growled. 'You will pay for this.'

Half embarrassed, Imira smiled coyly at me as one of her lovely breasts fell out of the sheet.

My brother and I stood outside father's door and Theseus, laughing now, jostled in front of me. He could be exasperating at times and didn't know when to stop.

'That makes up for the Etruscan Princess,' I said.

'I think the fire joke was unfair,' he said. 'So watch your back!'

'Come in, you two, and stop messing about.' Our father's annoyed voice echoed through the door. We pushed and shoved our way in. Father was seated in his favourite orichalcum chair but made us stand still in front of him. He was getting on in years. He had long salt and pepper hair with a bald patch above his forehead. His clean shaven face was showing many worry lines. Crow's feet grew from the corner of each eye. The white linen robe he wore had a dull red stain down the front as a result of an accident with a mug of red wine.

Our stone palace looked out over the fledgling city of Athens. I could see a mule train off in the distance, wending its way to the agora. Theban slaves hammered at massive sandstone blocks at the half-finished Temple of Zeus. I recognised one of the Spartan hoplites in the square. He had given me a thorough belting at sword practice, trying in vain to instil some fear into our cohort of raw recruits. I could still feel the bruise at the back of my leg where his wooden sword had almost hamstrung me.

Of course, Theseus, whose battle skills were much better than mine, did not have a mark on him.

'Callias, are you listening?' The king jolted me from my daydream.

'Yes Father, I was distracted by the hoplites outside,' was all I could think of.

'Well, I hope the two of you have been paying attention to your instructors,' he replied.

'Why is that, Father?' Theseus asked.

'I have a mission for the both of you,' the king said, seriously.

When my mother and I first came here, a flotilla of Minoan ships was standing off Piraeus. She told me that the Minoans had sent a diplomat ashore, demanding that we hand over the murderers of Androgeus, who was King Minos's arrogant son. Androgeus had won the bull leaping tournaments at Knossos and the Minoans had sent him to our first Pan Hellenic games. He outshone us all at the twenty stadia sprint, the wrestling and the hoplitodromus. He was found, mysteriously drowned in our sanctuary to Athena before he could return home. King Minos immediately assumed that he had been murdered by a bitter Athenian athlete, and demanded that we give up his assassin.

My father had no intention of giving up anyone. So every seven sun years, or great year as the augurs say, we are forced to give up seven youths and seven maidens to the wretched Minoans. This was meant to keep the peace between us. Fourteen of our finest young maidens and warriors, every great year, was a price too high.

As to the fate of the hostages, there were many rumours. Theseus told me that they were fed to a monster called "the Minotaur" in a labyrinth at Knossos. Mother was told that they were sold as slaves to the pharaoh. Many Athenians wanted answers. This could not be allowed to go on. The relationship with the Minoans was deteriorating and now, the seven sun years had come around again.

'The boule wants to find out the fate of our hostages,' announced the king. 'The third great year expires on the full moon. If we don't send fourteen of our finest to Knossos by then, Minos will attack. His mighty fleet rules the oceans, so we would only court disaster to defy him.'

He paused for a moment. 'The senate has ruled that we send two spies with the next batch of hostages, spies who will not betray us, spies who we can rely on to find the truth.'

Before Theseus or I could ask any questions, a cloud came over Father's face.

'But that is not all. The Sea People could attack Knossos,' the king carried on gravely. 'I have just received news from one of our triremes that the Peleset have carried out several attacks in Alasiya and Phoenicia and could be headed for Keftui. Minos's mighty navy is a great threat to them. The captain advises me that they have been causing great devastation; I'm told they are using new swords that are so sharp and strong, they can slice a man's head off in a single blow.'

Bemused, Theseus reeled, 'But is it not true that Knossos is so cleverly built, whoever sets foot in it cannot find his way out without a guide?'

'This is true of the labyrinth where the Minotaur lives, but the palace itself does not have high walls like Mycenae. '

'Do you think the Sea People could succeed in destroying Knossos and Minos?' I was beginning to feel a sense of foreboding. Ignoring my question, the King sighed, 'We live in treacherous times, and it does not please me to say this. I have no choice but to send my own sons to spy on Minos.'

Theseus looked at me, the thrill of adventure slowly lighting up his face. I looked at Theseus, filled with dread. We both turned and stared at Father.

'You will need all the skills the Spartan has taught you. You must find the labyrinth and kill the Minotaur. I want you to find out the fate of all the hostages. The five other youths and seven maidens have already been chosen. You will dress in common clothes and mingle with the others. They have been told to treat you like ordinary citizens.

'If the Sea People attack Keftui while you are there, your courage will be tested in many ways.

'One of our merchant ships leaves for Thira and Keftui in the morning. Talk to Daedalus before you go,' the king went on, 'he knows the layout of the labyrinth well'.

'How long …' Theseus asked.

'You must report back with information, one sun year from today,' the king said.

Terror clutched at me as my mind raced.

'Father, when we do find out what's going on, how will we escape?' My palms started to sweat.

'Do not worry Callias. I have a plan,' Aegeus said.

'Importantly, when you sail back, if you have killed the Minotaur, I want you to fly white sails. If you both die, the captain must fly black sails. If one lives and one dies, the ship will row into Piraeus with no sails. The hostages and the citizens of Athens are depending on you both. May the gods go with you.'

'Yes, Father.'

'Theseus, you may leave now. Shut the door after you. Callias, stay behind for a moment,' Aegeus commanded.

'You will see the white sails sooner than you think, father,' Theseus bragged as he walked out.

The king signalled me to come closer.

'Your brother is adventurous, a born warrior and is everyone's favourite son. He will make a fine king when I am gone,' the old king said in a low tone. 'But you, Callias, are a scholar. You have paid attention to your scribes and teachers.'

'Yes Father, but I am always walking in his shadow,' I replied.

'That may be so, but I want you to watch out for him. The two of you make a fine team. I have something else in mind for you, when you arrive in Keftui.'

My chest started thumping. *Killing the Minotaur and possibly being attacked by Sea People wasn't enough?* I secretly wished that no killing was required and I certainly had no desire to be confronted by Sea People. Their barbaric reputation was well known to us all.

'If you kill the Minotaur, I want you to find an excuse to stay behind. We have been humiliated often enough by Minos and his son, Gadeirus,' he whispered even lower. 'The elders want you to find a way of becoming immersed in the life of the Minoan palace. Tell us of their plans for Athens and the rest of Greece. Also, see if you can find out anything about the swords the Phoenicians speak of. Where did the Sea People get them? How are they made?

'You can read the Minoan scrolls. You might overhear conversations that will interest us. If you are caught, you will be sacrificed to their gods, but this mission is very important to our country.

'I have set up one of our merchants in Iraklion as your escape route. You must not tell another soul about this, especially your brother.'

The gravity of it all was hard to grasp. I could see myself in some dark Knossos side street with my throat cut. My palms were sweating. I wiped my brow with the back of my hand.

'How many years, Fath ...?' I stammered.

'This mission could be for a long time. You will be our eyes and ears in Keftui,' Aegeus went on.

'Father, I owe you and Athens for everything that I am. I agree to go for two sun years ... if I live that long. Then I must come home.' I tried to hide the shaking knees beneath my robe.

'I know I can depend on you. After two sun years, I will find a way to get a message to you through my contacts in Iraklion,' Aegeus said. 'Good luck. It is up to you to save Athens.'

I drew a couple of deep breaths and walked out the door. Theseus was waiting near a window overlooking the courtyard.

Had he been listening at the door?

'What did he want?' Theseus asked.

'He asked me to take particular notice of the layout of the Minoan palaces during our mission,' I lied. 'He wants to build one the same, here. Maybe when we find Daedalus ...'

'Who is Daedalus?' Theseus said.

'He designed the labyrinth at Knossos,' I replied.

We had stopped fooling around.

Chapter II

Knossos Palace, Keftui – 1200BC

Several black gannets dived into a large school of baitfish as the Athenian hostages sailed into Iraklion. Small trading vessels bustled about the port trying to dock in the small harbour. Theseus and I were dressed in nondescript linen robes. We mingled inconspicuously among the hostages who were instructed not to address us as "Prince" or "Your Highness" while on this mission. By the sound of the crowd, the Snake Goddess games were about to begin.

We were escorted to a prison in Knossos, and rather than being thrown into a dungeon or fed to the Minotaur, we were told to bathe and were given fresh food and colourful Minoan clothing. A palace guard, dressed in sandals and a loin cloth, escorted us back to our cell. He was about to lower the heavy wooden beam across our cell door when I saw a chance to question him.

'Guard. What is to become of us?' I asked.

'You are to choose two hostages from amongst yourselves, to entertain our citizens tomorrow. We will come back when the sun rises and escort them to the throne room,' he replied.

'Entertain? What do you mean entertain?' I asked.

'I do not know what is required of them, but the rest of you will remain here tomorrow.'

They didn't have much choice, I thought. *At least, we are not going to be fed to the Minotaur for a couple of nights yet.*

'I will go,' Theseus volunteered.

The other five youths all yelled at once, 'I will go', 'I will go,' 'I will go!'

Theseus held up his hand for them to stop. 'Now wait. My father has ruled that Callias and I are to find out the fate of our hostages, not any of you.'

They all groaned and started to argue amongst themselves.

'That's final. You can all stop muttering now,' Theseus said, looking about the cell. The roar of the crowd at the bull leaping contest echoed across the paving stones.

The next morning, four armed guards arrived and escorted the two of us up to the throne room.

A tall, dark, olive skinned priest, wearing a feathered headdress, sat on an elaborately carved royal chair. He was attended by several men wearing short linen loin cloths. Their long black hair, covered with coconut oil, glistened in the light. Two bare breasted women in coloured linen skirts sat, one on each side of the priest. The walls behind them were decorated with magnificent gold griffins and saffron crocuses. A wide, carved stone bowl, full of water, sat on the floor in front of the priest. Several palace guards, armed with long bronze swords, stood at the doorways.

'Before you may address this court, you must cleanse yourselves in the libation bowl. Remove your clothes and pay homage to the Snake Goddess,' the priest ordered.

These people have some strange customs, I thought.

We stripped naked, stepped into the shallow masonry bowl and splashed holy water over our bodies while the court looked on. As we stepped out, the cool water dripped from our skin and formed a small pool on the paving stones. No one handed us a cloth to dry ourselves. We stood as our mother's had made us, in front of the court.

'I am the high priest of Knossos and the ladies sitting alongside me are Princess Ariadne and Princess Kitane, daughters of the king. What are your names,' the priest growled.

'My name is Callias and this is my brother, Theseus, citizens of Athens.' I answered.

'King Aegeus hopes that our two great nations may remain at peace,' Theseus added.

I bent down to gather my clothes.

'Leave your clothes where they are,' the priest snarled. If he was trying to intimidate us, he was succeeding.

'We have remained at peace these last seven sun years, only because of our treaty and your hostages. But now, our king has a trial for you. You have heard the roar from the crowd at our games. The people are becoming harder to satisfy. They tire of wrestling and bull leaping. They need warriors to fight our champion'.

I had suspected something like this. 'Who is your champion?' I asked, but I knew the answer.

'Our champion is known by another name. Outside of our nation, he is called the "Minotaur",' the priest replied, an evil smile spreading over his face.

'So, our king was right. You are going to feed us all, one by one, to the Minotaur,' Theseus said.

'No. That is not quite correct,' the priest went on. 'You will be given one weapon of your choice. You will battle our champion – one at a time – for the pleasure of our citizens. Should you, by some remote stroke of good fortune, kill the champion, the remaining hostages will be released.

But should you die at the hands of our champion?' He shrugged his shoulders and smiled evilly.

'The rest of the hostages will be allowed to watch the contest tomorrow – chained to their seats.

King Minos is not unreasonable. If you kill our champion and manage to escape the labyrinth, the others are free to go,' the priest repeated.

'I advise you both to have the other youths ready to fight in case you are both killed.' A chill ran through me at this request. They were only boys. I started to weaken at the knees again.

'There is something our king would like to know, before we are all killed,' I asked. 'What has happened t ... to the other hostages who were sent here many moons ago?'

'Some were put to work in our palaces. Some were put to other uses,' was the stony reply.

'What were the other uses you speak of?' Theseus asked.

'You will need to ask the king what became of them, I do not know their fate,' the priest replied.

Lies. I wonder will we ever get a straight answer, I thought.

'You may pick up your clothes, now that you have dried off,' the priest sneered. 'We will see you at the labyrinth.'

Theseus and I were marched back to our cells. Beads of sweat broke out on my brow. Theseus, in his usual self-assured manner said, 'I'll go first, Callias. If I don't kill the bastardos, I'm relying on you to finish the task.'

'If you don't kill him, make sure you break one of his legs,' I responded nervously. 'Then I may have a chance. It's no good relying on these other boys, I am not going to send them to Hades.'

Theseus replied, 'Then it's just the two of us.'

We had finished playing games. We could both die here and father would never know what had happened. If I only knew more about the champion, we could work out a plan of attack. I rubbed the bruise on the back of my leg where the Spartan had hit me.

'What weapon will you choose,' I said.

'It will have to be a sword,' Theseus said. 'I wonder what their champion will choose?'

'From all the rumours, I don't think he needs a weapon.'

Theseus slapped me on the back. 'Don't worry Callias, I'm sure it won't be any worse than the Seven Entrances to the Underworld where I killed far worse beasts than the Minotaur.'

I hoped he couldn't sense the hollow feeling developing in the pit of my stomach.

'What is happening,' one of the youths asked, as the cell door clanked shut behind us. They gathered around, their innocent faces looking up at us.

'Their king wants Callias and myself to battle the Minotaur tomorrow, one at a time. If we kill the beast, you will all be released,' my brother explained.

They broke out in spontaneous cheering.

'Whoa! Wait a minute. We haven't killed it yet!' I yelled as I held up my hands.

'Is there any doubt?' the youngest, Alexandros, asked.

'None at all,' Theseus smiled, giving them all a hug.

Next day, the highlight of the Snake Goddess games finally arrived. Our group of hostages sat nervously chained to their seats. The five remaining youths were barechested and dressed in Minoan loin cloths. As was the custom with these strange people, the seven Athenian maidens were also bare to the waist. They sat frightened, as their small, white breasts caught the morning sun. I had visions of their pure white bodies and innocent faces being torn to pieces by the Minoan monster if we failed. Our hostages and the loud Minoan crowd were sitting high in a stadium cut from the rock. I could see how Daedalus had cleverly constructed the labyrinth to run through the bowels of the palace. We could see into the top of the high labyrinth walls but we had no idea what would take place in the many dark tunnels.

'Champion! Champion! Champion!' the Minoans chanted, knowing that the Minotaur always won.

I had found out more about the monster from one of the guards on the way to the stadium. At the last games, two Persian captives were tricked into following the champion into the fourth tunnel. When they became confused in the dark, the champion struck. Their remains were left all year to rot in the sun.

Upon hearing this, I learnt that the Minotaur had brains and could see in the dark. I told Theseus not to go into the fourth tunnel, but he wasn't listening. He was standing near the entrance to the labyrinth as the crowd roared.

'Do you remember what Daedalus told us?' he asked me at the last minute. 'Was it, "don't go left, don't go right, go straight ahead?". Or was it "go left or right, but not straight ahead?"'

I growled at him. 'It was "go straight ahead".' And don't be led into the fourth tunnel under any circumstances,' I said again. I looked at him in disbelief. *Does he ever take anything seriously?*

Theseus was still trying to figure it out when Princess Ariadne ran over from the royal box. She stood on her toes and I overheard her say to him, 'you won't get out of there alive. Tie this thread to your belt. I have tied the other end to a post outside. It will help you find your way out.'

She scampered back to the royal box before the crowd could see what was going on. Theseus's face remained blank. He looked resplendent in his Spartan helmet and leather cuirass. The helmet was adorned with short ostrich feathers which made him look even taller. The cuirass was made from hand worked auroch hide and his bulging abdominals made him look invincible.

A guard escorted us to the entrance to the labyrinth, where an assortment of weapons was laid out. Theseus picked up a sword and wielded it about, judging its weight and balance, checking its sharpness, before testing another. As he placed the second sword down, he noticed a blade shining, half-hidden by the tangle of weapons. Tugging the stubborn piece from the pile, he discovered an unusual leaf shaped sword.

'What do you think?' he asked as he handed it to me. It felt well-balanced as I swung it around. It was light and strong and I noticed it was made from a brightly flashing metal. I shaved some hairs from my arm and was totally surprised at the keenness of both edges.

Unlike our old, heavy bronze swords made only for chopping into flesh, this one could be used for stabbing and chopping. Aegeus would be most interested in this. I looked at the hilt, just below the handle – it was stamped with a boar's snout and fox's ears. Strange. The signs looked like something the ancient tribes would use. I could have sworn the fox's ears began to twitch. Was it the sunlight? It must have been just my shaking hands.

I held it by the blade and handed it back to Theseus. 'The Spartan would like one of these,' I nervously observed. 'May Athena be with you.' He gave a final wave and sprung down into the labyrinth.

'Don't forget to break his leg,' I yelled. The place stank of Minotaur skata and rotten food.

He turned to me, smiling. 'It's very light, the sword, I like it. I'll do better than break his leg with this.' He headed for the three entrances.

'Champion! Champion!' the crowd called to the Minotaur. 'Where are you?'

'Open the cage door,' Minos yelled.

One of our maidens pointed. 'There,' she said. I could see a rope and pulley lifting a heavy bronze grate above the top of one tunnel. The crowd went wild as they saw the champion bound out of his cage and run to the third bend. Theseus emerged from the middle tunnel and stumbled in the slime. As he regained his foothold, he picked up what looked like a white bone then felt around his belt for something.

The thread! Hades, I thought, Ariadne had not made the thread long enough. Theseus ran back to the central tunnel. He searched amongst the filth at the exit. He found the last of the thread and wrapped it around the bone. He dropped the bone back onto the floor.

The Keftui crowd roared, 'Champion, Champion, Champion, where are you?'

Theseus was growing smaller in the distance when suddenly, he stepped backwards and looked up, thrusting his sword up in defence.

There in front of him, stood the champion of Knossos – the Minotaur – watching him tie the end of the thread to the bone.

The crowd roared. I blinked twice, *was it man or beast?* It was completely nude and was much larger than a hoplite. Its face peered out of filthy black hair which hung to its waist. A grizzly lump grew from its forehead like a growth of some sort. It looked like the head of a bull from a distance; half man, half beast. Strangest of all, the champion had a huge right arm and a small, withered left arm. The right hand – like Hercules's – was the size of a dinner plate. I could see why the Minotaur had been hidden from the world for so long. One eye stared at Theseus; the other eye was a blank socket. It bared its black teeth.

If Theseus was caught by that right hand, he would make an early trip to the gods.

The Minotaur was cunning, though. Its physical appearance had obviously fooled many into thinking it was slow-witted. It ran back into the darkened fourth tunnel after Theseus spotted him. *This is a ruse. Did Theseus listen to my instructions?* The Minotaur was smart.

'It's trying to lure Theseus into the dark,' Alexandros cried.

'You *skata alogo* Minotaur! How many of our maidens have you raped. How many of our youths have you butchered?' we heard Theseus yell. 'I am not so easily fooled. You deserve to die. Come out of there!' The home crowd booed.

Could the beast even understand?

A deep throated growl came back through the tunnel.

The Minoans yelled with delight. Many of them were fanning themselves with palm leaves by now.

The champion crept out of the fourth maze into the daylight, realising that his ruse was not working. Theseus and the monster circled each other. Theseus lunged with his new sword but the beast easily sidestepped the blade. The champion darted into the fourth tunnel again.

The crowd were thumping their seats.

Theseus ran to the fourth entrance but checked himself just in time. He hid behind one of the large stone columns which held up the ceiling and listened. The beast doubled back through another tunnel and launched himself at the unsuspecting Theseus from behind. It grabbed Theseus's sword arm with his monstrous dinner plate hand, and twisted.

I felt the pain as my brother's arm cracked. Theseus sank to his knees, his cry of pain echoing through the stadium. The sword gave a metallic clang as it hit the floor. The crowd were ecstatic. Theseus's right arm hung loosely at a very strange angle as the Minotaur flashed an eerie smile to the crowd.

'Finish him! Finish him!' the crowd screamed at their champion while the guard smirked at me with annoying arrogance.

Our priceless maidens hid their faces in their lily white hands. The youngest maiden jumped up to see what Theseus was doing on the floor. She came to a painful halt as the chains jerked her back down again.

'For Hades' sake, get up! Get up!' I yelled. Theseus nursed his broken arm.

I thought, *this is it, Theseus has dropped his sword. There's no way he can win now.*

Then unexpectedly, a strong beam of light flashed across the Minotaur's face. Someone in the crowd was blinding it with a mirror. I looked with disbelief, glad that the guard was not distracted by it too. It was Princess Kitane. A bright shaft of sunlight from her bronze mirror burned into its one good eye. Theseus had woven his magic with a girl once again.

The champion lost its sight for a split second. Theseus grabbed the sword with his good left hand and drove the blade deep into the champion's leg. A rush of blood sprayed into Theseus's face as the beast let out a roar that filled the amphitheatre.

Theseus stumbled back towards us, cradling his broken arm with his good left hand. He plunged headlong into the middle tunnel. The champion's hollow roar echoed down the labyrinth behind him. I could see the long white bone. 'The thread! It's at the mouth of the middle tunnel,' I yelled, but I knew Theseus couldn't hear.

The beast half ran, half limped, dragging its wounded leg, only a cubit behind my brother, as they both staggered towards us.

The noise from the crowd was so loud, I'm sure the Titan Gods could hear.

Theseus tripped over the long bone and sprawled head-long into the kopria. The Minotaur fell onto my brother's back, its massive hand grabbing Theseus under the helmet. Its huge fingers clamped right around his neck and tightened. My brother was being slowly strangled.

I forgot about the nausea and the shaking knees. The image of those savaged Athenian maidens came flooding back. Driven by a mixture of anger and sheer terror, I pushed past the guard and raced frantically to Theseus.

The Minoans were nearly out of control.

'Kill him! Kill him!' they chanted in unison at their hero.

As Theseus lay crumpled and listless on the floor, I smashed headlong into the Minotaur. The beast let out a huge gasp as the air left its lungs. Hot Minotaur blood splashed over me. In my wild rush, I grabbed the long bone out of the filth. I smashed it down with every last fibre in my body. I heard the reassuring sound of bone crushing bone. The back of the beast's skull turned into a pulp of bone, blood and hair. The beast gave one loud grunt and slumped, lifeless, on top of Theseus.

The Athenian hostages were ecstatic. 'Athens! Athens! Athens!' I could hear them yelling. The Minoan crowd went quiet with disbelief, then started to boo. I looked over at the royal enclosure and saw Ariadne smile curiously at her sister. I pulled my brother's face out of the gore, tore off his helmet and thumped him on the back.

Theseus started to cough up lumps of black kopria. He was alive. I didn't care if he liked boys and girls, I didn't care if I was always in his shadow. He was all I had. I grabbed him by the shoulders and pulled him close. 'The gods aren't ready for you yet, Brother. Asclepius is with you.' I whispered a prayer to the healing god in his ear. His head lolled against my shoulder. I knew he couldn't hear.

The crowd booed and called for us to go back to Athens. I threw my brother's good arm over my shoulder and we stumbled back through the maze, as I remembered what Daedalus had told me and followed the linen thread to the safe exit.

As we lurched along, King Minos stood up and raised his hands. The crowd fell silent. He addressed them in his high pitched voice. 'We have not one new champion, but two. I want you all to applaud our visitors from Athens.'

The Minoan princesses stood up and clapped wildly. The rest of the crowd booed and yelled 'Go home, Greeks! Go home, Greeks!' I saw the Minoan blacksmiths walking up the stairway towards the hostages – the king had kept his word.

I dragged Theseus to the foot of the dais where Minos turned to us and said, 'The crowd is disappointed – they have lost their champion. We are not pleased. You are both to report to me at sunrise.' I nodded but Theseus was in a land near the Underworld.

I held my brother under a palace fountain for a very long time until the filth and the stench had left both of us. After the released maidens had dried us and wrapped us in clean loincloths, the Knossos pharmacea bound up my brother's broken arm. Theseus gulped down a draught of poppy elixir to deaden the pain. He wasn't quite in this world yet.

We all assembled on the balcony overlooking the bull leaping court. Someone had found a kylix of red wine and we all drank to our good fortune. The hostages were going home!

There was only one thing on my mind. *What excuse could I use to stay behind?*

As usual, I was engrossed in my own little world when the eldest maiden approached. She was taller than I, and gave me a huge hug. I looked up into her face.

'I still can't call you "Prince" but there are no Minoans about. You have saved our lives, Prince Callias.

'No, not me. Theseus saved our lives.'

'We need to thank you both then. But there's something else I want to tell you.'

'Oh, yes, go on,' I said.

'As you know, we were chained to our seats next to the princesses. After you killed the beast, I heard the older Minoan princess say to the younger one, "Thank the Mother Goddess, Kitane, that was close." The younger princess just nodded and smiled back. They both stood and clapped wildly when their father announced that Minoa had two new champions, but the rest of the crowd jeered and booed. I thought that was unusual, what do you think?'

I remembered the curious smile from Ariadne.

'I have no idea,' I replied.

I looked at her perfect face for a moment and then it sunk in. That would explain the thread, the mirror and the new sword. The Minoan princesses had set us up.

EPOCH II

'It is said, moreover, that as they drew nigh the coast of Attica, Theseus himself forgot, and his pilot forgot, such was their joy and exultation, to hoist the sail which was to have been the token of their safety to Aegeus, who threw himself down from the rock and was dashed to pieces.'

The Parallel Lives, Plutarch, Vita of Theseus 22, Vol.1, Loeb Classical Library, 1914.

CHAPTER III

Knossos Palace – 1199 BC

The next morning, Theseus and I stood before the king in the throne room. I was relieved that we didn't have to cleanse ourselves again. The chamber was decorated with magnificent frescoes of the king himself wearing a feathered headdress, long black, platted hair and a white linen loin cloth with blue trimmings. Around the painting were beautiful yellow crocuses and water lilies, griffins and bull leapers. The lilting notes of a lyre echoed through the chamber from somewhere deep in the palace. A male peacock spread his kaleidoscope of colours just outside the window.

'You succeeded in killing our champion,' the king said drily.

'I regret the death of your old champion,' I said.

'You misunderstood our arrangement. You were to battle our champion – one at a time,' the king rumbled. 'Two against one was not my instruction.'

'My brother only entered the battle when he thought that I was dying.' Theseus quickly chimed in. 'I was no longer a threat to your champion when my brother dealt the fatal blow.'

The king did not seem satisfied with our explanation.

Theseus's bandaged right arm had swollen to double its normal size. I started to feel nervous and I shuffled from one foot to the other. Minos obviously wasn't happy with the fight and I needed an excuse to stay on Keftui. Unlike my brother, I hadn't broken any bones. Frantically I hoped that one of the hostages would go missing or I could suddenly came down with a terrible illness. Acting was not one of my strengths.

Minos persevered, 'Because you have killed our champion, I have a problem.' He made sure his comment unnerved us by pausing unnecessarily.

'I know that you are the sons of Aegeus. It was very foolish of him to send his two most valuable men.'

'How did you …?' I asked.

'While you were celebrating, one of my guards heard one of your maidens address you both as "Prince" last night. It makes me suspicious that Aegeus is plotting something,' the king scowled.

He was trying to make me feel very uncomfortable and he was succeeding. Theseus didn't flinch.

'You say you thought your brother was dead, and so it may have appeared. But YOU,' he said pointing a goat's leg at me, 'struck a cowardly blow from behind!'

'Your champion was dead anyway, from his leg wound.' I was not going to be intimidated.

'You struck the fatal blow,' Minos roared.

My mind was racing, my knees were trembling.

'Because of this cowardly action, YOU,' he pointed the bone at me again, 'will not return to Athens for one year. You will make a valuable hostage.

'The youngest of the other youths will remain with you as a second hostage. The others may go.'

I couldn't believe it and hoped my relief did not show. My reason to stay behind had been handed to me on a plate.

'But, Your Highness, that was not our arrangement,' I complained. 'You swore to release all hostages and I have important duties to perform at Mycenae on the way home.'

'That is not of my concern,' came the arrogant reply. 'You and the other hostage will report to my son, Gadeirus, in the morning. You both can go.' He waved us away with his bone.

On the way out, Theseus winked playfully at me, 'The two princesses are very pretty'.

I wasn't interested in the princesses right now, though my mind was on Ariadne and Kitane – but for a different reason. As we walked out into the open, Theseus was grinning while I complained bitterly about being left behind.

I was confused as to why Ariadne and Kitane had helped us. It bothered me that Minos was suspicious of Aegus's plans and I wondered what was really going on.

There was one more matter which needed my attention before my brother left. The new sword – I desperately had to find it. As I swung it about yesterday, it felt like no other sword I had ever used; it was like an extension of myself. I wondered if this was the same type of sword the Sea People used in their recent attacks and if it was, we needed to send it back to Aegeus or to the alchemists at Pylos.

'Theseus, I have to attend to one small matter before you leave. There is something I want you to give to Father. If I have not returned by sundown though, don't wait for me.'

'I need some more poppy elixer, so good luck,' he slurred, nursing his swollen arm.

I ran back to the labyrinth and followed the thread back to where we had killed the Minotaur. The beast's corpse was gone. The sword must be further back into the maze. *Just where had Kitane's mirror woven its magic?* There seemed to be a trail of congealed blood spattered in places. I carefully back tracked, trying to remember my way back for the return journey.

I crept through the central tunnel and looked back to where the princess was sitting yesterday. This should have been about the spot where Theseus stabbed the champion in the leg. I found the pool of dried blood, but there was no sword. There were footprints everywhere – some from the battle, some from the person who had taken the sword – I couldn't tell which.

Frustrated, I ran back to wish Theseus a storm-free journey, but his ship had sailed. It cut a fine sight as it coasted out of Amnisos harbour, but to my dismay, it was flying black sails.

* * * *

The ladies-in-waiting fluttered around the dock. Some held their hands up to their heads and moaned uncontrollably. Their white rouge was streaked with small rivulets of tears. The matron was gesticulating wildly at the harbour master. I couldn't make out what was going on.

'What's all the commotion?'

'That cowardly hoplite has kidnapped Ariadne. The king will see this as revenge and will be so angry,' she wailed.

Straight away, I realised this had put me in a very precarious position.

'That cowardly hoplite is my brother and too popular with the maidens for his own good. How do you know that the Princess Ariadne did not happily jump on that ship to be with my brother?' I challenged.

'The Princess Ariadne would never behave as you suggest!' the old matron hissed as she stormed off.

* * * *

I lay awake in my quarters that night wondering what Minos and Gadeirus had in store for us. Alexandros tossed and turned in his sleep. I felt sorry for his parents. They would be expecting him to walk off that ship with Theseus. Now that Ariadne had been kidnapped, our circumstances had changed. *Would Aegeus keep her as a hostage until Alexandros and I returned?*

I could see how the situation could escalate if it wasn't handled properly, and the last thing I wanted was a war between my father and King Minos. I was sure Theseus had woven his spell over Ariadne at the labyrinth, broken arm and all. If I could convince Minos that this was an affair of the heart and not an act of revenge, we may not be treated so harshly. Alexandros sat up suddenly and yelled out, 'not that tunnel!' I threw the woollen cover off him and sat on his bed.

'It's only a nightmare,' I said softly and stroked the back of his head. His eyes were glazed and stared at nothing. 'You'll be home soon.' He looked blankly at me and slumped back down onto his goat skin mattress.

The sword was missing. The palace guards were still using the heavy bronze swords and I hadn't seen any of their warriors sporting the new weapon at the games. We needed to find the sword and establish what kind of metal it was made of.

If I could find my contact in Iraklion, we could get a message on a clay tablet to father in our own tongue. Even if the Minoans discovered the tablet, it would mean nothing to them as they were still using the old writing. A hundred and one thoughts jumbled together kept me from Hypnos.

It was just then, in the blackness, that I noticed my candle flicker. There was no breeze. Maybe it was the soul of the Minotaur fluttering through the rooms. The table shook and my bronze water cup clattered to the floor. I quickly said a prayer to Demeter and the vibrations stopped. I was wide awake now and Alexandros mumbled something about his mother.

The first rays of light struggled through the linen curtains, as I watched the trail of water running under my mattress.

* * * *

Already the vast palace was buzzing with activity. The delicious smell of fresh honey-cheese plakous wafted through the rooms. Many slaves swept the floor with their spelt brooms. A flock of shrikes had taken up residence in the gardens and their high pitched calls signalled a new day. One of Minos's guards appeared at our doorway.

'You, Athenian who killed our champion, will come with me. The boy is to stay here,' he ordered coarsely.

'No. Where I go, the boy comes with me,' I said, surprisingly sounding braver than I felt. Realising that I no longer had Theseus to back me up, forced me to stand up for myself and my young charge.

'He is to be put to work in the stables, so he will be well looked after by our slaves,' the guard replied.

'He must be sent back here to sleep each night then. I am his father for as long as we are both held hostage.'

'I will see to it,' the guard said. 'Now hurry up, Athenian, as the king is waiting.'

We hurried past the Hall of the Double Axes, through the central court and stood at the doorway into the Throne Room. *Not more cleansing for the Snake Mother*, I hoped.

'Enter,' the chief priest said.

I was marched into the brightly frescoed room, past the libation bowl and the dark Nubian guards and stood before Minos. His younger daughter, Kitane, sat on his right hand side and the chair where Ariadne would normally sit, was empty. His eldest son, Prince Gadeirus, sat next to the empty chair.

I expected the worst.

'Your brother has kidnapped my daughter, Prince Callias. It was a cunning scheme that you both contrived, after our last meeting,' the king said.

'I can assure your majesty that we contrived no plan,' I replied. 'In my opinion, your daughter has eloped with my brother. She was not kidnapped!'

'They only knew each other for two moons. Do you think that they fell in love in two moons?' the king responded sarcastically.

'My brother is popular with the maidens, your majesty, that's all it would take for him to win a girl's heart,' I smiled.

'Ariadne spent a long time bandaging his broken arm,' Kitane cut in.

'Enough time for him to beguile her,' I emphasised.

'I have made arrangements for her to marry the king of Alasiya. To elope with a prince of Athens will ruin my alliance,' the king went on. 'You and the boy will not be released until she is returned to me unharmed.'

'She may not want to return,' Kitane broke in.

'Why not?' Frustration was showing on Minos's face.

Kitane's eyes could not meet her father's gaze.

'So you and your sister have been scheming,' the king said looking across at his daughter.

'I knew nothing of her plans, Father,' Kitane replied. 'But I do know that she does not want to marry that fat Hittite king of Alasiya!'

Kitane had his attention.

'Did you help her escape?' the king asked her, crossly.

'No, Father, I did not. I don't think she was kidnapped because I saw her riding away from the palace with her slave, only one sun before the Athenians sailed.'

My mind was working overtime. *How would she be returned unharmed if she didn't want to return? Was Minos going to keep Alexandros and myself here past the one year he had promised?*

43

'You will return to Athens, find my daughter and bring her back here, undamaged,' Minos said, pointing his leg bone at me again. 'I have the boy to guarantee your return. She must marry the king of Alasiya in exchange for a shipment of aforinium.'

'Aforinium?' I asked. I had never heard of it.

'Yes. To make new weapons,' the king answered.

New weapons? I panicked. *What was Minos planning?*

'I sincerely hope Your Highness does not see the need for new weapons to fight against King Aegeus. The Athenians are eager to keep peace with you. Until now, we have kept all the conditions that you have demanded of us when sending our youths over every seven sun years.'

'It is not the Athenians who trouble us – it is the Sea People. They grow more ruthless every year and now, we believe they have swords that are much stronger and sharper than ours.'

I almost choked at this news and tried to remain calm.

'Does the king of Alasiya want the princess as payment for this aforinium?' I was incredulous.

'That is part of our agreement,' the king went on. 'There are some other arrangements.'

So that's all daughters were good for. Trade goods. My father would want this information, I had to get to Athens.

'I will sail with the next merchant to Athens, Your Highness, and return with your daughter on the full moon,' I claimed boldly.

It was a promise I could never hope to keep.

* * * *

As we pulled in to Piraeus, the port was ghostly quiet. A lonely smoke column drifted towards the sun. Normally a hundred wooden ships from all points of the ocean would be moving up and down with the swell. Slaves would be loading olive oil and pottery, purple dye from the murex snail and bronze goods from Pylos. Other slaves would be unloading bags of durum from Ugarit and rolls of fine linen from the Nile. I counted only ten ships and nothing moved. As our twenty slave rower thumped into the timber wharf, one of the Minoan seamen sprung over the handrail and tied the bowline. A few pelicans dipped their heads gracefully into the water searching for fish.

In the distance, I could hear something. I looked at the captain and held a finger to my lips. The faint sounds of a funeral dirge drifted across the bay.

'I think it's a funeral, Captain,' I said quietly. 'Leave the men here. You and I will investigate.'

We found a couple of mules munching oats in a timber yard, threw the halters on them, and trotted off in the direction of the smoke. As we came over the ridge between the port and Athens, we could see most of the population gathered around a flaming pyre in the valley before us.

As we neared, I saw my mother and Theseus with their hands lifted towards the heavens. The priest's incantations to Thanatos, the guardian of the Underworld, echoed through the hills. I could see the flames licking at a shroud-covered corpse at the top of the pyre. The chief priest was invoking Charon, the ferryman, to row the deceased across the Styx, to eternal paradise. Tears dropped from my mother's face onto her black shawl. Theseus gave me an ashen look as we dismounted.

'What on earth …?' I mumbled to my brother.

He was so distraught he just sobbed, 'Father …'

'Oh no, not …' the tears welled up in my eyes. The flames grew higher and higher and the white shroud floated into the sky on the way to the Elysian Fields.

The shock gradually dawned on me and I began to feel a deep pain. Aegeus who had treated me as his own son; Aegeus who had spoken to me about all the battles and all the gods; Aegeus who had sent me to Pylos to learn the art of writing; it was hard to believe that he was no longer with us.

The hymns to Charon grew louder and louder and I collapsed on the ground in front of Mother. The flames turned in on themselves and the burning logs crashed down. My mother's sobbing echoed somewhere far away. The priests chanted the sacred hymns as they sacrificed ten sheep and a bull to help father on his journey. Demeter and Persephone would be waiting for him on the other side. The priestesses fed the flames with holy olive oil. I staggered to my feet and tried to comfort mother. Theseus sat by himself, his head bent, not wanting to meet anyone's eye. He was not himself.

'Well, Brother, do you want to tell me what happened?' I sobbed.

'It was my fault,' he mumbled as he took a sip of water from a bronze cup.

'Yes, go on,' I said.

'Remember when we returned from Keftui, Father told us to fly white sails if we killed the Minotaur, black sails if we were both killed and to row in, if one died and one lived?' Theseus sobbed.

'You didn't … you didn't … change the sa …' my horror was quickly replaced by sad realisation.

'I was so excited about killing the Minotaur, when we left Amnisos, I forgot we were flying black sails,' he said quietly.

'You WHAT!' I yelled. 'You were with that Minoan princess, weren't you? It was the same when Daedalus told us about the labyrinth. You are so full of your own importance, you never listen!'

'Yes, you can yell and scream, but it won't bring Father back,' Theseus went on.

'Well, how did he die, then?'

'He threw himself off Mt Pentili when he saw the black sails,' my brother replied. He hid his face again and started to sob. I felt worse myself for losing my temper and just shook my head in disbelief. Maybe this would teach him a few things about himself that he could not come to terms with. I walked away.

The spying mission that King Aegeus had given me, what would I do now? I decided I would not reveal any of it to Theseus for now, I needed time to think.

If my brother was to become king, I would have to place all my trust in him. Aegeus and mother also had a son, Prince Medus, another of my half-brothers. He was still playing with toy soldiers. *Would his presence make trouble for us?*

I still had to find Ariadne and return to Knossos. I wouldn't be getting much sleep tonight again. A lone hymn echoed through the palace and the oil lamps flickered out.

A barn owl swooped down on an unsuspecting mouse as the moon peeked over the horizon. Visions of the smoke column blurred my mind as I forced my eyelids to close.

CHAPTER IV

Athens Palace – 1199 BC

Theseus had pulled himself together overnight and did not seem so guilt ridden this morning. I had calmed down after a disturbed night, but decided not to apologise to him. I meant everything I had said.

'What brings you to Athens?' Theseus asked. 'I thought you were a hostage.'

'Minos has sent me to find Ariadne. He has Alexandros, to guarantee my return,' I replied. 'He suspects you have kidnapped her and he will not release us from our bond until he has her back.'

'She does not want to go back,' Theseus smiled.

'Where is she?' I asked.

'In a safe place,' he replied.

'She is promised to the King of Alasiya,' I said.

'Yes, she told me. That is why she does not want to return.'

'Look, Brother, there are higher matters at stake here; agendas more important than you and the princess,' I said.

'Just what agendas are you talking about?' he asked.

I had to make a decision then, to trust him with Father's mission.

'Who is to succeed Father? Will it be you or Medus?' I asked.

'It was Father's wish, that I be crowned the next King of Athens. Medus is too young to rule yet, but I hope that the two of you will help me run our land,' he said.

'I would be honoured to accept but will not be of much use until Minos has released me from his bond,' I replied.

'That may be sooner than you think,' Theseus said.

'What do you mean by that?' I asked.

'I have plans which I cannot reveal just yet,' he went on.

'If we are to run Athens together, you and I must discuss everything before any important decisions are made,' I said.

'All in good time,' he replied.

'If you are to rule Athens, I have some information which cannot leave these four walls,' I said.

'Are these your higher agendas then?' he asked.

'Yes. Concerning the King of Alisaya,' I said. 'When father sent us to battle the Minotaur, he asked me to find an excuse to spy on the Minoans. I was to infiltrate the palace and be his eyes and ears. So, as it turned out, it was a stroke of good fortune that it took the two of us to kill their champion and that I was kept behind.'

'How is that so?'

'I discovered some important information – about the Sea People and Minos – and I need to know where Ariadne is. It is important that I take her back to Knossos with me to marry the King of Alasiya.'

'Why is that so important?' he said.

'Brother, I ran back to the labyrinth to find that sword. I was going to give it to you to give to Father. Unfortunately, I could not find it.

'That sword was definitely different to our bronze swords; it was stronger and sharper. Minos told me he needs to make new weapons to protect Keftui from the Sea People. He said that they have been using swords that are stronger and sharper – a description that fits the one that you used to kill the Minotaur.'

'It also fits the description of the weapons the sea traders warned father about!' Realisation dawned on Theseus.

'Yes! I think that sword was made of a new metal which Minos called aforinium. Apparently the Alisayans have an aforinium mine and Minos has agreed to exchange Ariadne for a supply of this new metal. If the Hittite king doesn't marry Ariadne, there will be no new metal.'

'Mmmm … so I have to decide, which is more important? The princess or new weapons of war?' Theseus thought out loud.

'We will also need the new metal if we are to stop the Sea People from invading,' I said.

'Ariadne and I had some wonderful times at Naxos on the way home,' Theseus admitted. 'I promised not to tell a soul where she was.'

'I will call there on my way back. You must give me a written papyrus explaining that you are to be king of Athens and that father had arranged for you to be married to a … a … Boetian princess,' I said. 'She may come back with me then.'

'You have a lot to learn about women, Callias, lessons which I cannot teach you,' he said. 'She will probably cry her eyes out, become furious with me and seek some sort of revenge.'

'I'll take my chances,' I said. 'Please dictate a letter to a scribe and convince her that you cannot see her again. When I return with her, Minos will have confidence in me again.'

'I hate politics, Brother. I was beginning to fall for her. But for the sake of Athens, I will do as you ask. I may meet her again someday under different circumstances,' Theseus added quietly.

'Father set me up with a contact in Iraklion – Mother knows who it is. Use our own tongue if you send any messages, as the Keftuins will not be able to read it,' I said.

Theseus adjusted the sling holding his right arm and went off to find a scribe. I walked out into the sunlight to find the captain and our mules. The city was gradually coming back to life. A sombre tone hung over the place as the citizens went about their business. The agora was deserted and the usual raucous laughter, from traders in the square, could not be heard.

* * * *

The north star dropped below the horizon behind us and the sparkling plankton splashed each side of the bows as our small ship cut through the water. The slaves hauled the oars inboard and Arpactias pushed us past Kea and Paros. The Keftui captain had sailed this route many times and used the island landmarks to keep his bearings. The slaves rowed into Naxos as the sun's rays climbed over the horizon. A small fleet of sponge divers sailed out of the bay on the way to their dangerous waters.

How much trouble was Ariadne going to make?

I shoved Theseus's papyrus into the folds of my tunic and sprang onto the wharf. Ariadne had smiled at me once, at the labyrinth, but I had never spoken to her. I was sure that she would not be the shy, retiring type. The captain and the first mate came with me in case she needed some persuasion. I said a prayer to Demeter under my breath as we walked up to an old fisherman sorting his catch.

'Kalimera, kyrie,' I said politely. 'We are looking for a certain Keftui maiden, would you know her whereabouts? She is olive skinned with long black, curled hair, Horus eyes, and she wears a long murex coloured ...'

The old Cyclades fisherman looked up from cleaning his fish.

'No need to go on. I know who you are, Your Highness. I saw you with Theseus at the funeral pyre.'

'Yes, a very sad day for us all,' I said. 'I need to find this girl urgently.'

'The Keftui maiden as you call her, I know she is the Princess Ariadne. Your brother and the princess ran past my boat on their way to that villa up there. They didn't emerge for a very long time.'

He grinned knowingly and nodded towards a white stone hut with a sky blue roof, set into the side of the mountain. 'She should still be there with her slave. I haven't seen her leave the house since Theseus left.'

I gave him a small lump of silver to show my appreciation and walked up the narrow, paved path. There were no secrets in these islands. I saw a curtain suddenly drop back into place as we drew near the hut.

'Go away, Callias! I know why you are here,' a female voice yelled through the door.

'Ariadne, I know you are in there. I have a message from Theseus, but you will have to let us in so I can read it to you,' I said.

'Pass it under the door. I can read your signs,' she snapped.

'Our father is dead, Ariadne. Theseus has some important words for you, words which you will not understand,' I said.

I looked at the captain and the first mate for moral support. 'Don't pass it under the door or we will never get in,' the captain whispered.

We could hear a wooden beam being slid from behind the door. The rusty hinges creaked as she opened the door a hand's width.

'How did you find me?' she asked.

'Theseus,' I said.

'The traitor! He swore ...' she snapped again

'If I could just read you his message, you will understand.'

'You can come in, Callias. Leave them outside,' she ordered.

I looked at my two companions and held up my hand. They nodded.

The hut was sparsely furnished, most unlike what she would be used to. A tiger skin rug warmed the cold paved floor and coloured Egyptian linen curtains hung across each window. A small fire surrounded by bronze cooking pots filled the kitchen and pithos jars of water and olive oil stood in the corner.

'Show me the message,' she demanded as soon as I stepped inside.

She glanced at the inscriptions.

'I can read my name, I can read Theseus's mark and something about a father; *'pa ... te'* and a king; *'wa ... na ... k'*. Is that right?'

'If you would just give it here,' I took the scroll back from her.

I started to read:

My Darling Ariadne

I dream of being in your arms once again someday. The days and nights at Naxos were the best of my life and I could have grown to love you. But sadly, we are not fated to be together.

Most unexpectedly, my father has gone to meet the gods and I am to be king of Athens. Please forgive me, my beautiful princess, but, because of an ancient alliance, I am to be betrothed to the daughter of the King of Boetia.

Ariadne's mouth dropped. I stopped for a moment. 'There's more,' I said.

You are to be wed to the king of Alasiya. My heart aches for you, but please do not come to Athens as it will only bring further pain to us both. Your mother and father are suffering, and long for your safe return. Please go with Callias.

Always yours,

Theseus

I invented the part about her mother and father.

She started to sob. Her slave threw her arms around her and started to stroke Ariadne's long hair. 'I have been ww ... waiting for him to return,' Ariadne cried. 'Why couldn't he marry me? Doesn't he need an alliance with Keftui?' Her blood shot eyes pleaded with me to provide some better answers.

'Our father and the King of Boetia arranged this marriage, eons ago,' I tried to explain.

The letter was having the opposite effect to that which Theseus had forecast. She hadn't lost her temper, nor threatened revenge. He didn't know all about women after all.

I chanced a suggestion, in between sobs. 'There's nothing for you here now, Princess. You must come home with us.'

'And marry that fat oaf from Alasiya!' she howled.

'I don't know anything about that, Princess,' I lied. 'You will be better off with us than raped by pirates or held to ransom by the Sea People once they find out that you are here.'

She started to regain her composure. Her slave handed her a clean scarf to wipe the tears away. Her lovely eyes were streaked red and the black galena eye shadow made small tracks down her cheeks.

'I saved him from the labyrinth ... and this is my reward,' she sniffed.

'We are in your debt, for that, Ariadne but maybe what my brother suggests is for the best,' I said.

I breathed a sigh of relief. Ariadne started to throw a few things into a goatskin bag. Her slave scraped some food scraps from one of the bowls and dowsed the fire.

'I'll come quietly,' she said. 'I'm sure father sent you to find me'.

* * * *

We showed Ariadne and her slave to their quarters below decks and told the crew to bring them fresh wine and some freshly cooked octopus.

We set sail toward Keftui once again and I tried to find some shade under the captain's quarters at the stern.

I thought about her comment that she had saved Theseus from the Minotaur. *Why did she want the beast dead? The Minotaur could have been used to entertain the masses for many years to come. Minos had spent much gold to design the labyrinth. What would Minos do with me when I returned?*

Theseus wanted to know everything about Keftui; the size of the Keftui fleet. Did they have massive stone walls around their cities, as at Myceneae and Tiryns? How many warriors could the Minoans muster at short notice? And so the list went on.

It was then I heard a loud female groan from below decks.

I ran from the handrail and looked through the porthole into Ariadne's cabin. She was lying on the floor, holding her right eye.

'I didn't mean for you to hit that hard,' I heard her say. Her slave had an odd smile on her face as she stood over the princess.

I shoved the door open and rushed to Ariadne's side.

'What on earth,' I cried. 'I'll find a wet scarf.'

I reefed the scarf from around my neck, dropped it in a bowl of water and held it to her eye. She pulled it away from me and threw it on the floor.

'Guard, lock up that slave,' I yelled.

'I don't need your help,' she said. 'And, don't you touch my slave.'

'In my household, there is only one sentence for a slave who strikes her mistress,' I replied.

'This is not your household,' she said. 'I have come to an arrangement with my slave. You may leave now,' the princess said to me.

* * * *

A royal welcoming committee was waiting for us at the docks of Keftui. Ariadne and her slave were first to jump across onto the wharf. Minos's wife, Queen Pasiphae, ran along the old planks, and hugged her eldest daughter. Ariadne's small sister, Phaedra, squealed with delight as she followed the Queen. Kitane kissed her older sister on both cheeks. Minos took one look at Ariadne. Her eye was black as thunder where the slave had struck her. She also now had a large tear in her linen skirt and her hair was tied in knots.

'Oh, by the gods, what have they done to my daughter?' the king cried.

I was a slow learner. The black eye, the torn skirt, the slave in the cabin. I remembered my brother's words now.

'Eloped, you said! She jumped on your brother's ship of her own free will, did she! Theseus won her heart at the laby-rinth did he?' the king was livid.

'I ... I ... can explain, Your Highness. Just give me a chance,' I said.

'You Greek filth. You will pay for this!' he swore.

Thinking quickly, I tried to play along with this. 'I am greatly shamed Your Highness. I have rescued her from my brother's clutches. She is still alive but a little damaged, I am afraid,' I stammered.

I glared at Ariadne. She looked away.

'For this betrayal, Theseus now has a great debt to pay.' Minos put his arms around his daughters and marched them off towards the palace.

Ariadne turned to her father and started talking. 'Theseus locked me in a stone prison at Naxos. He told me that I would not be going home until you released Callias and Alexandros. Several hoplites held me down while he entered me ... several times ... It hurt, Father ... I ... I ... cried and cried and asked them to stop ...' Ariadne's voice trailed off as they walked away. Minos kept shaking his head.

I will need to watch that one. She is dangerous.

I gathered up my few things from below decks and walked dejectedly back to the palace. I had expected to receive a good reception from the Minoan royals, not female treachery. I would have to put a lot more effort into gaining their trust.

When I opened the door to my quarters, I noticed Alexandros's bed was neatly folded in the corner and his few belongings were gone. There was no sign of him. I ran down to the stables, but the stable master told me that he had never worked there.

The guilt of leaving him behind began to set in. I walked quickly to Gadeirus's chambers and waited while his slave announced me. After a considerable time, the king's son sauntered into his interview room and slowly sat down in his griffin chair.

'You hold no favour with me Callias, after what your brother did to my sister,' Gadeirus went on.

'I apologise for my brother, Gadeirus, but I did deliver her back to you as requested,' I replied.

'How did you rescue her from Naxos, then?' he asked.

'We had to overwhelm the guards while Theseus was at my father's funeral,' I lied.

'Rather too late, by the look of her,' he said, not even commenting about father.

'Well, Theseus no longer has a hostage, and she is alive,' I went along with the ruse.

I didn't want to dwell on this any longer. The more lies I told, the greater the chance of slipping up. I had to win their confidence somehow. The lilting sounds of a distant lyre had a calming effect on the conversation.

'Yes, we have to thank you for that, I suppose,' the prince grimaced.

I began to wonder what Ariadne would think when she realised that I was going along with her story.

'I have not come to discuss your sister,' I said. 'I have come to ask what has happened to the boy?'

'Which boy?' he replied.

'Alexandros.'

'We had to move him to safer quarters while you were away. He was having nightmares and we thought he may do himself some harm without you to comfort him,' the prince said.

This sounded unconvincing.

'I want the truth, Prince,' I said.

'That is the truth, Callias. He is with the tribal mothers.'

'If you could tell me where that is, I have a message from his own mother,' I went on.

'That won't be possible,' Gadeirus said. 'He is safe and sound, and we don't want you upsetting him with stories from his mother.'

Although I didn't like what I was hearing, I decided not to push the matter.

'If he is in good hands, I trust your tribal mothers will look after him.'

I secretly swore to Persephone, to find him myself.

'He is in good hands and has other youths to amuse him,' the prince replied.

These people lived on half-truths and deceit. Minos promised to release us all, once the Minotaur was slain. No-one would explain the fate of the hostages taken many sun years ago. Ariadne instructs her slave to give her a black eye to get even with Theseus. And now Alexandros had disappeared.

I was learning fast. I needed all the cunning I had to avoid being trapped by the Minoan's trickery.

'What are your plans for me while I am a hostage?' I asked.

'What skills do you have, Callias?' Gadeirus said.

'I have been schooled in reading and writing by the scribes at Pylos,' I replied.

'You would be of use in the palace records room, then,' he suggested.

'Yes, I could help the scribes.' My luck was in.

'I will see to it,' he replied.

* * * *

The snake mother Xoanon looked down on the feeble offerings her subjects had placed at her feet. The moon cast long shadows over the central court of Knossos and light from a single oil lamp danced a thousand dances on the altar. The kernos stone held the ritual ingredients of sage, wine, milk and unwashed sheep's wool. Her faience eyes flashed and the bronze snakes in each fist writhed in the firelight. Warm olive oil dripped off her clay feet and the white Mt Juktas stones formed a sacred circle around her.

The snake mother and the bull Rhyton formed an alliance to control the people of Keftui. The mortals had killed their servant, the Minotaur, and now they would pay. She shook her right fist and the snake squirmed to escape. The earth around Malia Palace gave a shudder. The apothecary was on his knees, bowing and scraping. He poured more olive oil over her feet but she shook the snake in her other hand. The earth shuddered again. Mere wine and wool would not placate her now. Her glazed eyes stared at the shiny sword, *Blood Seeker*, which the mortals had used to kill her servant. The fox's ears pricked at her visions of hot blood. The apothecary grovelled at her feet as the sweet incense slowly twisted around the room.

He crawled away from the altar. Maybe a fattened calf would appease her next time. Another rumble from far below the palace turned the calm flames into flickering firelights.

* * * *

CHAPTER V

Malia Palace, Keftui – 1198 BC

The scribes and I were up to our ears with piles of clay tablets. Records from the other palaces had just been delivered and they sat in a pile in the records room. The field managers from the Malia wheat paddocks had been queued at the door all day, giving us counts of pithos jars of wheat and barley from the plentiful harvest. There were only the three of us, so we had no one to share the load. Each town and each field had to be recorded before the clay dried and I noticed one of my fellow scribes taking a few shortcuts. He wasn't using the correct marks for barley so that the grain inscriptions all read as "wheat" and when recording livestock, he didn't differentiate between "rams" and "ewes" or "bulls" and "cows". I made a mental note that his records were not accurate. The tablets had to be left in a cool place to dry, so that they didn't crack and ruin the inscriptions. Once they had dried, we filed them by town and district in separate baskets.

I was carefully recording the talents of wheat from Lisithi when one of the shipwrights from Amnisos walked in and told me that they had finished ten of the new slave rowers, bound for Thira.

After some careful questioning, he told me that they were designed to ram enemy shipping. A gangplank, which foot soldiers could run across, could then be dropped onto the enemy's deck. These were the latest design but had not been tried in battle. The new warships also had drop-down linen covers which could stop enemy arrows from striking the deck crew. I noted this vital information on a spare piece of papyrus and asked, 'How many have you finished, again?'

'We have finished ten ships and are waiting for more supplies of cedar and pine before we can start on the next ten,' the shipwright went on.

'The palace will be very impressed with your efforts,' I said. 'When will you deliver them to Thira?'

'I think we are due to sail on the full moon. The Thirans will be doing the final fit outs,' the carpenter went on.

'I will note all this on a separate tablet when I get through some of that pile over there. The king will probably want to launch the ships himself,' I said.

'Yes, he wants to make a sacrifice before they sail,' the shipwright said.

I hurriedly left what I was working on and started to inscribe this new information on a wet tablet. I had to make two copies: one for the palace records and a secret copy for Theseus in our own language. I had no idea what Theseus may do with this information once he received the tablet, but that was his business. I sharpened the brass inscribing tool and started scratching the wet clay. We didn't have a file for "new ships" so it sat in a basket by itself, ready for the palace treasurer. Luckily, my two workmates were busy with the wheat and barley records. I pretended to re-organise some baskets we had filled earlier in the day while I wrote this new information in our script on some fresh clay. Some scraps of papyrus lay on the floor. I pretended to tidy up and wrapped some papyrus scraps around my wet tablet. I dropped the new message in the folds in my tunic.

As I walked back to my quarters, the shadows were growing very long.

Gadeirus still had not told me where I could find Alexandros and I began to worry that the tribe mother story was also lies. The oil lamps flickered through the many windows in the stone buildings, as slaves, farmers and klaretoi made their way home from the fields. I desperately looked for somewhere to hide the tablet. I decided to chisel my way through the soft mortar behind my bench, pull out a small block and make a secure hiding place. I was just patching up the mortar when Princess Kitane walked in. She was carrying a round object wrapped in a linen cloth.

'Hello Callias. What are you doing?' she asked, smiling across the room at my rear end.

I looked around, startled. 'Just patching some blockwork.' *How much had she seen?*

'Haven't you finished your work for the day?' she said.

'I am so busy in the archives, I have little spare time,' I replied, getting to my feet.

'I came to thank you for rescuing my sister,' she said. 'I don't believe her story about your brother, but she won't tell me the truth. I saw the way she looked at him in the libation room and again at the labyrinth, so I know that she was definitely not kidnapped.'

'And I need to thank you for that flash of blinding light at the labyrinth,' I replied.

'You wouldn't have escaped from there without our help,' she went on.

I still couldn't work out why the girls had wanted the Minotaur killed. She held out the round bundle.

'I found this in the labyrinth,' she said.

I carefully unwrapped the white linen. It was Theseus's bronze helmet. It had been highly polished but was still a little worse for wear. Several dents in the top showed where he had nearly gone to the gods.

'Theseus should have this as a memento of your struggle,' she smiled. 'Ariadne and I owe you a great deal.'

'I think it is my brother and I who owe you our lives. Why did you help us?'

'Our deformed brother was a great embarrassment to us. My sister and I decided that it was time that he was stopped being used as entertainment,' she said. 'But we nearly lost you and your brother.'

I didn't believe all of this. There must be something she was not telling us. I decided to let it slide but there was one other thing on my mind.

'The sword that Theseus used, do you know what became of it?' I asked. 'I ran back to find it, but it was gone.'

'No,' she replied. 'I wasn't looking for it. Why did you want it?'

'It was light and strong – well balanced. I have never seen a sword like it,' I said.

'I don't know what became of it. It was most likely returned to our armoury,' she shrugged. 'Father wants to see you again in the morning.'

Oh, Hades, what has he found out now? I dropped my brother's helmet into a goat skin bag and thought that it could go, along with the tablet, to my contact in Iraklion.

'What does he want of me?' I asked.

She just smiled as she turned on her heel and walked away.

* * * *

I was beginning to feel like a traitor after talking to Kitane. She was a very pleasant girl, unlike her scheming sister. I

would need to invent some excuse to escape from the archive room for a few suns. I wasn't ready for another of Minos's tirades. I had that hollow feeling in the pit of my stomach again.

A shudder ran through the grand staircase as I slowly climbed to the throne room. *Was it my imagination?* No. The stairway shook again. A faint puff of mortar flew in a small cloud from a crack in the blocks. I burst into the king's ante chamber, eager to leave the stairs behind. A palace guard stood at the door to the throne room. He stared straight ahead with an expressionless look on his face. Sweat ran in rivulets down his dark torso and stained his loin cloth.

'Did you feel that?' I asked.

'Sit,' he said. *A man of few words.* I sat on the hard stone bench which ran along the wall. As I anxiously waited, I buried my head in my hands. *Demeter, please get me out of this.*

A small bronze bell rang in the next room and the guard grunted, 'You may enter now.'

Minos and his three daughters sat in their carved stone chairs on a raised platform. The morning sun shone in a yellow shaft on the tiled floor. My mouth was dry. I wiped my palms on the back of my loin cloth and prepared for the worst. I looked up and to my amazement, the princesses were smiling.

'Father, this Athenian is a lot paler than us and his hair is brown,' Phaedra said. She wore a thick, plaited wool necklace which just covered her small, dark breasts. White lotus flowers were interwoven through her long hair.

'Quiet, girl, I am not concerned with the way he looks,' Minos said.

'Prince Callias, I hope your work in the archives is keeping you busy.' The king sounded hospitable.

'Yes, Your Highness, we have more records than we can handle,' I replied.

'Without your assistance, our own two scribes would be overwhelmed,' he said. 'Unfortunately, they will have to manage without you for several moons.'

My spirits picked up. The royal axe still hung on the wall behind him.

'As we know from your bad behaviour at the labyrinth, your brother chose our new sword as his favourite weapon to kill our champion. We only had one sword made from new metal which comes from Alasiya. Over there, they call this weapon a "xiphos". The new metal is worth more than gold. Some time ago, I sent my son to Alasiya to find out where the metal comes from,' the king went on.

'The king of Alisaya has a mine on his island, but won't reveal its whereabouts. Of course, he will sell us what we want, but at a high price. He will supply us with one hundred talents of ore in exchange for five of our new ships, the same as we are sending to Thira. In addition, I have agreed that he can take one of my daughters as a bride, to cement our alliance with Hatti.'

Why was he telling me all this? Had he changed his mind about Theseus?

'You are one of only three scribes who can record the formula for making the new weapons. I want you to go to Alasiya with Kitane, find an alchemist who is making these weapons, and bring the formula back here. You will also accompany a shipment of the new metal from Alasiya back to Zakros.'

I looked over at Ariadne. Her black eye had disappeared. I remained wary of her and found it odd that she was smiling at me.

'But, I thought Ariadne was to marry the fat ...' I stammered.

'No, no, the king of Alasiya asked for one of my daughters. I have other plans for Ariadne,' he said. I have decided Kitane can take her place. It is about time she took a husband.'

Phaedra piped up, 'Father, I could go to Alasiya with Kitane?'

'Be quiet, girl,' Minos said. 'King Mutallu only wants one daughter. You are not ready for marriage.'

'But I could come back with Callias,' she persisted.

'No, it is too dangerous. You could be kidnapped by the Sea People. You will stay here, my girl,' he said.

'But, Father,' Phaedra kept on.

I wiped my forehead and breathed a sigh of relief that none of this concerned what Kitane may or may not have seen last night, or Theseus spiriting Ariadne away. The banter going on between Phaedra and her father amused me.

On the beach below us, a couple of small fishing boats hung out their nets to dry.

'Why not send Gadeirus back?' I asked.

'Gadeirus cannot read or write. If they have a complicated formula, how will he remember it all?' Minos said. 'Besides, I need him here to run the palaces now.'

'So I am to escort Kitane on the voyage to her new husband, accompany five of your warships to Alasiya, supervise the exchange of one hundred talents of ore for your daughter, find the formula, record it on a tablet, and sail back here with the ore,' I asked incredulously.

'One more thing. If you encounter any pirates, you will make sure my daughter is not taken prisoner.'

I presumed that meant, "don't come back here alive if she is taken".

'We will meet you at the wharves at sunrise, two moons from now. Take what you need from the archive rooms to record the formulae and ask the armourer to give you one of our bronze swords. You may need it,' Minos said.

There was still the matter of the missing Alexandros. Still, I decided not to push my luck. I was not headed for the snake pit and I would soon know how to make the aforinium sword. I was also sure Theseus would be very keen to know.

'I'll do my best, Your Highness,' I replied as I backed away.

'But Father, you said we could go sailing soon!' Phaedra whined.

* * * *

The streets of Iraklion were jostling with traders from all over the Aegean. The Phoenicians sold grain, exotic herbs and spices from Canaan and Labu. The Carthaginians bought bronze weapons and cooking pots from Carthage, the Iberians made the finest silver goods and hand crafted leather, and the Achaeans traded pots, wine and olive oil. Most goods were exchanged on the barter system but the wealthiest had small pieces of silver, copper and gold which could be used to buy anything on display.

I pretended to buy a goat's bladder water bag for my trip to Alasiya and a new bronze dagger from an Iberian silver-smith. The hard clay tablet rubbed painfully on my skin as I walked about. Theseus's helmet bounced along in the bag on my back. I kept looking behind but there were so many people, it was hard to tell if I was being followed.

I was to maintain contact with Theseus through Father's spy based in Iraklion.

Theseus had told me to ask for a wine called nykteri at the taverna nearest the wharves and someone would contact me there after one sun. No other person on Keftui knew that the taverna sold nykteri and my password would be "passing the night away". The security sounded far-fetched for two nations which were meant to be allies.

If I was caught with a Malia tablet outside the archive room, that would be enough to commence a torture session with Minos's guards.

I sat at a long, carved pine log which acted as a table, and ordered a mug of nykteri from the portly woman who served me. She acted as if it was just another order. She held her hand out for a small clip of copper and disappeared within the bowels of the kitchen. In a short while, she reappeared and said in a loud voice, 'We don't seem to have any of that particular wine, sir, but if you would come this way, maybe you could choose something else.'

The large woman led me to an alcove inside. She said out loud, 'If you would like to take a seat, I'll see what I can find.' I dropped the helmet on the seat but kept my right hand on the new dagger. I was about to leave when a light skinned, northern girl sat down opposite me. She had a veil pinned across her nose. Those eyes certainly looked familiar. She dropped the veil as she handed me the jar full of delicious wine.

'Remember me!' she whispered.

'Imira, what on earth!' I smiled.

'What have you been doing?' she asked.

'I've been killing Minotaurs and rescuing Minoan princesses,' I said.

'What is the password, you fool?' she laughed.

'Oh, yes, "passing the night away". I would make a poor spy,' I laughed as well.

'Theseus and I still owe you for that arrow!' she said.

'As long as it's not in the back,' I replied.

'We used to have some fun before your father died,' she continued. 'Now it's all hush, hush and serious politics. I don't see your brother anymore.'

'You would need to be extra careful now that Theseus is married to the princess from Boetia,' I said.

'Oh, he doesn't bother with me now. He only sends me on these dangerous missions to get me out of the way,' she replied. 'We do make a small profit selling wine to the pagans.'

'It's such a surprise to see you again,' I said. 'But there's no going back.'

I took a sip from the wine jar. 'Won't you join me?' I asked.

'Oh, no,' she said. 'I would be under the table all day if I had a drink with every warrior who asked. Now, what did you come to see me about?'

'I work in the archives room at Malia palace now. While recording talents of grain from the palace farms, a shipwright came in to record the completion of a number of new Minoan galleys,' I told her quietly. 'I have recorded, in our own tongue, on this tablet, the number of ships, the date and the time that they are to be delivered to Thira.' I slid the tablet under the table. 'Theseus will need to get a scribe to read it to him.' My hand touched one of her bare knees.

'Is that an invitation?' she smiled.

'Imira, be serious. Get this to Theseus as soon as you can,' I looked around to see if anyone was watching. She slid the tablet, still wrapped in the white papyrus, under her linen skirt. I handed the bag containing the helmet across the table to her. 'We found this helmet in the labyrinth. Could you give it back to Theseus,' I said loudly 'He will remember it from the labyrinth.'

I said quietly, 'Please tell the king, that I am going to Alasiya with Kitane tomorrow to find where the new metal comes from. We are sailing new ships to Alasiya to help the king repel the Sea People. So, I will need to meet you back here again to pass on what I have found,' I said.

'I'll be here,' she said.

I took another swig of nykteri from the bronze mug. 'Imira, you are a shining light in a dark sea, but do not cause trouble, please,' I said.

'Ariadne, does the fat king not desire her now?' she asked.

'No. King Minos has decided that he has other plans for her,' I said.

'I do not like the sound of that. I do not trust her – she is far too fond of Theseus.'

Her frown was quickly replaced by a smile.

Before I could protest about Ariadne's fondness for Theseus, the portly woman loudly interrupted:

'Hurry up, girl – clean up that kitchen!'

'Don't forget the password, next time. And I still owe you one, Your Highness,' Imira said. I waited until she had disappeared into the kitchen, drank the rest of my wine and rose to leave. As I left the taverna, I glanced over at some linen traders from Aegyptus. A dark haired Minoan girl was haggling over the price of a bolt of material. She had white crocuses in her hair.

* * * *

Several gannets flew overhead on their way to a school of fish near the shoreline. The crowd at the wharves jostled to catch a glimpse of Minos and his daughters as Kitane kissed her mother on both cheeks and clung to her for a long time. Ariadne and Phaedra were teary eyed and Minos tried to hold himself together.

The fat Hittite doesn't deserve a girl like Kitane. The new metal must be very important to Minos or he wouldn't be doing this – using the princess as trade goods.

The other four galleys were lined up alongside us. Zephyrus bellowed the sails, eager to send us on our way. The slave rowers, ten per side, sat waiting for their captain's signal to start rowing out of the harbour. Kitane finally walked across the gangplank towards me, her white and rouge cheeks streaked with tears.

'We grant these five ships to Alasiya to form a mighty alliance between Hatti and Minoa. We give our sacred daughter to King Mutallu as a sign of marriage between our two great nations. May Poseidon bless these ships and all who sail in them,' the king said, and nodded to the chief priest. A quick slash of a knife severed the neck of the white goat and an attendant rushed to collect the warm blood in a bronze bowl. The attendant presented the bowl of hot blood to Minos. The king dipped his fingers into the bowl and sprinkled droplets over the prow of our galley. Priests intoned sacred hymns to the god of the sea. The blue and white evil eyes, painted on our bows, gave a stern warning to all sea spirits to let us pass.

'Cast off,' the captain yelled. I looked at the princess and her blood shot eyes told me that she was not happy with this. She waved and waved as her family faded to specks on the shoreline. The wind caught the white, woollen sails and the slaves hoisted their oars inboard.

'Cheer up,' I said to her. 'I hear that Mutallu has many Minoan court officials and concubines, so it will almost feel like home.'

This only made matters worse, and she buried her face in my shoulder. It felt good. I stroked her long black hair and tried to think of something more comforting to say. I couldn't think of anything. One of her ladies-in-waiting ran over and pulled her away from me.

'I'm sure the Prince of Athens does not want you messing his robe, Your Highness. Come below deck and we will tidy you up,' she said.

I told her to leave Kitane where she was, I liked having my robe messed up.

Keftui faded below the direction of Zephyrus and the other four galleys stood in line astern as we headed across the open sea. Our ships had a crow's nest and the keenest young eyes were sent up the main mast to keep watch for pirates. The blue dolphin flag meant "all clear" but a red flag flying above the main sail meant "danger".

It was times like this when I wished that I had Theseus with me. He always knew what to do. Sometimes he made the wrong decision but no matter what, he stuck to his decision. Unlike me, indecision was not in his make-up. I had learnt to read and write from the scribes at Pylos but I was of little use with the sword and spear. I kept a sharp lookout for red flags.

CHAPTER VI

Alasiya, Island of the Hatti – 1197 BC

The surface of the sea split apart as our galley cut a path to Alasiya. Our royal companions – the dolphins – splashed happily beside us for many stadia, frolicking in a race to nowhere. The lookouts watched for any sign of bird life which meant we were near land.

I wondered how Kitane was holding up. I hadn't seen her on deck for a long time and decided to pay her a visit to relieve the monotony.

There was only one room below deck. I dropped through the hatch and knocked on her door. Her slave asked who it was disturbing the peace and I quietly answered, "Callias". I heard some voices from inside and the heavy lock slid away. Her slave ushered me in to the sparsely furnished cabin. A kylix of freshwater stood on a roughly hewn cedar table and a change of clothes hung from a hook on the wall. Some water dripped through the gaps in the deck and splashed into a small amphora on the floor. Kitane was sitting on her bunk brushing her hair. She smiled as I came in.

'Leave us,' she said to her slave. 'Come back when the sun sets.'

Kitane had a calm, relaxed way about her; her long, black hair glistened as shafts of sunlight shone across her face.

'Your father will need to fix the gaps in the deck in the next line of ships,' I joked.

'Then, what will I do for sunlight and water?' she said, smiling.

'He will need to make a porthole, so you can see the outside world. And also install a wash basin,' I laughed.

'Yes, it's not a room fit for a princess, but, after all, they are fighting ships,' she replied. 'How much longer before I meet my new husband?' she asked.

'The lookouts have not sighted any birds, yet, so it will be a while,' I said.

'No pirates, either, thank the gods,' she smiled.

'Yes, I think five Keftui fighting ships in one place are enough to keep the pirates away,' I said. 'Besides, we have a valuable princess to protect.'

'Oh, where is she?' Kitane laughed.

'I came down to cheer you up, Kitane, but I think it's me who needs cheering up. I'm afraid, I wasn't born with Greek sea legs,' I said.

'Well, we all can't be sailors,' she teased. 'But you do have many other talents.'

'Yes, that's why I'm here, I guess. Your father wants to know how to make these stronger and sharper swords.'

Then she said something which caught me completely off guard.

'I saw you with a lovely Achaean girl at the taverna. Are you to marry her?' she asked. My heart skipped a beat.

'No. She is a lady-in-waiting at Theseus's palace,' I quickly covered my tracks. 'Remember, you said to return the helmet to Theseus.'

'Oh, I see, yes. I saw you hand it across the table to her.' *Did her father send her to keep an eye on me?*

As if she was reading my mind she said 'I just happened to be with the Aegyptus traders, buying some cloth for my trip, when I saw you.'

I just nodded.

'Kitane, I can't see you with that fat king. Why didn't Minos send Ariadne?' I said. The words didn't seem to come out properly.

'When the new ships are built, he is sending her to Thira, to Akrotiri. Father told her that she is to rule there until a suitable prince is found. I was not considered for that job. Of course she jumped at the chance so that she could be closer to your brother,' she said.

I thought Ariadne hated Theseus.

I walked over and sat on the bunk next to her. She kept brushing her hair and didn't move away. 'How am I going to get you out of this mess?' I asked.

The fast moving ship hit a patch of rough sea and the bows crashed down into a trough. Kitane dropped her brush and for a moment, lost her balance. I reached out to stop her falling and she landed against me. Aphrodite was kind to me today. The feeling of her bare breasts against my chest was more exquisite than I could have possibly imagined. She went to say something but I smothered her lips with my mouth. For a wonderful moment, she kissed me back but then pulled away, shaking her head.

'Don't do this, Callias,' she whispered in my ear. 'I am spoken for. Let's not start something that cannot be.'

I didn't take any notice. I pulled her to me and her tongue searched for mine as Eros took control. I reached behind her back and pulled the linen tie holding her skirt. We fell onto the soft goat skin rugs on her bunk. The galley hit another trough but we felt nothing.

'We shouldn't be doing this,' she cried but Aphrodite had us now.

I tore off my toga and my hard manhood found its way to the soft, exquisite place between her legs. I gently pushed into her and she gasped.

'Callias, don't do this,' she whispered as her long legs wrapped around me. 'We better stop now.'

'Kitane, I'll find a way to get you out of this,' I murmured as she pulled me further in to her exquisite place. The warm juices spread over us. We were one. She sucked on my earlobe and I almost lost control. I could just feel my seed starting to flow, when there was a loud knock on the door. My hard manhood suddenly deflated. She wouldn't let go.

'Your Highness. Open up, you two,' her slave said loudly. 'The lookout has spotted some petrels.'

'Go away,' Kitane said, loudly.

'Let me go,' I whispered.

'No … oo. Come back. My slave can wait,' she cried.

Her dark eyes looked pleadingly up at me as I tried to extract myself. Her make-up was badly smudged. She slowly unlocked her legs and let me go.

'Just wait,' she yelled to the slave, as we quickly stepped back into our clothes.

'I'll find a way,' I whispered as I snatched one last kiss. 'I'll get a message to you at the Hittite palace before I leave for home. I'll give this ring to the messenger, so you will know it's from me.' I held up my right hand to show her.

'I know I can trust you,' she said.

My spirits should have soared, but instead, I became overwhelmed by guilt at having been party to Kitane's unhappy situation.

We were not greeted like royalty at the busy Alasiyan harbour of Salamis. The city was the meeting point of traders from all points of the compass. Exotic spices and silks from China and India were shipped across from Byblos, valuable cedar from the Levant was stacked in neat rows along the wharf, bags of grain from the Great River of Aegyptus were being stacked in a warehouse. Bustling Phoenician merchants loaded goods to all points of the ocean. Alasiyan copper bowls and drinking vessels were piled high in several crates. I noticed some unusually shaped, heavy copper ingots, being loaded onto an Aegyptus merchant ship. I had seen them before at Pylos. They were shaped like a cow hide, with a handle at each corner. This made them easy to carry.

The Hittite royal family and their bodyguards lined the dock. They were dressed in bright linen cloth and wore head-dresses of bird feathers. King Mutallu sat in a woven reed chair, his enormous stomach glistening in the hot sun. Nude slaves on each side of him waved large palm fronds, trying in vain to keep the king cool. Several of his wives chatted eagerly as we approached the dock and some small, dark skinned children played hide and seek amongst their mothers' skirts.

I waited at the handrail as our captain – along with Kitane, her slave and lady-in-waiting – walked across the gang plank towards the king. She looked around at me and gave a weak smile. The look in her eyes said it all.

'King Minos sends greetings to Your Majesty. May I present Princess Kitane, daughter of our king,' the captain said. King Mutallu nodded to one of his bodyguards, who then walked over and took her by the arm.

'Our king wishes to inspect you,' he said to the princess. The guard then grabbed her by the right arm marched her over to the king.

'Turn her round,' he said from his chair.

She looked back up at me, despondent and helpless. *A royal inspection, to make sure the goods weren't faulty,* I thought.

The fat malaka. The king's other wives eyed her off and giggled amongst themselves.

'She is too skinny,' one murmured. The royal children played a game of hide and seek in their mothers' skirts.

'She'll do,' Mutallu said to the captain. 'Take her to the palace and dress her in some proper clothes,' he said to one of his wives.

It was then, I saw red. Visions of the Minotaur choking Theseus, raced across my eyes. I strode down the gangplank up to the sweating king.

'If she is to be treated like a sack of grain,' I said. 'The deal with Minos is off!'

The hands of two of his bodyguards flew to their swords, as I yelled at their king.

'Who would you be?' Mutallu asked.

'I am Prince Callias of Keftui, envoy of Minos, and we will sail away with these ships and our princess, if she is to be treated so badly!'

My warriors started to finger their swords. The Alasiyan guards looked at their king for an order. Kitane did not move. One of the king's wives tried to pull her away.

'You will apologise to her NOW. She is a royal princess,' I yelled. The fat animal probably didn't know the meaning of the word apologise.

I could feel the tension in the air, but I didn't care. Even the petrels stopped squawking. I kept my hand away from my sword. The dock workers stopped and waited for the king's reaction. Somewhere in the distance a slave dropped an oar on a wooden deck and a loud thud broke the silence.

Kitane looked at me, shaking her head. 'Please don't do this,' she mouthed the words to me.

'Ahh, I think the prince has affection for the princess,' Mutallu said sneeringly. 'I have no interest in affairs of the heart. I want to make sure I am getting a fair deal.'

'She deserves to be treated better,' I said, my heart beating wildly with anxiety. 'Apologise to her, NOW,' I repeated.

Mutallu gazed over me condescendingly as if summing me up and running different scenarios through his fat brain. His beady eyes looked across at his older sons, then at his bodyguards and his wives. There would be a lot of blood spilt if he made the wrong decision. He stroked his black, goatee beard and looked at Kitane.

'I apologise for treating you like a sack of grain, Princess. You are the nicest bag of grain I have ever seen.' His entourage burst out in nervous laughter. The warriors took their hands away from their swords.

'Once we are married, you will be put in charge of the royal household. You will be given your own private chambers,' he said to her with a forced smile. 'You can keep your slave as your companion. This will be your new home.'

A sigh of relief went round the docks. *He must want these ships badly*, I thought.

I knew I desperately had to do something to rescue her.

One of the dark Nubian wives asked Kitane politely, if she would like to follow her, she would be shown some Alasiyan clothes and her new chambers.

'Thank you, Your Majesty,' I said. 'Minos loves his children, dearly. He has asked Kitane to report on every full moon, telling him how she is being treated in the kingdom of Hatti,' I lied.

'Now regarding the shipment of aforinium?'

After our confrontation at the wharves, relations between the king and ourselves seemed to thaw. He gave us a guide to conduct us to the copper mines at the foothills of the Troodos Mountains. I ordered our captain to supervise the loading of the Alasiyan merchant ship with the bags of ore and to make sure that the fat king did not trick us. The training of the

Hittite captains would take several moons which would give us time to inspect the mines and talk to the alchemists.

I decided to take Pirithios with me. He was a mercenary in the Keftui guard and could handle a sword far better than I could. He was born in Attica, so we both spoke the same native tongue. He had decided to stay on at Keftui after being sent by Aegeus to train Minos's warriors.

The tracks around the island were well worn. We could see evidence of Thutmose and Seti's hieroglyphs carved into stone boulders before the Hatti had arrived. Some people still lived in the old stone round houses built by the ancients. The Alasiyan farmers harnessed heavy horses and pulled strange metal objects which ripped up the soil. In some places, the corn grew higher than a man. In other fields, weeds were torn out of the ground by these new implements. We stopped beside a small stream and I made a sketch of these strange contraptions using a piece of charcoal and dried goatskin.

The smoke from the Troodos furnaces hung low around Mt. Olympus as we rode in. There were no bird calls, while the mountainsides had been stripped of trees. An eerie, blackened landscape greeted our small party.

Several gangs of slaves laboured at the tunnels which were dug into the side of the mountain. Clouds of dust spewed from the tunnel entrances as they followed the seams of copper into the ancient formations. Further down the slope, several small furnaces burned ferociously, as the Hittite alchemists smelted the copper ore. The impurities were skimmed off the top of the large clay crucibles and the molten copper was left to cool in flat moulds with a copper handle at each corner. These were the same as the large, flat, cow hide ingots, which we had seen at the wharves.

They were using a similar system to that used at Pylos. The difference was that Alasiya mined the copper ore but we only smelted the copper ingots which we bought from them. Our alchemist at Pylos told me that he used one part tin to ten parts copper to make our bronze weapons. I basically knew this process. *But, where was the aforinium mine? Were they going to show us how they treated this new ore?*

Several of the slaves had stopped work and were doubled over with choking coughs. Our guide explained that the copper ore gives off a poisonous gas when it is heated. These slaves didn't live very long.

Sparks flew into the sky as a metalworker poured the molten copper into a stone mould. One of the coughing slaves fell – face down, into the black dust. The overseer pushed him over with his sandalled foot to see if there was any sign of life. Satisfied that the slave was dead, he ordered two others to dump the corpse into an old mine shaft.

If there was a Tartarus on earth, this was it, I thought.

'I would like to speak with the foreman,' I said to the guide.

The foreman looked up from the molten metal and our guide beckoned him over.

'What do you want?' he said to our guide impatiently.

'This is Prince Callias from Keftui. We are selling them one hundred talents of aforinium. He wants to speak to you.'

'What did you want to know?' he said again looking at me.

'Could you tell me where the aforinium mine is located?' I asked.

'I have never been shown. I don't work with the new metal' he said. 'I have another batch of copper nearly ready. I must go.'

'Do you treat this new ore here?' I asked quickly.

'No. Of course not. We can't generate enough heat here to melt the aforinium. You will need to return to Amathous to see how it is done.'

'*Sas efcharisto,*' I replied.

I turned to the guide. 'I need to return to Amathous to find out how this new ore is treated.'

We rode south to the new village of Amathous, which was named after Adonis's mother. Many of my countrymen had settled here but they spoke a different language called "Pelasgian" which I could not understand.

I could see as we rode in that Amathous was another mining town. The village was built high on a cliff face and most of the time the wind howled in off the Sea of Aegyptus. Smoke from large fires at the top of the cliffs constantly blew over the town. The workers huts were solidly built from the surrounding stone and a freshwater spring gurgled through the village. We found a mine worker's family willing to take overnight guests and dined on a delicious meal of goat stew and dark Alasiya bread. Our host, an Ionian miner, told us that the fat king had sent one of his Hittite alchemists to Amathous, to take charge of smelting the new ore. We would find him in the metal workers' building at sunrise.

I lay in bed wondering about Kitane. The lovely musk smell of her travelled with me always. I thought about how that fat pagan would try to make love to her. The thought filled me with revulsion. My rescue plan was beginning to take shape. I felt guilty about spying on Keftui, but I had decided, that, from here on, the princess came first. Would her slaves be brushing her long shining locks, preparing her for a visit from the royal globule?

Orion, the hunter, sparkled in the clear night sky as I lay with my eyes open. If only Hera's Scorpion would find the fat king, she would save us all a lot of trouble. My rear end ached from far too much contact with a donkey's back, and my eyelids gradually succumbed to Hypnos's magic.

'Wake up, you lazy hoplite!' I said to Pirithios as the sun's rays burst through our window. 'Some bodyguard you turned out to be. The Persian Immortals could be attacking!'

'I sleep with one eye open, Callias,' he said, yawning, lazily.

'You must be blind in one eye then, or you would have seen those Alasiyan guards walking towards us,' I replied. I pointed out the window to the three figures approaching our hut.

Pirithios jumped up from his goatskin stretcher and grabbed his sword.

'I think they are friendly. They have our guide with them,' I said.

'I wouldn't trust this lot as far as I could piss,' Pirithios said. 'That reminds me.' He headed out the rear door.

Our guide knocked on the front door.

'We have come to escort you to the workshops,' he said. 'The alchemist wants to make sure that no harm comes to you. We have bandits around this town.'

'He doesn't want us poking around by ourselves, more likely,' Pirithios said as he stumbled back inside.

'Just a moment!' I yelled through the door.

We threw our dirty clothes on, strapped on our baldricks, and walked out into the bright sunlight. The view over the ocean towards Ugarit was magnificent. Several small fishing boats bounced over the waves, their woollen sails billowing as they made their way back to shore. Dozens of seagulls squabbled over fish guts where the fresh fish had just been cleaned. I could make out several dolphins surfing in the clear blue waves.

Most unusual of all, several huge funnels ran from sea level up the face of the cliffs. The funnels appeared to be constructed of fired clay and were about ten cubits across. There was a small stone building at the top of each funnel. Slaves, like so many black ants, buzzed around the fires which were driven by the concentrated wind rushing from each tube. Some of the flames were blue.

'I've never seen anything like this,' Pirithios said.

'Take a mental note of everything you see,' I said. 'We will need it.'

The guards escorted us up to one of the stone workshops. We could hear the clanging of metal as we approached the door. Pirithios and I looked at each with raised eyebrows.

'You there, throw more wood on that fire,' a foreman yelled.

'Careful, you fools,' another yelled as two men handled a red hot metal bar.

The wind from the southern ocean blew through each funnel underneath each fire. As the wind hit the fire, the flames roared through holes cut into the rock at the top of the cliff. When the wind blew at its strongest, some of the flames turned blue. The clay crucibles on top of the holes contained red hot ore with a dark scum on top. The furnaces at Troodos were hot, but these were much hotter.

A fair skinned man, covered with a thick woollen apron, came to the door.

'Come in, come in,' he said as we were ushered into the workshop. 'I am Cinyrus, Mutallu's chief alchemist. He has instructed me to show you our smelter.'

Word spreads fast over here, I noted.

'I am Callias of Keftui and this is Pirithios, my bodyguard. As your king is giving us one hundred talents of aforinium, we will need to know how to process this ore when we get home,' I said.

'Where would you like to start,' the alchemist replied.

'Where do you mine this new ore?' I tried again.

'We ...' he almost started to tell me and then backtracked. 'That is a closely guarded secret, Your Highness. The Sea People have attacked us and succeeded in stealing the swords of some of our dead warriors. The Sea People have caused much trouble, so if you will forgive me for saying, our king is wary of spies.'

'I can assure you, we are not spies,' I replied.

'I am not permitted to tell anyone about the source of this new metal, but if you would like to purchase more of it, I'm sure King Mutallu will oblige,' the alchemist said.

Egyptian traders must have learnt their craft from these Alasiyans, I thought.

'Then, could you explain the reason for the funnels outside?' Pirithios asked.

'The fires at Troodos that we use for making bronze, are not hot enough to make good quality aforinium. The fires there will melt copper and tin but they aren't hot enough to heat the new metal. I did a few experiments at Salamis, and I found that if I made the fire much hotter, the impurities in the new ore will bubble out. The impurities can then be scraped off the top of the ore to make a much harder metal. We use bellows in here to heat up the hard lengths of metal to make the swords.

''What are bellows?' Pirithios asked.

'Bellows? Yes. A goat's stomach with two handles which can make a strong air flow,' he explained. He reached down under a bench and handed a well-worn set of bellows to my bodyguard.

Pirithios pumped the two wooden handles and a blast of air shot out the gullet.

'Now that would be good for cleaning my hut,' Pirithios laughed.

'I get it. The funnels up the cliff face act like huge bellows,' I said.

'Amathous was the windiest place we could find, so we decided to set up here,' Cinyrus explained. 'It was easier than trying to construct huge bellows, and then trying to work out how to pump them.'

'How much hotter does the fire need to be?' I asked.

'The fires here, with a strong wind blowing, are much hotter than Troodos. Of course, we have to wait for a very strong wind to turn some of the flames blue.'

'Do we have a suitable spot on Keftui?' I asked Pirithios.

'The windiest place that I know of is Kato Zakro, so we could try one funnel there to start with,' he answered.

The sounds of clanging metal from the forming room drowned out what I was trying to say. I counted ten craftsmen hammering at long lengths of red aforinium. The sweat dripped from their noses as they heated and reheated the metal, flattened it out with heavy hammers and shoved it back in the fires.

'After we have skimmed off the slag, or impurities, we turn the hot metal into bars. These bars can be reheated later on, by the blacksmiths, or left to cool and transported away. Many more hours of sanding and polishing are required before we produce a finished product,' he went on.

He reached under the bench again and pulled out a long wooden box. I opened the lid slowly. Lying on white woollen cloth was the finest sword I had ever seen. It was about one cubit long and had a beautiful, carved, ivory tusk handle. It was the same as the one which we had used to kill the Minotaur. The highly polished metal glinted as the sun's rays bounced off the blade. It didn't have the strange engravings on the hilt.

'This is what we can do with this new metal,' he said. He reached for the box. 'We gave one of these to your king, when we made these new arrangements about the ore. We call it a "xiphos".

'Did you make any strange symbols on the blade?' I asked.

He looked at me rather puzzled. 'No, what sort of marks?'

'A boar's snout, for instance,' I replied.

'No, why do you ask?'

'My brother and I killed their Minotaur with one of these. It had a boar's snout and fox's ears engraved on the hilt,' I said.

Someone from Keftui must have made those marks after he gave it to the king.

'They may have been symbols from one of the Keftui ancient gods,' the alchemist replied.

I let it rest. 'You have been of great assistance, Cinyrus. We will find a place on Keftui to build one of these funnels, but we may need to return.'

'I am always here,' his withered face belied the words as he showed us the door.

The Alisayan guards and our guide were waiting outside when we emerged in the bright sunlight. We walked away from the metal worker's hut to escape the hammering. The wind had died down and several of the smelters had stopped working. A crowd of people had gathered around the fishing boats away in the distance. A thin column of smoke rose from a fire on the beach. Fresh fish for the evening meal; my mouth watered. We were escorted back to our sleeping quarters, guards in front and behind. We flopped on our stretchers. I felt like joining the party on the beach but did not want to cause a scene with the escort.

'Do you get the feeling there is something they are not telling us?' I asked Pirithios.

'Yes, and why the armed guard?' he asked.

'Maybe there's something they don't want us to see,' I replied. 'I think we should take a look around after sundown.'

'I agree,' Pirithios replied.

'I hope you remembered all that he told us today,' I said.

'Well, what I have forgotten, I am sure you will remember,' he smiled. 'You better write down what we have seen before I forget.'

I unrolled the piece of dried goatskin and made a sketch of one of the funnels next to the drawing of the weed killing machine. My artwork was not the best, but if Minos or Theseus was looking at the drawing, they would get the idea. An Alasiyan slave knocked on the door and placed a beautiful platter of fresh seafood on the large tree stump between our beds. Several cut limes were placed among the fish and a slave placed a jug of mead and two brass mugs beside the food.

'A feast fit for two kings,' Pirithios smiled as he reached for a piece of grilled octopus.

'They are making sure that we do not venture outside,' I said.

'And they're hoping that we will fall asleep quickly. I would not drink that mead. Only the gods would know what they have put in it!' Pirithios said.

The hot Aegean sun sunk below the horizon. We tipped the mead into a crack in the stone floor and pretended to be deep asleep when the slave returned for the dirty plates. After she had gone, I risked a peek out of our single window. I noticed that one of the furnaces was still firing. 'Let's go,' I said and crept out the back door with Pirithios close behind me.

The moonlight appeared and disappeared as the night clouds sailed across the sky and we had to be careful that we didn't get caught in the open. The furnace glowed in the distance, but it took a long time to get there, ducking and hiding in the shadows. We could see a few metalworkers silhouetted against the orange glow and saw that their attention was focused on the fire. There shouldn't be any guards but we didn't take any chances. A particularly dark cloud drifted across the moon and we headed for a stone wall built off the metal working shed that we had been in this morning.

I poked my head over the wall and almost came face-to-face with a slave carrying a bucket of something black. Fortunately, he was heading for the fire and his eyes weren't adjusted to the dark. I put a finger to my lips and pointed over the wall. I waited until my heart had stopped thumping and ventured another look over the top. Pirithios craned his neck to see what was going on. The ore in the furnace was red hot and Cinyrus was carefully adding the contents of the bucket to the red semi-liquid. Another slave was waiting with a full bucket of the substance. When Cinyrus added the black powder, the mixture sent a shower of sparks high into the night sky. We ducked down as our hiding spot was temporarily lit by the sparks. The first slave, now with an empty bucket, headed back towards us for more black ash.

'Count the number of buckets,' I whispered.

We watched as four more buckets were tipped into the red hot aforinium.

'Quick, let's get out of here,' I said and pointed back to the trees. I grabbed a handful of the black powder and dropped it into my pocket as we ran past.

'What did you make of that?' I asked Pirithios when we were safely back in our cabin.

'That alchemist told us nothing about adding something to the ore,' Pirithios said.

'Yes. What do you think it is?' I asked, as I held some in my hand.

'It looks like black ash to me,' he replied.

'Why would he be adding ash just after he had skimmed off the slag?'

'I have no idea,' Pirithios said. 'You better make a note of it on your goatskin.'

'Did you count how many buckets he threw in?' I asked.

'He added four after you asked me, plus the one where the slave nearly caught us,' he replied.

'Mmmm...five altogether, but how many before we arrived?' I said.

'Can't be sure. And he could have added more after we left,' Pirithios said.

'Well, we found out what they didn't want us to see. The important thing is that they were adding ash to the ore. We have no idea what for, but maybe our alchemists can find out,' I said.

Alongside my sketch of the funnel, I drew a bucket and wrote: black ash – five, orichalcum – two hundred?

Back in our hut, I lay in bed with my eyes open. My heart was still pumping after our excursion and the animal skin stretcher seemed as if someone had forgotten to remove the animal from it.

My thoughts drifted to the princess and how Mutallu had treated her. Herein may be the solution to my problem. Maybe if she wasn't "a perfect sack of grain", she could accumulate some faults which the fat king could find repulsive? I dwelt on this for quite some time. Just what faults would make her so undesirable that she would be returned to her father? Hypnos overcame me and my back moulded into the lumps and bumps in my mattress.

* * * *

Pirithios woke before me and saw an opportunity to get even after my Immortals joke. He grabbed a bronze bucket and

91

made a trail of oats leading from my bed to where my donkey was tethered. The animals were always eager for their first feed early in the morning. He undid the halter. The donkey happily munched his way along the trail, through the large doorway, leading to my bed. The animal reached a small pile of grain dumped next to my head. Pirithios sat back, watched and waited.

I was dreaming. Something warm and soft nuzzled my neck. The movement would stop for a short while and then start again. It was a lovely feeling. I was back with my princess in the cabin. I smiled in my sleep. I threw my arm over to hold her closer and grabbed the unfortunate animal's head. It let out a startled bray, bucked and knocked everything over on its way out. I sprang up and instinctively grabbed my sword, half in this world, half in the next.

'You skata' I yelled. I was wide awake now. 'That bloody animal could have torn my ear off,' I said. I was not amused.

Pirithios eventually gained some self-control. 'That is one story for the palace guards,' he spluttered.

'You had better watch yourself, from now on, Pirithios,' I said sternly.

After we had come to our senses, and were on speaking terms again, we packed up our few possessions, rounded up the donkeys and waited for Mutallu's guide to show up. As we rode along the dusty track back to Salamis, mule trains passed us heading to Amathous with wagon loads of ore. A fast despatch rider galloped past on a bay pony and mining slaves trudged along with their heads down. Large forests of trees were no longer large forests. Naked stumps stood as forlorn reminders of the need for fires, boats and buildings.

After a couple of suns had passed, I started thinking about my problem with Kitane.

'King Mutallu, I gather he has quite a harem,' I said to the guide.

'Oh, yes. He has fifteen or twenty concubines in the palace,' he replied.

'He would have fathered a lot of children, then?' I asked.

'The king has eunuchs watching his concubines. He uses his traded princesses, like the Keftui princess, to breed future princes and princesses so that they are of royal blood,' he explained.

'So, he likes to implant as many other princesses as possible, to add to his large family,' I observed.

'Yes. If the women with blue blood don't fall with child from one full moon to the next, the king does not want them in his palace,' the guide went on.

'He is becoming so large, it amazes me how he manages to implant them,' I said.

'It appears that the poor princesses have to do most of the work!' the guide smiled. I shuddered at the thought.

After many more stadia and chafing of my nether regions, we rode over the crest of a hill and could see the busy port of Salamis away in the distance. Our five galleys were tied up at the wharves, so I assumed that my captains had finished training the new commanders. An old Phoenician merchantman, heavily laden with ore, sat low in the water.

Our Keftui slaves were now Alasiyan slaves, to power the Hatti ships. I had to ask the Hittite captains with their new warships to sail with us for some time until we were away from dangerous waters. I had one more duty to perform before we left. I needed a prostitute. Mutallu's guide smiled knowingly at me when I asked about the classiest girl in Salamis.

'Ah, I see,' he said. 'You have been away from home for a long time.'

'Yes,' I laughed. 'I need a girl before I sail back.'

'My lord's favourite girl is Puduhepa – not her real name, of course. This was the name of a queen of Hatti but our Puduhepa is the queen of the night. She will show you a good time,' he said, winking.

'You will find her in the taverna behind the wharves.'

I stowed my woollen bag and goatskin drawings in the Phoenician merchantman and told Pirithious that I needed a woman.

'Does she have a friend?' he asked.

'No,' I replied. I needed to do this by myself.

I sat at the long wooden bench in the taverna and ordered a mug of wine. The olive oil lamps flickered against the mud brick walls and some inebriated sailors from Byblos started singing a loud sea shanty. The serving girl placed a bronze mug, brimming with wine, in front of me and I asked her how I could find Pudahepa.

'She is busy at present, you will have to wait,' she replied.

'I'll wait,' I said.

I had just swallowed the last of the wine, when a dark skinned Nubian girl sat down next to me. A faint aroma of rose petals drifted past me and her bone white teeth flashed a smile.

'Would you order me a drink?' she asked.

'Of course. You must be Pudahepa?' I asked. 'Beautiful, strange women do not normally sit down next to me.'

'Yes, I am the queen Pudahepa, but I do need a drink. Nothing to dull the senses, mind. Just to quench my thirst after my last customer.' she said.

I beckoned for the serving girl and the queen ordered a glass of fresh lime juice. Lapis lazuli beads hung in rows around her neck and her small breasts were visible through a thin, white linen jacket.

'I am very expensive, but I am worth it,' she invited.

'Could we go somewhere a little less noisy?' I asked as the Byblos sailors grew louder and louder.

'Yes, I have just the place. I'll just finish my drink,' she smiled across at me.

She grasped me by the hand and led me up a set of stone stairs to a lavishly furnished room above the taverna. We could still hear the noise below but we could speak without yelling at each other. The soft mattress on the floor was covered in bright cushions and pillows, and the flame of a single candle flicked placidly on the walls.

'My price is a piece of gold,' she said, very business-like. 'What is your name?' Her eyes moved ghostlike in the firelight.

'My name is Callias, from Keftui,' I replied.

'Oh, yes. I was told about your unfortunate meeting with Mutallu when you came ashore,' she said. Now, where would you like to start?' She started to take off her linen jacket.

'No. Don't undress,' I said. 'I haven't come for that.'

She looked amused. 'Oh, you prefer to just talk? Please tell me what is troubling you. My fee is still the same.'

'I am not here to just talk, but I will keep you in mind when I need to talk,' I said. I am here for some personal information and need to ask you to carry out a small task for me. I sail in the morning, so I cannot attend to it myself.'

'You intrigue me,' she said.

'I hope you don't become offended, but how do you stop yourself falling with child every time you make love with a client?' I asked seriously.

'Why do you want to know?' she asked.

'As you may have gathered after my confrontation on the wharf, I am in love with a certain Keftui princess,' I smiled at her.

'A princess who will soon be married to our royal fatness, Mutallu!' Pudahupa laughed.

'I have found out that Mutallu's wives must all bear him children within one sun year, or they are expelled from the palace,' I said.

'No need to explain further. I understand!' the queen laughed again. 'I use an old recipe from Aegyptus. It can be bought from our herbalist. He has told me that he grinds dates with acacia tree bark and honey and the liquid mixture is soaked in cotton wool. We insert a fresh cotton pad every night, and so far it has worked like a dream.'

I breathed a sigh of relief. 'I have to get this recipe to the princess before the king gets to her. I know this is not your usual line of work, but I am willing to give you ten gold pieces if you could buy some of these herbs for me, take them to the princess and tell her how to use them?'

'I need to visit the palace occasionally to accommodate the chief of the guards, so this task should fit in nicely. I will need to think of some excuse to see her, but leave that to me,' she said as she buttoned up her jacket.

'Please give this ring to the princess when you see her. She will then know that I have sent you,' I said. I dropped the ring and ten gold pieces into a small cloth bag and handed it to her.

* * * *

'What was she like?' Pirithios asked when I opened the door into our cabin.

'She's definitely not your type,' I said. I remembered the donkey. 'She's got class and likes an intelligent conversation.'

* * * *

The hot Aegean sun burnt relentlessly into the deck of our loaded Phoenician merchantman. The one hundred talents of aforinium were stowed in the hold and acted as ballast to keep us on an even keel. The sails of the five Hittite warships trailed off over the horizon as they patrolled for Sea People and pirates. The birds had left us now, so soon our escorts would head for home. The five Keftui captains played dice below decks and now and again I could hear their raucous laughter as someone's number came up. Our sails luffed as they struggled to catch Apeliotes. Oars splashed rhythmically into the calm sea as the slaves kept up a steady beat.

I stood aft with the steerage oarsman and gazed across the endless blue water.

Where was home? I asked myself. *It used to be Attica, then Pylos, then Athens. Now Keftui. Where did my allegiances lie? I didn't feel like a spy. Why was I sending secrets to Theseus? Am I going to help Minos make these new weapons when we get back? What will I do if Theseus wants me to sabotage their furnaces? I have the formulae and drawings saved on goatskin. Maybe I could give the king the wind funnel drawings but not tell him about the buckets of ash.*

I could feel the small ash sample in a coin bag bulging my pocket. Then there was Pirithios. *Would he keep his mouth shut if I asked him? If the Sea People attacked, I would fight with Keftui. If Theseus attacked Knossos, I would fight with ... I couldn't answer the question.*

Most importantly, there was Kitane. *Did Pudahepa get to her in time?* Oh, Aphrodite, what a twisted game you play.

The bow of the merchantman slid down the front of a wave and slammed into the bottom of a trough. It brought back lovely memories of the trip across.

'The Hittites have changed course.' Pirithios's voice jolted me from my daydream. 'We are on our own.'

'Pirithios,' I ventured. 'Do you remember what we saw that night at Amathous?'

'Which night was that?' he asked.

'Remember, the buckets of ash?' I said quietly.

'Yes, I recall you asked me to count the buckets.'

'Yes that's it. Can you forget what you saw?' I said.

He looked at me with a strange expression on his face. 'Forget what I saw?'

'Yes. As one Athenian to another. Forget that you ever saw it,' I repeated.

He looked at me, in a different light then. 'Callias, my friend, I've already forgotten. We've been together for a long time, but I still don't know you.'

'We'd best keep it that way,' I smiled.

CHAPTER VII

Island of Thira, Southern Aegean – 1197 BC

'Ships to starboard!' the lookout yelled.

They were still many stadia away from Thira when the captain of the new Keftui ship looked up and cupped his hands. 'How many?'

It took the lookout a while to count the dots coming from the north. 'At least ten!' he yelled back.

'Stand to!' the captain yelled at his small detachment of warriors. 'Ships on the horizon.'

The twelve warriors threw on their ribbed vests, grabbed their figure-of-eight shields and bronze swords and formed up on deck.

'Hoist the red flag,' the captain ordered.

The second warship, sailing in line astern, saw the lead ship's red flag under the sign of the dolphin and followed suit. The same procedure followed down the line until Minos's five new warships were on full alert.

The lookout peered into the haze and waited for the other ships to draw near. They were close enough now to make out some detail. Each ship had twenty rowers per side and they weren't slaves. Their sails were lowered but the rowers kept up a steady pace, heading straight for the fleet.

'They are Athenian ships, Captain – our allies. I can see the flag of the lion,' the lookout yelled.

'Very well. Everyone, stand down. Hoist the green flag,' the captain ordered.

The Athenians kept coming. The white foam from the oars splashed their decks as each ship pulled alongside each of Minos's new galleys.

The captain of Minos's fleet stood watching and wondering as the Greeks pulled alongside. Without warning, grappling hooks flew across from the Athenians and locked the ships together. Fully armed hoplites ran across the boarding planks.

The Keftui captain screamed, 'Ambush! Ambush!' It was too late.

'You traitorous dogs …' was all he got out, before a Mycenaean arrow caught him in the chest.

Minos's guards had just finished taking off their armour. They were cut to ribbons. The sea ran red as butchered Keftui warriors were thrown overboard. Some sailors dived into the ocean to escape, but the Greek archers used them for target practice. One hoplite missed his footing while jumping onto a deck and screamed as the two ships squashed his body to a pulp.

Theseus ran to the foredeck of the lead ship. 'The augurs were right,' he yelled.

'Athena was with us!' His troops cheered as he waved his dripping sword in the air. Throw those carpenters and sailmakers overboard. Poseidon can have them. I want no prisoners!'

The gagged and bound tradesmen made little splash as the Aegean swallowed them.

'Leave their slaves chained together. Throw a few overboard and they will drag the rest down,' he yelled.

'Now, throw that bag of Sea People headdresses in after them,' he yelled. 'Make sure they float so that a Thiran search party finds them.'

Theseus's hoplites cheered as they threw the feathered Peleset headdresses onto floating debris and timber.

'This will give Minos an excuse to attack the barbarians but it is our revenge for all those hostages of ours which he has taken,' the new king exclaimed. 'Now, let's sail these new warships home!'

Another loud cheer echoed across the sparkling blue waters.

* * * *

Minos was more than pleased with my efforts in Alasiya. One hundred talents of the precious ore were locked in a magazine room at Kato Zakro.

We walked around the old copper and bronze furnaces there and I explained that they were nowhere near hot enough to smelt the new ore. I stretched my goatskin drawings on a rock and pointed out how the Alasiyans created such hot fires. The palace at Kato Zakro was much closer to Alasiya, should we need more aforinium. Stiff breezes from the Aegean howled up the cliff faces there.

Gadeirus and Pirithios agreed that Kato Zakro would be better than Malia to build a test funnel. But the site was a long ride from Malia and in a place which we could not monitor on a daily basis.

Minos listened carefully to all our arguments and asked many questions about how the ore was smelted. We had a ready-made workforce in the village surrounding the palace and slaves could be brought in by sea from Iraklion and Phaistos. We could continue to make bronze armour from nearby copper mines at Chrysokamino and use the harder aforinium to make new weapons.

We walked down to the magazine room where the ore was stored and the guard unlocked the door.

'So this has cost me a daughter and five warships,' Minos said as he ran some of the red earth through his fingers.

'If it will win wars, Your Highness, it will have been a small price to pay,' Pirithios said.

'So, if we build new funnels, you can guarantee that the fires will burn blue?' he asked looking at me.

'I cannot guarantee the heat of the fires, but this is very similar to Amathous. Our timber is different but the strength of the wind will be the same,' I replied.

'All we need to do is produce the blue fires and we can make a weapon the same as that given to me by King Murappu,' Minos said, still looking at me. I forgot to mention the buckets of charcoal.

Pirithios opened his mouth to say something but I shook my head.

'Yes, Pirithios, you were about to say?' Minos asked.

'They have skilled swordsmiths at Salamis and Amathous. They are used to working with the new metal. Maybe we should ask the Hittite king to lend us a few of his men?' Pirithios replied.

I breathed a sigh of relief.

'Yes. I only hope that they don't cost me another daughter!' the king joked. The assembly chuckled at the king's rare attempt at humour. He looked thoughtfully at the pile of aforinium bags for a few moments and turned to his entourage.

'We are far behind the Alasiyans by now. They have known how to turn the new earth into hard weapons for many moons.

'We also hear that the wretched Sea People have stolen some of the new swords from King Murappu's men. We need to act quickly and construct a test funnel on a cliff face here and find out how hot we can entice the Keftui pine to burn. Callias and Pirithios will supervise the construction. I will send my chief alchemist from the workshops at Knossos to take charge of the test firing.

Gadeirus will sail back to Alasiya to ask the Hittite king for two of his technicians and to check on Kitane. More slaves will be shipped around from Iraklion to help with the work, and we will need more carpenters and masons to build huts and workshops.'

The king stopped to draw breath for a moment. A gaggle of excitement went round the officials. He held his hands up for silence.

'If we are to survive in this savage world around us, we need the latest ships and weapons and highly trained warriors. The Hittites now rule Persia, the Babylonians have overrun the Tigris and Euphrates, and the Achaeans have sacked Troia. We will need to keep an eye on all of them. Our old ally, Ramesses is under siege on all fronts. Hattusa, Alasiya and Ugarit have been attacked by the Sea Scum and they will not stop there. We need new ships and weapons to protect us all. I ask all of you to do whatever you can to help make this happen.'

A loud round of applause went up for the king, clapping and cheering. Gadeirus, Pirithios and I suffered much thumping on our backs with wishes of "well done" and "good luck".

I felt like a traitor, knowing full well that I would be passing the formula on to Theseus and the Athenians.

Pirithios took a sideways glance at me. Maybe we should tell the king about the ash. Or maybe not. We had at least several months until King Mutallu's swordsmiths arrived. I had no idea of the quality of the weapons which we would turn out without the ash.

Minos's batch of new slaves and his alchemists from Knossos set to work and after many moons of sweat and orders barked by the overseers, the new Zakro wind funnel was completed. The first firing was a disaster because Apeliotes was not with us. The flames at the top of the smelter would not change from orange to blue.

'Maybe we should sacrifice a maiden as Agamemnon did before sailing to Troia?' Pirithios suggested.

'That is a very poor idea, considering what our hostages have been through,' I growled.

'A goat then?'

'Find a fatted goat in the village, and we will see if the wind god is watching,' I said.

* * * *

Many moons went by and the huge funnel project lay idle as the wind gods ignored our sacrifices. Minos had sent a new weapons committee around from Malia to inspect our progress but we had to fob them off. The dejected committee boarded their small skiff for the return journey, dreading what the king would say. We had stockpiled large trunks of Keftui Cypress in drying heaps. These had to be dragged all the way from Mt Dicti and the Lassithi Plateau. We cut down hundreds of oak trees but I suspected that they would not burn very hot. Slaves dragged mules and carts to old villages, tearing down ancient timber buildings. This timber would not last long if Minos was going to smelt large quantities of ore. We made sure our timber stockpiles were tinder dry and tried burning different timbers we had collected from far and wide. We found that the pine trees burnt the hottest but used up the most fuel. One of the Knossos alchemists, who had been making bronze for many moons, suggested that we make a vent in the funnel to regulate the flow of air blasting the fires at the top of the cliff face. This proved to be a great success. At last, Apeliotes answered our sacrifices. A stiff wind blew across the ocean from Alasiya. Our long hair lashed our faces and gannets floated motionless above the rocky shore.

'Light the fires!' I yelled.

Four Iberian slaves touched their glowing firesticks to the kindling. Soon the dry Keftui pine was burning red and orange.

'Open the flue,' said an alchemist, pointing to a large lever.

After several anxious moments, one of the smelters started to burn blue tipped flames.

'Throw more timber in!' Prithios yelled.

The red dust in the clay crucibles turned to liquid and a grey, black scum formed on the top.

The other alchemist scraped off the scum, and there underneath was the rarest metal on earth – pure aforinium.

A thought crossed my mind. *How good was this going to be without the charcoal? We would soon find out.*

'We've done it,' I cried. 'We've done it!'

Pirithios hugged the alchemists. I pounded a foreman on the back. Even the Iberian slaves started to smile.

* * * *

We had embarked on a long journey and only Zeus knew where it would end. There was a lot of work to do yet; a lot of trial and error. I was beginning to feel more and more Minoan, torn between two worlds. I should get this information, plus the small bag of the secret ash from Alasiya to my brother. Pirithios had not mentioned it since the voyage home. I would have to decide one way or another before the Alasiyan swordsmiths arrived. They would soon know that there was something wrong.

* * * *

Minos padded up and down in front of us. All our tests had gone to plan and we were ready for the second firing. He had decided to sail from Knossos to inspect our progress but we had been fore-warned by one of the slave ships. I could see by his stern countenance, that he had other things on his mind. He wasn't wearing his feathered headdress or blue and white skirt; he had thrown on a white linen robe for the journey.

'Callias, did you tell anyone that five of our new galleys were going to Thira? You were in the records room when the shipwright came in, were you not?' He looked me straight in the eye.

He had caught me completely by surprise.

'Sorry, Your Highness. I don't understand what you are asking,' I lied.

'When you took the other galleys to Alasiya, DID YOU tell anybody about the other five ships?' he asked again.

'No. I had no idea where they were going. I thought you were going to use them to attack the Sea People!' I said indignantly.

'What about you?' he said pointing his goat leg at the captain.

'I only carried out your instructions to deliver five of the ships to Alasiya. I ... had no idea about the rest,' the captain stammered.

Pirithios stared at me. He was beginning to see the light.

'I'm sorry, Your Highness. If you would just explain the question,' I said quietly.

'We have lost five of our finest ships, plus all the crews. Ariadne waited for seven moons for them to arrive. The trip from Knossos takes two moons!' His anger escalated. 'There were no storms and the crews were all hand-picked by myself.'

'Poseidon has some strange ways,' I said.

'Don't bring your useless gods into this! Poseidon does not wear a feathered headdress,' he snarled at me.

'The Sea People,' Pirithios said straight away. 'The Peleset tribe wear feathered headdresses.'

'Then how did they know the exact time and date and which part of the mighty Aegean to strike?' the King answered angrily.

'I have found that they have lookouts and spies on many islands, Your Highness,' the captain said.

The king turned to the palace guard. 'I want those spies found urgently. They will make excellent sacrifices to the Snake Priestess now that the Minotaur is no longer with us. Put out our own spies. Find out who is betraying us. This can't be allowed to happen again,' the king raved on.

'Now show me this new fire.'

A column of smoke billowed up from our furnace. The choking smoke swirled over the small town and I held a wet rag to my mouth. One of the king's servants ran up to him with a wet scarf but he waved it away. Pirithios and I tagged along behind the royal party like a pair of lapdogs. The wind gods blessed us this day and soon the flames burned like the fires of Tartarus, only hotter. The fires danced below the new metal and the dancers wore blue headdresses.

'Did you know what he was talking about?' Pirithios mumbled through his wet scarf.

'I had no idea.' I couldn't look him in the eye.

'You are treading on dangerous waters, my friend,' he replied. 'Be careful that you don't become snake food.'

'Don't worry. They have nothing,' I murmured.

CHAPTER VIII

Malia Palace, Keftui – 1195 BC

The central courtyard was covered in shadows as the half-moon glided in and out behind the clouds. The shadows of the gods danced on the walls as the oil lamps flickered. The priests chanted the dirge handed down to them a millennia ago by the Great Bull rhyton. The hymn echoed through the palace walls and the king's servants and slaves sank to their knees and joined in the chorus.

The apothecary led the fatted calf through the rows of priests as they invoked the Snake Mother. The calf was resplendent in its murex coloured neck collar and silver halter. Each priest bowed to the calf as it was led past. The intensity of the hymn increased to a high, constant drone. The high priestess stood with razor sharp *Blood Seeker* in her right hand. It was fresh from tasting Minotaur blood. She raised her face to the Snake Goddess xaonon and the sword glinted in the firelight. Her apprentice held the sacred kantharos, waiting to receive the warm blood. The priestess wailed in her high pitched voice:

> *Sacred Mother*
> *Power of the Earth and Heavens*
> *Queen over mighty Zeus*

We pray that this offering will appease the restless souls shaking the Underworld
So that you may banish them to Erebus for Eternity

The apothecary placed a bowl of fresh oats on the raised platform and the calf bent its neck to nuzzle at the fresh grain. The high priestess poured some warm wine over the calf's head and it nodded its approval to be sacrificed. She plunged *Blood Seeker* into the calf's neck. Its front legs buckled and blood pumped from its throat. Its hind legs kicked wildly in its death throws. The hot blood ran along a stone drain into the kantharos. The chanting reached a crescendo as the high priestess poured the hot blood over the Earth Mother's clay feet.

The apothecary fell to his knees and looked up into her faience eyes. She stared out over the mortals. The shadows danced on her face but she did not blink. The snakes did not move.

The sacred butcher started to skin the calf and burn the entrails. The line of priests started to chatter amongst themselves, happy that the offering had appeased the Mother. The earth had stopped shaking. A cooked piece of meat from the calf would ensure that they were empowered. They sat around the fire happily chatting in low tones as the slaves handed out the roasted meat. King Minos and Pasiphae smiled at the high priestess and began shaking her hand.

The light played tricks as the celebrations went on. Minos stared at the snake in the Snake Mother's right hand. He thought he saw the snake's forked tongue dart in and out as the light from the cooking fire bounced off its head. *There, some of the scales moved as it tried to escape.* The goddess stared out over the feast. She was not impressed. She shook her right hand and the earth under the palace shook again. The chatting

109

stopped. A metal plate holding a piece of cooked meat clattered to the floor. A deathly silence fell over the ceremony.

'We ... have one final sacrifice that may appease her,' Minos whispered to the priestess.

* * * *

'Callias', Gadeirus said out loud. 'What are you doing?'

I was in the records room when I felt the shudder. The Minoan prince startled me. None of the other scribes were with me. I was bent over a soft tablet, trying to remember the signs for the formulae from Alasiya. Gadeirus had just returned from there, recruiting some experts to help with the new swords.

'Did you feel that?' I asked, ignoring his question.

'No,' he replied. 'Feel what?'

'The gods are shaking the earth once again,' I said, relieved that I had successfully changed the subject.

'I've been looking for you everywhere. I've arranged for two of King Mutallu's metalworkers to come over by the full moon and give us a hand with the new swords. It cost us a ship load of olive oil and an amphora of murex royal purple dye, but it will be well worth it.'

I did some quick calculations in my head and worked out that I had fifteen moons to tell Minos the truth about the black ash. *Would Mutallu tell his metalworkers not to divulge the information about the charcoal?* They would not want Minos to know.

'We have several ingots of aforinium ready to be forged,' I replied. 'Your sister? Any news of her?'

'Which one?' he replied.

'Kitane.'

'She has been put in charge of the king's concubines and has many slaves at her disposal,' he said. 'She has put on some weight.' My heart sank.

'She's not …?'

'She's not what?' he asked.

'You know, w … with child?' I was dreading the answer.

'You are acting strangely, Callias. I didn't ask her. If she has a child with King Mutallu, it will further cement our alliance with Alasiya. Why should it interest you?'

Slowly, Gadeirus began to see the light. He looked me straight in the eye. 'You are jealous! She is married to Mutallu; you have no claim over her.'

'No. But I didn't like the way Mutallu treated her like a sack of grain. I challenged him.'

'We are looking for a husband for Ariadne, though,' he replied. 'She is getting lonely at Akrotiri all by herself. You are a fine specimen. What do you say?'

That scheming shrew, I thought. 'No, Ariadne is not for me. She is too … feisty … and I fear I would not be able to tame her. She requires a strong hand. I'll ask my brother to pay her another visit,' I said.

'I don't think that would be wise,' Gadeirus said. 'He has kidnapped her once. Father detests him and Theseus has just been betrothed to Queen Helen of Boetia.'

'He didn't kidnap her.' I was getting sick of this accusation.

I was relieved that he hadn't asked about the tablet. Although it didn't matter if he saw my inscriptions anyway, he couldn't read them.

'I'll just finish up here,' I said as casually as possible. 'I'm indebted to you for the information on the swordsmiths.'

Gadeirus disappeared back up the passageway. I scratched the information about the blue fire and the ash on the tablet and dropped it into a small pithos jar for safe keeping. I made a small 'X' at the top so that the reader from Pylos would know where to start.

* * * *

After losing five warships at Thira, Minos had sent many spies to mingle with people in the shops and wharves of Iraklion. A sailor lolling against the post or a girl in the doorway pretending to be a prostitute, could be one of Minos's spies.

The sun dropped down behind Palaikastro and I pulled the cape over my head. I stopped every block or so to see if I was being followed. I had a large linen bag slung over my shoulder. I dropped it into the dirt a few times before filling it, to make it look like a working man's carry bag. As far as I knew, no-one suspected what I was doing on Keftui, but I needed to be careful as I continued toward the taverna.

'Nykteri please?' I asked the same serving girl.

After several minutes she returned and said out loud, 'we don't seem to have any nykteri, but if you would come this way, maybe you could choose something else'.

I stood up and followed her inside. My nerves were on edge. The taverna was alive with customers. I could tell by the raucous laughter that someone was telling a good story. A huge Nubian sat quietly in a darkened corner, drowning his sorrows. A group of Phoenicians – born traders and scoundrels – were using their fingers to tally up their latest shipment of something.

'What have you been doing?' a female voice said behind me.

'Passing the night away,' I replied.

Imira laughed once again. It was so good to hear her voice.

'You remembered!' she smiled.

'Imira, it's so good to see you. What news of my brother?' I asked.

'We were almost caught by his wife last full moon,' she laughed again.

Joining in her laughter, 'I see my brother has not changed his ways then.'

'No.'

'Imira, remember I told you about sailing to Alasiya in Minos' new ships? Did you pass that onto Theseus?

'Yes – just as you asked.'

'Do you know what Theseus did with that information about the Minoan ships?'

'Yes. He used it to capture them all,' she was starting to get serious.

'And killed everyone on board,' I said.

'I believe the Sea People got the blame,' she replied.

'That is what Minos told me. Theseus could have spared the sailmakers and carpenters,' I said.

'And what, have them tell the truth if they made it to Akrotiri?' she said.

'I see – that would be disastrous,' I said.

'Theseus is not happy with the way Minos has treated us since the Pan Athenic Games. He thinks his father was too soft. He has plans.'

'I was recruited by Aegeus to find out what had happened to the hostages and to make sure the Minoans were not going to attack us. I didn't suspect Theseus's motives when Father died,' I went on.

Imira was not laughing now. She was far more than a lady-in-waiting; she had some influence with Theseus, from all those nights spent in bed together.

'These filthy pagans have murdered our youth for many years. You have rescued some, but where are the rest?' she asked.

'I'm still trying to find out,' I said quietly.

'Whose side are you on?' she asked.

I could see her dark side now. I didn't know what to reply.

'I'm an Athenian, first and last, but the Minoans have grown on me. They have many more troubles than just Athens. I simply don't like to see unnecessary killing,' I replied.

'Why did you come to see me?' she asked.

I made a note to be more careful with her from now on.

'I have information about making the new swords. You remember the sword which we used to kill the Minotaur?' I said.

'Yes,' she replied.

'It was made of a special ore called aforinium which is mined on Alasiya.'

'Does the ore make a better sword?'

'Yes.'

'Do you know where to find the ore?'

'Yes. Minos sent me to Alasiya with Kitane to deliver the rest of the warships and bring back a load of the new ore. While we were on the island, Pirithios and I inspected their smelters. The Alasiyans have worked out how to smelt the metal at Amathous and I have made a drawing of a new type of furnace I saw over there. The Minoans have also built an experimental furnace at Kato Zakro. I have drawn both these furnaces on goatskin and marked in the dimensions,' I explained as I rolled out the skins.

'Then you would be able to make swords that are much stronger and sharper,' she exclaimed.

'I have also inscribed a tablet, written in our tongue, explaining the heat of the fire and the amount of black ash which the Alasiyans added to the ore,' I went on. 'Pirithios and I did not have time to check the ratios in the formulae, but I have a small bag of the ash here. Can you give that to Theseus and let me know what it is. We think it is only charcoal.'

'Did you give all this to the Minoans as well?' Imira asked.

'No,' I replied. 'They do not have the information about the ash.'

'It's getting too complicated for me,' Imira smiled again. 'Theseus will have to take all this to Pylos and let the alchemists and scribes work it out.'

'He will have to find a source of the new ore and start building a furnace as soon as possible,' I said.

'Why is that?' she asked.

'The Sea People have attacked Hattusa, Alasiya and Ugarit. Mycenaea and Athens could be next,' I said. 'As far as I know, they don't know how to make the new weapons – yet. But they have stolen some from Mutallu so it won't take them long to find out. Mutallu is using five of the new Minoan galleys to fight them off, the same type of ships which Theseus commandeered near Akrotiri.'

'You have much information, Callias,' she went on. 'Thank the gods you are with us.'

'One other thing Imira, Ariadne is now Princess of Thira. She is feeling very lonely.'

'Now that's one piece of information Theseus won't be getting,' she said. 'She can stay lonely.'

My wickedness paid off.

I looked around the noisy taverna to see if anyone was paying particular attention to us and then handed her the dirty linen bag. I sipped some sweet nykteri and memories of Attica came flooding back. Imira and the bag disappeared into the noisy night.

CHAPTER IX

Malia Palace, Keftui – 1195 BC

I sat next to the head of the palace guard when the Lukkan prisoner was brought in. Minos had doubled his counter spies since losing his five precious warships and ordinary Minoans were starting to look over their shoulder and whisper to each other. I wasn't too sure just who Minos feared: the Athenians and Mycenaeans; the Sea People; or all of them. He still had strong ties with Ramesses because he had just sent some of his finest artists to Karnak and Alexandria to decorate the pharaoh's temples. So Aegyptus was not to be feared. I had my parchment and quill ready to note down the important parts of the interrogation. I just hoped that there would not be too much screaming and blood.

'What were you doing hiding in our new sword room at Zakros?' the head of the palace guard asked.

'I … I was hiding from a large Nubian,' the prisoner squirmed.

'Why?' the torturer asked.

'He caught me kissing his wife,' the Lukkan said.

A murmur of laughter went around the court.

'A likely story, you sentina. What is your name and where are you from?' the torturer wasn't amused.

'I am Ibanus, from Lukka, near Hatti,' he said.

'What are you doing here?' the guard said as he twisted the prisoner's arm.

'I heard that Minos was looking for freed slaves to build the new smelter. I help to heat the ore.'

'So you knew where the new swords were kept,' the torturer went on.

'Yes, I knew,' the prisoner admitted.

'Bring him closer to the pit,' Minos instructed.

The prisoner looked down into a pit. The Snake Goddess looked up at him. The vipers jockeyed for positions around her bare breasts and outstretched arms.

'Hold him over the pit,' the torturer ordered. 'Now I'll ask you once again, and we want the truth this time.'

The Lukkan's face went white as he looked down. The snakes were silent. The room fell silent. Minos nodded and the guards moved to throw him in. He screamed. 'Stop! No! Not the serpents. Chief Lydus sent me!'

'Chief Lydus? Who is Chief Lydus?' Minos asked.

I scratched the symbols for "king" or "chief" on the parchment "*wa … na … ka*" but for "Lydus", I had to scratch the sounds for "*li … da*" and "*us*".

'He … he is the king of Lukka. He sent me to find out how to make the new weapons,' the prisoner sobbed.

'Will we let the serpents have him now?' one of the guards asked.

'No. Not yet. We need more information,' the torturer went on.

'Your chief, Where is he now?' Minos asked.

'He is with our starving people at Mira. A black cloud darkened our sky for a very long time. Our crops have died and our people have starved. We have eaten all our sheep and cattle and now have no animals to breed. Please spare me. My children are dead because their mother has no milk. Our corn has withered and many of our wells are dry.'

'This dark cloud that you speak of, describe it to us,' Minos instructed.

The prisoner took a gulp of air and sobbed further. 'Many moons ago, a dark cloud came over our land from the north. The cloud blotted out the sun and it rained grey ash. We had nothing to eat so we had to kill ewes and cows for food. The gods have forsaken us. '

I felt sorry for the prisoner. Surely they wouldn't sacrifice him now.

'When the gods were young, it rained ash on Keftui and Thira also. But, we did not attack our neighbours,' Minos said. 'Did your Chief Lydus kill our sailors and steal five of our new ships?'

'No. No. No! Your Highness. We have not stolen any ships,' the prisoner pleaded.

The torturer sneered.

'Were you going to use this information about our new weapons to attack us?' Minos asked.

'No. No. No.' the prisoner pleaded. 'We need the weapons to conquer the Hittite scum who have mistreated us for eons.'

The guards pushed him forward. The Lukkan gasped as he caught sight of the snakes again.

'I don't know anything about your ships. We are not going to attack Keftui,' the prisoner screamed.

'We found many feathered headdresses floating in the water,' Minos went on.

'They are not ours. They belong to the Peleset.' The prisoner's feet were dangerously close to the pit now. 'I am a Lukkan from Lycia. I know nothing of headdresses or missing ships.' A stream of urine ran down his leg and made a pool on the edge of the pit.

'Pull him back,' Minos ordered. A look of disappointment spread over the guards' faces. 'I have a job for him.'

'I have decided to let you live, Lukkan,' Minos said. 'Should you try to leave Zakro or escape to Lycia, you will be immediately given to the serpents. You are to act as a spy for us amongst all of our furnace workers. If you hear of any acts of treason or see someone acting suspiciously, you are to report to the guard immediately. Is that clear?'

'Thank you, my lord,' the prisoner bowed to the king.

'If your Chief Lydus should contact you, you are to report to us. You will tell him that we are only making the same old bronze weapons at Kato Zakro. Do you understand?' the king continued. 'If we find that you have betrayed us, your wife will never have any milk again.'

I scratched his name, *"aye … ba … nas"* from *"li … ch … a"* and the name of his hometown *"mi … ra"*, on the papyrus and nodded to Minos. 'I have all that down.'

'Store that with the names of the other spies,' Minos said to me quietly. 'We will give him a few moons and then feed him to the snakes.'

'Release him,' Minos ordered. 'And give him a bucket to clean up that mess on the floor.'

* * * *

I dropped the scroll with the other papyrus in the archive room and counted the number of spies on Minos's list. They ran into the hundreds. Maybe it was time to make a decision. I didn't want to make it onto that list.

If Theseus pulled me out of Keftui, though, I would never see Kitane again. *And where was Alexandros?* I still hadn't discovered his whereabouts or the fate of the missing hostages. Just thirty more moons. With a bit of cunning, I should survive that long.

The files were lined up by palaces, Knossos, Malia, Palaikastro, Zakros and Phaistos. Several tablets were filed in the wrong place and I bent down to fix them up. I was just blowing out the last of the oil lamps when I noticed one yellow oil lamp flicker. There was no breeze in the magazine rooms. Suddenly, the flame went out and the room went pitch black. I heard a couple of tablets clink to the floor. I ran into the passage – it was still lit. My legs started to tremble. The whole palace began to shake. A bull's head rhyton crashed to the floor and several pithos jars overturned, spilling grain across the passage. The small amphora, where I had hidden some tablets, broke into many pieces. I didn't have time to pick them up. A distant rumble from Erebus growled up through the floor.

Their useless pagan Snake Mother. How many wasted animals had been sacrificed?

The walls down here were two cubits thick; they had been rebuilt many times. The top storey had only been added just before Minos had been made king. Some of the new walls collapsed above me. A couple of bronze workers ran past and yelled to get out. Several Hittite slaves from the kitchens dropped their saucepans.

I headed for the grand staircase, trying to find my room in the half-light. A few musicians coughed past me going in the opposite direction.

'Don't go up there, it's caving in!' one of them yelled.

I ignored his instructions and held my scarf over my nose.

My tablets. I had hidden a few in the hole in the wall in my room. I had to find them. I kicked my shin on a large block and limped to the door. I frantically scratched through millennia of rubble but it was fruitless.

'Get out of there!' someone yelled.

I grabbed my goatskin bag and limped toward the relative safety of the central court. I could just make out the Snake Goddess sanctuary through the haze. Some of her priests and priestesses were dusting themselves down. A high priestess lay motionless on the paved courtyard. It looked as if she had been struck by a falling block. One side of the sanctuary was caved in and I could see the sacrificial altar. The white body of a naked teenage youth was trussed on top. His heels were pulled back behind his legs and his arms were tied behind his back. A blood streaked xiphos had been dropped near the victim's throat. A track of congealed blood ran down into the sacrificial bowl.

I stumbled through the haze to get a closer look. Peering through the dried blood on the sword was the strange boar's snout engraving – the same weapon which we had used to kill the Minotaur. The one I couldn't find in the labyrinth. Now I knew why they wanted it back – it had a special use – sacrifices to the Snake Mother. A priestess must have engraved those ancient symbols into the hilt.

The victim's head fell back, almost severed from the torso. His mouth fell open. His eyes gazed into eternity. It was Alexandros.

I forgot about the pain in my leg. I forgot about the choking dust and the falling mortar. I grabbed the xiphos and slashed it across the throat of the nearest priestess. Her blood spurted down onto her bare breasts as she sank to her knees.

'Go to the crows you heathen skyla. You sacrificed that defenceless boy for what?' I screamed. 'The earth still shakes!'

I sunk the xiphos into the back of an apothecary and he reeled forward onto the floor. 'Alexandros is safe with the tribal mothers, is he?' I yelled, looking for another victim. The other priests scattered. I chopped the blade into the neck of another priest and his head dropped sideways onto his shoulder, as he went down. A couple of the palace guards drew their swords and started to run towards me in the panic. Their peacock feathers cut through the dust and smoke.

Another wall collapsed and sent up a huge cloud. I hung onto the xiphos and used the cloud for camouflage. I didn't want to battle the whole palace guard. My fate had been decided. I needed Hermes now.

I glanced back. The top floor of the palace was alight. The town beside the palace was burning. The shaking went on as I ran through the night toward Iraklion.

I stopped and listened. No-one followed. Hermes was with me.

I don't remember running to Iraklion.

Please, Imira. Be home. The window rattled as I carefully knocked on the timber shutters.

'We are closed,' a female voice echoed from inside.

'I need nykteri badly,' I said quietly.

'Just a moment,' the voice said.

A moment later a shutter opened and a pair of eyes I knew very well, peered through.

'What have you been doing?' Imira asked.

'Imira, open up quickly. I haven't got time for games,' I said urgently.

'Come around the back,' she said.

'There's been a bad quake at Malia. The palace is in ruins and the town is alight,' I gasped.

'Why aren't you ...?' she asked.

I cut her off mid-sentence.

'Imira, I'm in trouble. I've killed a few of their priests.'

'You what?' she replied.

'I discovered what they were doing with our hostages,' I said. 'I became very angry.'

'What were they ...?'

'They sacrificed Alexandros to their Snake Mother,' I gasped. 'I found him with his throat cut.'

'Why would they …?'

'To stop the earth shaking!' I almost cried.

'It obviously didn't work,' Imira said.

'Of course not!' I said. 'It wasn't the Minotaur that was killing our hostages. It was their Snake Mother.'

'Theseus has plans for these pagans. We best get you home.'

'After tonight, I am serpent food here,' I said. 'Do we have a ship in the harbour?'

'Minos's spies will be all over Iraklion wharves after what you have done,' she said. 'I will have to get you to Agia Triada. We have several traders down there.'

I could see why Theseus had chosen her. There weren't too many like Imira left in this world.

'I haven't been to Athens yet, after your last visit,' she said. She went off to find my dirty linen bag.

'That's good. Put this cursed xiphos with the other things and I will take them with me,' I said as I calmed down.

Blood Seeker smiled as he was shoved in amongst the goatskins. The Minotaur and the Athenian youth had been good for his habit. It wouldn't be long before his thirst was quenched again

* * * *

Imira packed me into the roughest wooden cart on Keftui and I squirmed under the animal skins and rolls of woollen cloth which the sailing ships needed at Agia Triada and Piraeus. My skin started to itch uncontrollably but every time the driver saw a movement from his load he thumped his horse whip down on top of me. I bounced around on the hard wooden floor as the journey seemed to take an eternity. The roads were chaos with victims, carrying their meagre possessions, were trying to escape the shaking earth and fires at Knossos and Malia. We weren't stopped by Minos's palace guards as obviously they had more important duties than searching for a rogue Athenian prince.

After many stadia of pain and itching, we arrived at the busy port of Agia Triada on the opposite side of the island. The cart driver told me that I was worth a double headed golden axe to anyone who turned me in. I said a silent prayer to Demeter. A couple of sun-wrinkled, Athenian sailors rolled me up in a bundle of woollen cloth, bound for Piraeus, and dumped me in the hold of their merchantman.

EPOCH III

Achaeans

*Relating to **Achae** in Ancient Greece, especially in Homeric contexts. The **Achaeans** were amongst the earliest Greek-speaking inhabitants of Greece, well before 12th century BCE. May be identified with Mycenaeans of the 14th–13th centuries BCE.*

Elizabeth Knowles, **The Oxford Dictionary of Phrase and Fable.** Oxford University Press, 2006.

Chapter X

Pylos Palace, Messenia, Peloponnese – 1195 BC

The old master, who had taught me many years before, was bent over a wet tablet, making inscriptions with his inscribing tool. The novices were trying to follow the lesson but I could tell by their baffled looks that they weren't taking it in.

I had shown the Myceneaen scribes what I had learnt in the archive rooms at Malia but we had modified the old Minoan tongue to suit our modern tongue. The novices would need to be able to read both languages so that they could read both the old Minoan signs and the new Mycenaean signs when the need arose. My brother organised a reception committee on the wharf at Piraeus, when he knew I was on my way home.

Imira had set sail for Athens the day after I had murdered the priests. Minos's armed guard had stopped the ship but found nothing. Imira had warned Theseus that I should be on my way home – before the full moon – if I escaped Minos's guards, but I had a price on my head. Demeter had been kind to me since I left Iraklion.

Theseus and I had done a lot of catching up since then, but our carefree days were long gone. The welcome home reception was well under way and I had the thankless task of addressing the mothers and fathers of our missing hostages. The sad news, that they were sacrificed to the pagan Snake Mother and that they would never be coming home was enough to cause severe pain amongst them.

Many mothers clawed at their faces until their fingernail tracks dripped with blood. Some fathers burst into fits of rage and wanted revenge.

The lost hostages were now declared heroes of Athens and their names were to be inscribed on a large bronze plaque. A tomb in their memory would be built on the outskirts of Athens and Theseus was preparing a public inscription for the plaque.

My description of the hostages' sad fate and the gruesome details of the people who had died at the hands of the Minotaur further enraged the citizens. I spelt out the urgency of attacking Keftui while Minos was crippled with earthquakes and most of his navy was away fighting the Sea Scum at Alasiya. The shipwrights at Piraeus were working by lamp light to modify Theseus's galleys to the same standard as the captured Keftui fleet.

True to his word from pre-spy days, Theseus announced at the feast that I was to be elevated to co-regent with him and that all decisions would be jointly made. A loud cheer went up from the guests.

The decision about invading Keftui had been made while I was away. The news about the fate of Alexandros and some of the other hostages made the decision more resolute.

'Do you want to be scribes? I said to the novices. We need you to decipher Keftui tablets and to keep records for our king. If you would rather wield a sword than a scribe's tool, now is the time to speak up.'

One of the students decided that he had had enough.

'I didn't know it was going to be this difficult. There are so many different marks, different symbols for different sounds, I don't think I can continue.'

'You can go back to your unit and I'm sure you'll make a fine warrior.'

'Thank you, Prince,' he said. He heaved a sigh of relief and walked out of the room.

Was there something other than killing that we could teach these young men?

I had tried.

'Anyone else?' I asked.

My old teacher broke in. 'No. I don't think there's anyone else. The rest want to learn but maybe my teaching is not what it used to be. Maybe you could also teach some of the class? You lived at Malia for quite some time.'

'Mmm … if you give me a class of the slowest learners, I will see what I can do.'

I looked at several tablets still on the drying racks. Quite a few mentioned some strange people called "Danaoi" who were sighted by our lookouts. They were spotted sailing down the west coast of Messenia towards Kythera. *Now where were they headed?* I made another note to ask one of the lookouts if the Danaoi were wearing any special head wear.

The Lukkan spy, who nearly ended his days in the snake pit, had said something about invading Hattusa and Ugarit. He knew of some people called the Peleset who I had never heard of.

Theseus also knew of the Peleset as he had used their strange headdresses as a decoy. And now, our coast-watchers had spotted some people called Danaoi. I wondered whether they could be somehow related. I needed a novice to keep tally of all this.

* * * *

'I am not having that woman live under the same roof!' Queen Helen of Boeotia yelled at Theseus. Half the palace could hear the row going on in the royal suite.

'She is not living under the same roof as you!' Theseus replied.

'When she returns from Iraklion, she is not to live under this roof,' the queen ranted. 'Why didn't you marry your lady-in-waiting?'

'She means nothing to me, Helen. You and I can make Athens great again. Imira is essential to us in Iraklion,' the king said.

The kitchen slaves were listening. The musicians were listening. The palace guard had stopped pacing up and down. I stopped dictating messages to my scribe.

That was a slip of the tongue, the remark about Imira and Iraklion.

'I'll make a deal with you, Helen. I will go down to her now and ask her to stay with her mother at Koele, when she is here. I will promise not to see her again, if you will promise not to see that Etruscan prince when I am not here!' Theseus said loudly.

'How on earth …? He is nothing to me.' She turned her face away so the guilt would not show.

The palace staff looked at each other with glee. My scribe grinned. 'This is better than watching the Immortals!' he smiled.

'I know about your prince, and that he is alone in your room with you when I am away. It is enough to set all the tongues in Athens wagging,' Theseus went on.

My scribe started to say something but thought better of it.

The queen burst into tears and all we could hear were her loud sobs. Even the musicians had stopped playing. A lone crow's warning call set the atmosphere.

'Do you AGREE?' Theseus yelled.

This would be a big wrench for both of them – Theseus to give up Imira and the queen to give up her lover.

My novice nodded his head, anticipating her answer. We couldn't see the queen's reply, of course, but we heard a door slam and Theseus came storming out.

The noise of slaves and staff going about their duties abruptly started again. The calming notes of the musicians came wafting through the air, again. We heard a succession of doors slamming as Theseus made his way to Imira's room.

I wanted to talk to Theseus about our planned invasion. Now would not be a good time.

'Make a note about those Messenian lookouts, and find out when I am required for classes,' I said to the scribe.

'Why don't we follow Theseus down to Imira's room?' he suggested, teasingly.

'Just get on with your work and forget what you just heard,' I growled.

* * * *

The festival of cold Poseidon was long gone and the warm hues of Anthesteria had taken over the land. The Pithoigia had begun with great hilarity. Masters became slaves and slaves became masters for a day. Many jars of wine were drunk.

During Choes, the wine was blessed and some serious drinking competitions started. Many a lord and master were drunk under the table by a slave. I had been caught by all this foolishness before.

I gave way to some superstition and chewed on some bitter buckthorn leaves to ward off Keres, the ancestral spirits. I gazed out of my private chambers at a flock of shrikes resting before their long journey to Mitiline. Some wood warblers hopped here and there with uninhibited dexterity as they tended to their offspring. We still had trees around us, unlike the birdless furnace towns I had been to. The metal workers no longer heard the joy of a yellow wagtail in the mornings. I remembered that day in the hut with Pirithios, when I opened my eyes, my scarf was dead still and the grey smoke hung in the air like a vast unwanted smell. The price of progress was a heavy cost to pay.

Some young maidens, who had fallen victim to the pleasures of Dionysis, squealed as they were pushed through the air on their swings. They tried to sing the song of Erigone and laughed and shrieked at each other as they struggled to remember the words. The flock of shrikes took fright and darted back and forth in a cloud, before they settled again. The girls squealed some more as the boys pushed them higher and higher and Minos seemed a world away.

Theseus was determined to seek revenge against the Minoans. This was the calm before the storm and some of those happy maidens may not have a father after the new moon.

* * * *

I could see Theseus walking quickly towards the agora to join a group of Festival of the Vine revellers. He would stay sober long enough to present the garlands to the winners of the drinking competitions and then probably drown his sorrows with the losers. It would be a few moons before they all came to their senses. So I decided to round up the slow learners tomorrow; that is, those who were sober.

Some non-drinkers took advantage of the festivities to mend the thatch on their rooves, while others replaced fallen mortar between the rocks on their huts. The paved roadway from Piraeus to Athens was in a mess and the chief mason had requisitioned one hundred Theban slaves to make repairs.

The shipbuilders had also caught the Dionysian disease. Many of them had entered the wine drinking competitions so the shipbuilding had also stopped. If one of our deadly enemies planned to invade us, now would be the time to strike. They would be met with jars full of wine, senseless hoplites and singing maidens being swung through the trees.

A fat calf bellowed for its mother as it was led toward the altar for the evening's sacrifice. The Basellinna danced her way toward the boukolion for her ritual marriage to the God of Wine after sundown. Her fourteen maidens joined in the revelry. Everyone knew that the groom was actually her archon husband wearing a bronze mask and dressed as Dionysis.

I could just make out Theseus waving to her as she danced towards the agora. She spotted him in the crowd, reached into her basket and threw him a bunch of grapes. *Oh no*, I thought, *not her as well*. The komos carried on all night but Hypnos caught up with me as I sunk into my woollen mattress.

Several moons later, I managed to assemble my brother and the tribal chiefs into the main hut at the agora. Some of them looked the worse for wear but, on the whole, they had recovered enough to vote on any important decisions.

Some Phoenician merchants outside were haggling over the price of bronze pots and the guards told them to move away if they wanted to continue the argument. Six or seven hoplites patrolled around the large stone walls to make sure that nothing discussed inside could be heard on the outside.

The ten tribal elders of Athens, Attica, Boeotia, Messenia, Myceneae and Sparta were all trying to talk over each other when Theseus held up his hands for silence.

'Kalimera, my friends. I hope that you all have enjoyed the hospitality of Dionysis and have recovered sufficiently to think clearly. We have welcomed Anthesteria this spring and the augurs have foretold a plentiful Hekatombaion. We now have my brother, Prince Callias, back with us from Keftui.

As you will know by now, Callias risked his life for us all. For many moons, he has been assisting King Minos in the records rooms at Knossos and Malia. He has found out a lot of important information about the Minoans. During an earthquake in the month of Poseideon, he found our much-loved, Alexandros, sacrificed at the altar of their pagan Snake Goddess. We have all suffered at the hands of Minos over the past years. Many of us have sons and daughters who have not returned. Thanks to Callias, we now know their fate.'

The chiefs grunted in agreement.

'Since the drunken Androgeus drowned himself at our Panathenic Games, the Minoans have dictated our lives. We have already decided that this state of affairs cannot continue any longer. Now that we know the fate of our missing youths, we must teach them a lesson. Their palaces are in ruins and Callias tells me that most of Minos's navy is away at Alasiya fighting the Sea Scum. One of Minos's daughters is married to King Mutallu, so he has an obligation to help the Hittite king. Now is the time to strike,' Theseus continued.

'Also, thanks to Callias, we have five brand new Minoan galleys in our fleet. The other twenty ships are almost ready and we have made about one hundred new xiphos. The swords are made from a new metal called "aforinium" which is meant to be sharper and lighter than anything else we have. I have my doubts. Do not throw your old faithful weapons away just yet. These new xiphos are only an experimental batch from Pylos and not everyone will be issued with one. The Minoans report that the Sea Scum stole many of these swords from Alasiya during their last attack, but we don't know whether they have the knowledge to make them, just yet. The Minoans are also making them, but they do not have the correct formulae, so their weapons will be faulty. It is essential that we are the first to equip our hoplites with the new xiphos as the metal to make our faithful bronze swords is running out fast.'

'I can't wait to try one on the priests who murdered Alexandros!' one of the Athenians yelled.

A "here here" rose ominously from the gathering.

'You may have the opportunity sooner than you think, my friend,' Theseus smiled. 'I propose that we attack Iraklion while Minos is away battling the Sea Scum. We kill any of his army left behind and take the women and children as slaves. They will have a treasury hidden somewhere in one of the palaces and if we find it, the spoils will be divided equally among us.' A loud cheer went up from the elders. 'We can also use Keftui as a base to stop the Sea Scum from attacking our homeland.' A further round of clapping went around the room.

'Callias has a different plan, a plan that may save lives. But I say that the wretched pagans have it coming to them. It is time to take revenge. Before we decide, I want you to listen to what Callias has to say.'

I held up my hands for some quiet and waited until the muttering had stopped. Much to my surprise, my hands weren't sweating and my knees were solid as a rock. My time in Keftui had hardened my nerves.

'I am pleased to be with you once again. I recognise some older faces from my own village in Attica. Theseus and I have sailed many stormy seas together,' I smiled over at my half- brother.

'I have lived with the pagans for a long time and they aren't all bad. I became friends with Minos's son and daugh-ters and they are normal people like you and me. Minos can be very difficult at times, but he loves his family. The Keftuins have many other troubles and their palaces vie with each other to rule over their own lands. Ramesses is Minos's one true ally and that is one foe we won't be challenging.

'The Minoans have become so complacent after ruling the Aegean for so long, their palaces are not fortified. They will be easy game. Their greatest downfall is their wretched gods, the Bull Rhyton and the Snake Mother, which demand human blood. Now that the Minotaur is dead and we do not have to send fourteen of our youths to Minos every seven sun years, they will have to start sacrificing their own youths.'

'What is your plan?' demanded one of the chiefs.

'I am getting to that, if you will bear with me for a moment. After so many years, we have a lot in common with the Minoans. They have settlements all around us.

'They will be easy prey at the moment. So do we need to kill everyone and take many slaves, as we have done in the past? I say we take them into our empire and make valuable allies of them.'

I ploughed on. 'I propose to take a delegation to them under a white flag.'

A murmur of restlessness went around the hut. Old, weather beaten faces turned to each other and nodded. The young warriors shook their heads. I could read the mood. They wanted revenge. They wanted their day of reckoning. I held my hands up for quiet again.

'Hear me out. Hear me out.'

'What exactly will this delegation say?' a voice yelled out.

'In exchange for sparing their lands and their people, we take control of their empire. Their royal family will answer to us and we take command of the palaces and headquarters. They will be made to offer up their treasury, some of which can be shared among us, but we will need gold to run this empire.

'In addition, we will not enslave their people but they must send fourteen hostages to Athens. This will ensure that they keep to the agreement,' I explained. 'This could save years of bloodshed, it could save many of our young warriors from the depths of Erebus and, as my brother has said, the alliance would make a solid wall against the Sea Scum.' Then I sat down.

A loud buzz went around the hut. I watched with interest the reactions from the elders. The older chiefs nodded in agreement with each other but the Spartans wanted blood.

Theseus rose again and stood waiting for quiet. 'Well, what do you think?' he asked.

One of the young lions said from the back of the hut, 'If they don't agree to your proposals, Callias, and they call on Ramesses for help, we are doomed.'

'Ramesses is a great distance away and the Aegyptus have enough problems of their own. If we act quickly, they won't be able to come to Minos's aid; it is a chance that we will have to take, though. We will have to block the Keftui ports and make sure that no ships escape to the Great River.'

'What about our youths who have been sacrificed?' another yelled out. 'We want to even the score!'

'I propose that we leave it be. If we are to be allies, their hostages will be enough,' I said.

A few of the young lions did not agree.

Theseus held his hands high once again. 'This could go on until the sun sets,' he said.

'Callias's proposal does have some merit, especially to counter the threat of the Sea People. But we will not have the opportunity to teach the pagans a lesson.

'This is what I propose: We continue to prepare for war. We arm some of our hoplites with the new weapons and we bypass all of Minos's small settlements near us. We sail for

Keftui on the new moon and wait far enough off their beaches so that they can see our armada. We send Callias and two chiefs ashore to talk to their leader.

'If they agree to an alliance, our ships will sail into Iraklion and take control of the palaces. Some ships will remain off-shore, in case there is any resistance. If they do not agree with our proposals, we invade the island as planned.'

'What about the hostages?' a young Spartan yelled out.

'They will give up fourteen hostages to be brought back here. They will be sacrificed to Zeus as a reprisal,' Theseus said. A loud cheer went up at this suggestion.

'I say we teach the heathens a lesson that they won't forget,' one of the young chiefs cried out. 'Callias is being too soft!'

'Those in favour of sending the delegation ashore first, show your hands,' Theseus asked.

Five hands slowly went up.

Theseus looked across at me. 'Well, are you in favour of your own proposal?'

'Of course, yes!'

'Well put your hand up.'

I quickly raised my right hand.

Theseus, after considerable thought, also slowly raised his hand.

'That's it then,' I smiled. 'Five chiefs in favour of sending the white flag first, plus the two of us. That makes it seven to five. The "ayes" have it.'

The mood of the meeting seemed to be in favour, but the Spartans shook their heads in disagreement. 'If one Snake Priest even blinks at me, I'll have his head,' I heard one of them say. I knew the feeling.

I stood up waiting for silence again.

'I have a presentation for my brother. He is a great warrior. He leads from the front and is fearless in battle. The blood of

Zeus flows through his veins and he probably has fathered more offspring than Zeus!'

A loud cheer went up. I continued.

'I present Theseus with this xiphos. It is the exact sword which he used to kill the Minotaur. I rescued it from the pagan's temple on the night of the earthquake. It hasn't been tested in battle yet, but I'm sure he will soon rectify that.'

Blood Seeker smiled from inside his goat skin bag. The fox's ears twitched as he heard what was being said. *Not long now*, he thought to himself.

I slowly drew the magnificent weapon from the bag which I had carried all the way from Imira's taverna on that fateful night. I grabbed the tip of the blade and presented it to him, handle first. He grasped the hilt and swung the sword about in the air, just as he had done at the labyrinth.

'I am ready for another Minotaur,' he laughed.

The tribal chiefs all rose to their feet, clapped and chanted 'Theseus, Theseus'.

He shook my hand. 'Without you, brother, I would be with the gods.'

* * * *

We were walking back to the palace when one of the young lions caught up with me. 'Hi, Callias. My name is Idas of Sparta. My young brother was one of the hostages you rescued.'

I pulled my toga up over my shoulder. 'I'm glad that he was delivered in one piece,' I replied. 'Now what can I do for you?'

'I didn't vote for your proposal. I was the one who said that you were being too soft,' he said. 'Nonetheless, we will help you with your plan. We volunteer to sacrifice the fourteen Keftui hostages to Zeus at the next games.'

'That is if they hand them over,' I replied.

The thought of slitting the throats of youths from Knossos and Malia didn't appeal to me.

'I listened carefully to your proposal, Callias. I would like to know more about the new weapons. What makes ours better than anything the Minoans have?'

'They contain a vital ingredient. I brought a sample back from Alasiya. Our alchemist told me that it is powdered charcoal,' I said.

'Charcoal?'

'Yes. Charcoal. We spotted the Alasiyans adding charcoal to their molten ore. They were trying to keep that information from us,' I said.

'Surely, charcoal would ruin the ore,' the Spartan said.

'Then why were the Alisayans adding it to their mix?' I didn't expect an answer.

He kept pace with me as we walked along the cobbled street towards my records room. In the distance, some piglets, marked for the sacrifice of the Lesser Mysteries, squealed as they fought over an old pumpkin. A small, slave boy kicked a roll of wool between our legs.

'How do you know it is a vital ingredient?' he went on.

I explained further. 'Idas, it is only early days yet. I have given the alchemist details of what Pirithios and I saw, plus a sample, which I stole that night. The metal workers are experimenting with it. They have made a couple of mixtures with differing amounts of charcoal added. I know that some swords made from the new metal are so soft that they bend in battle; they are worse than bronze. We are trying to find the reasons why.'

'This is interesting. We have our own bronze smelter at Sparta. I know the tin mine near Troia is almost exhausted so we need this new metal badly. We have melted down a lot of old bronze pots to replace our boar's tusk helmets with bronze helmets. The one hundred new xiphos that Theseus spoke of, are they much better than bronze?'

'Why don't you meet me at Nestor's Palace the sunrise after tomorrow and we will see what the alchemist has found?'

We reached the front door of my records room. I could see my learner scribes waiting.

'See you at Pylos then,' he said, as I went inside.

* * * *

I left Theseus and the fleet commander to attend to the details of preparing the armada. Now that the Dionysian madness was over, we might get some work done.

The shipbuilders and sailmakers had gone back to Piraeus and they only had fifteen moons to finish the alterations to our galleys. My scribe made a list of provisions which we would need to take to Keftui, and he gave it to the quartermaster to organise.

I left the warriors to Theseus while the other prince from Sparta stayed behind to arm them. We had no idea who was running the Minoan empire while their fleet was away. If Pirithios was still alive, he would be a great source of information. We had to be prepared for some of the palaces to put up a fight, especially if they hadn't been damaged by the earthquake. Imira had told Theseus that Iraklion was still functioning as a port but Amnisos, Malia and Knossos were in ruins.

She didn't know about Kato Zakro, where we had built the first wind funnel. She couldn't give us any information about Phaistos and Agia Triada either. I knew that if we occupied Malia and Knossos, the rest of the island would be ours, as it was governed by these two palaces.

I would like to get into the archives, if any had survived. The tablets stored there would yield all sorts of information.

This is where my class of scribes would prove useful. If I could get Gadeirus or Pasiphae to see some sense, I could save a lot of lives.

Minos would be another matter. He would not give one cubit. I'd have to deal with him when the time came.

The early morning sun brought the yellow wagtails back to life as I waited for Idas. The olive harvest was over but farm workers and slaves chipped weeds amongst the trees and cleared new fields for planting. I hadn't had time to show my brother the sketch of the large soil machine from Alasiya. Maybe when this was all over, we could build one at Pylos.

We seemed to be constantly at war. But still, armies needed to be fed. We needed to sort out this vital ingredient before we sailed. We may not be back for a long time and we may need many thousands of weapons.

* * * *

We heard the clatter of the horse's hooves on the paving stones before we saw the Spartan. The alchemist and I were discussing the xiphos I had given to Theseus. It had not been used in battle, only to slaughter innocent youths and kill a Minotaur. *Would it bend or break if struck by a bronze weapon?*

'Kalimera, Idas,' I said as the Prince dismounted. 'This is Prince Idas of Sparta,' I introduced him to the alchemist and my novice.

'You have produced some fine bronze swords from your furnaces at Sparta,' the alchemist said to him.

'Yes. Thank you. I don't know for how much longer,' the young man replied.

'We are having trouble with the supply of tin. I have heard the Iberians are sailing all the way to the island of Albion, the Land of the Saracen Circle, to find tin,' our alchemist replied.

'We will also need to sail there soon, if we can't find another tin mine,' the Spartan went on.

Fortunately, Apeliotes was blowing strong across the sea from Italia, and the new furnace was running hot. The Pylos workers were still trying different mixtures, using the records from Alasiya which I had given them.

'Why don't we have a look at our aforinium smelter before the wind dies down, and Prince Idas can see for himself, just how we are making the new swords.'

We walked over to the roaring flames. One of the clay crucibles was red hot and the ore inside was not quite molten, but had a consistency of thick glue. A dark scum was forming on the top and one of the workers scraped the black scum on to a pile on the ground. When the ore was almost liquid, another worker gradually added a bucketful of ash. The sparks leapt high into the air leaving small smoke trails behind them.

'What is he doing?' the Spartan yelled above the roar.

'That is powdered charcoal. It is partly burnt pine,' the alchemist yelled.

'What does it do?' the Spartan yelled.

'It makes the metal very hard. Stops it from bending, we think.'

'How much do you add?' the young prince asked.

'That is the question that we would all like answered!' the alchemist said loudly. 'We are still working on it.'

'What happens to the thick ore after you have mixed the charcoal with it?' the young prince asked.

'We let it cool in long bars, ready for the swordsmiths to reheat and hammer into swords. This can be done anywhere as long as you have a forge. We have a few swordsmiths here, but we have set up most of them at Tiryns, where they are close to our warriors at Mycenaea. You will also need trained polishers to finish the weapons and add the handles. The swordsmiths follow a few different designs depending on what Theseus has ordered.

'Our latest designs have a horned handle to deflect the enemy's blade away from your hand,' the alchemist explained. 'Follow me over to the swordsmiths' hut and I can show you a xiphos being made, similar to the one Callias gave to Theseus.'

The loud hammering sounds that I knew so well from Alasiya, echoed across to us, as we approached the workshops. Two swordsmiths worked over a forge of hot coals. Now and then they pumped some large bellows. Blue tipped flames sprung from the super-hot coals. The craftsmen pushed long pieces of dull grey metal into the inferno. After a short while, the grey aforinium turned red, and one man pulled the rough blade out of the forge and started hammering the metal into the shape of a xiphos. *This is far slower than making bronze swords,* I thought. We only had to pour the bronze into a mould.

The tradesmen wore sweat-soaked, blackened shirts. I held my hand up for one of them to stop belting the metal. He shoved the piece of metal back into the coals and looked up at me, sweat dripping from the point of his nose. 'Yes, Lord.'

'How long does it take to make a sword in the rough?' I asked.

'It depends on the design, whether the king wants ridges up the centre or a horned handle. Possibly one to two days per sword. And then, of course, they need to be sanded and polished,' the master replied. 'You will have to call at Tiryns to see that.'

The Spartan prince turned to the grizzled face of the alchemist. 'I am most impressed with what you have shown us today, but I am still wondering about the bucket of ash. How many buckets did you add to the molten ore?'

'Callias and Pirithios thought that the Alasiyans added charcoal at the rate of about one-to-one hundred, or two-to-one hundred. They were not sure because they did not see the beginning or the end of the mix. So we have used three mixtures in the swords which you will have at Keftui. The finished swords all look the same.

'The swords with no stamp on the hilt have no charcoal; the swords with a one mark stamped on them have one-bucket-per-hundred of ore; and the swords with two marks stamped on them have two-buckets-per-hundred.

'Watch this,' he said.

He had a large melon set on top of one of the many thousands of blackened stumps.

'This is one of our prototypes,' he said as he pulled a gleaming weapon from under a bench. He swung a wild blow as if to separate a head from a neck. The blade effortlessly sliced through skin and flesh and the top half of the melon landed at my feet. Seeds spewed everywhere over our feet and sandals.

'What do you think, My Lord?'

'This is all very well, but a melon is not a Minoan's head!' I retorted, shaking my foot.

'Perhaps My Lord, you could help us test these weapons in battle?' he asked. 'Maybe the Spartans could help?'

'We would be happy to help, alchemist. As long as you don't give us any faulty swords,' Idas growled.

'How will we know, Prince? I think it best if you don't reveal what the marks mean, but take a record of which hoplite is issued with which sword,' the alchemist went on.

'My men would be happy to help, I'm sure. I am intrigued myself. Will I use a zero mark or a one or a two? We will soon have the opportunity to try them out,' I replied.

* * * *

'Well, you all know as much as I do, now,' the master finished up. 'Good luck with the attack, and I think it only fitting that Prince Idas takes this prototype with him into battle.' He handed the new weapon to Idas.

'What number does it have on it?' he asked.

'A lucky number Your Highness, number two, the sword master replied.

'We shall see,' the Spartan growled again. They were not known for their sense of humour.

We made our way back to Nestor's palace. The limestone walls shimmered in the midday sun as the heat waves split the air. The hammering echoed behind us and I realised why these tradesmen shouted at each other all the time. They must be all deaf.

CHAPTER XI

Knossos and Malia – 1185 BC

Aided by the power of Boreas, Theseus pointed our armada, made up of forty galleys, towards the land of our oppressors. It was reprisal time. We had dreamt of this moment for a generation and the warm water of the Aegean splashed across our bows as a beginning to the dream. Most of the ships were rowed by line after line of hoplites and warriors.

My merchantman was driven by slaves who we would need to run the palaces. I had also selected six of the brightest from my class to work in the archives.

The morale of the men was high. The sweat glistened off their tanned chests as the oars splashed back and forth. They had removed their cuirasses and new bronze helmets to man the oars. Their highly polished greaves caught the sunlight as their legs shifted with each pull.

The Spartan prince had armed the men with bronze lances and round metal shields emblazoned with their tribal emblems – a grizzly bear, a fox, a galloping horse, a gruesome face – anything to strike fear into the enemy. A scallop had been cut from the lower section to allow the men to run while carrying their shields.

The luckier section commanders were issued with the new Pylos swords but most were still equipped with the old bronze weapons. Each man had a small, hemp sack which could be hung from his lance while marching. This contained his essential rations, a goatskin water bottle and replacement spear points. The two ships from Messenia were loaded with specially trained archers who could rain death from above.

Our royal escorts, the dolphins, raced us across the Sea of Keftui, as if to warn the enemy. Boreas, god of the northern wind, was kind to us today. Our woollen sail billowed as it caught the wind. I looked around and saw two lines of oars pointing to Orion as the slaves took a rest.

My scribes huddled around a block of wet clay. I had set them a task; a problem to be solved before we reached Keftui. If we had forty warships, each manned with thirty hoplites and the hoplites ate a mina of food, and drank half-a-kab of wine per moon, how much food and wine would we need to stockpile at the palaces to last thirty moons? I would check the inscriptions and totals and they would need to be correct before they could step ashore. My novice had taken charge of the exercise but some of the advice he was handing out was not correct. The arguments over the numbers raged on, as the ocean rolled by.

As we sliced through the sea, I started wondering how fast we were going. The captain had told me, back at Zakros, about their crude method of measuring the speed of a ship; tying knots in a piece of rope, tying a log onto the end of the rope and throwing the log overboard. The navigator then had to count how fast the knots unravelled off the ship.

There had to be a better way.

'Your Highness,' my novice yelled above the arguments of the others. 'What rations do we have?'

'Each hoplite will have one-third meat, one-third grain and one-third olive oil.'

That should take them many stadion of ocean to work out.

My scribe was a neodamodeis, or a freed Spartan slave. He had served his master well in several battles with the Persians. As a reward, his hermoioi – the Spartan lord – had given him his freedom. He went on to tell me how the lords had overrun his tribe in Messenia when he was a child. They had killed his father and taken his mother, his sister and himself as slaves. In the early days, the Spartans declared war on them once a year and slaughtered hundreds of innocent Messenian youths.

They were brought up as helots, as the Spartan slaves from Messenia were called, and were mostly set to work growing food for their overlords. This released the lords from the menial work of farming and growing food.

The fortunate helots were drafted into the army to serve their masters, sharpen their swords, polish their sandals, prepare their food and sometimes fight alongside their masters.

My scribe had seen enough blood and killing to last a lifetime, so after he was set free, he decided to seek another profession. He could see that his previous tormentors did not have any way of recording facts of everyday life. A scribe at Pylos had shown him the clay tablets so he had decided to take the writing back to his own people at Sparta.

I gazed across at the armada. It was four ships wide and ten ships in line astern; a formidable sight. I couldn't make out the last ships in the line – they were below the horizon behind us. Of course, my brother's flagship was out in front.

He had re-fitted many of the monoremes which we had used against the Troians many years ago. They were long, lean and fast. Each ship had a bronze battering ram which could smash through an enemy hull below the water line. With thirty strong men at the oars, each ship could smash through a thick oak hull with ease.

While the square woollen sails billowed like King Mutallu's stomach, the hoplites who were rowing took a well-earned rest.

The ships were also equipped with boarding ramps which could be dropped onto the enemy's deck after ramming. Thick rolls of cloth ran down the length of the stern. These could provide shade and shelter and could be rolled out to deflect enemy arrows.

The steering master sat in a lattice work cage on a small deck at the stern. He used his steering oars to guide the ship through fair and foul weather. The mast could be raised to catch the wind or lowered for rowing speed.

I wondered what Minos would think when he saw his five galleys leading the fleet. It didn't matter now – we were in charge.

I kept an eye out for gulls and cormorants, but the skies were clear.

'I make it ten mina of meat, ten mina of grain and ten mina of oil for each soldier,' one of my students held up ten fingers.

'Note that down on that clay,' I said. 'Now how many soldiers are there?' They were still working on the calculations. *Were these my brightest?*

It was then I saw an albatross. It was flying from Zephyrus to Eurus – that was a good omen. They could soar a long way from land. No need to get excited until we saw some land birds. *Who would be our welcoming committee?*

I prayed to the gods that Minos was away at Alasiya fighting. Gadeirus wasn't so bad, I could reason with him, but given the circumstances under which I had left Keftui when

I killed the priests at Malia, I expected to be greeted with vengeance and an arrow in the chest.

If the women were running the country, I had a chance. *Would Kitane be with them? Oh Hermes, I hoped not. I was a traitor and a spy. She wouldn't want to lay eyes on me ever again.*

My eyes followed the albatross towards Eurus and it was then that I saw a fine white speck against the blue. The shadows from the mainsail had gone and my crew were dozing under the canopy. As we grew closer, the white speck flapped its wings – a kestrel out looking for food.

I looked over at the flagship. The red flag was up. Battle stations!

'I make it one thousand hoplites,' one of my brightest had a flash of inspiration. He was wrong.

'Leave that you idiots! Look at those flags!' I yelled back. They dropped the wet clay on the deck and fell over each other looking for their armour. I didn't feel like laughing, but I couldn't help myself.

* * * *

We anchored about ten stadion offshore. We spread the fleet across the horizon to make us appear twice as large. I could just make out Iraklion, Amnisos and Malia from my ship. There was no smoke from the furnace at Amnisos. There was no smoke from the palace. A few deserted ships lolled lifelessly in Iraklion harbour. A faint plume of smoke meandered into the sky from far away in the hills. That could be Knossos. There were no brightly coloured fishing boats or merchant ships from Iberia or Phoenicia. Nothing. I couldn't see the outlines of any buildings.

A small row boat with Idas and one of my tribal chiefs from Attica bumped into our hull. 'Hurry up Callias,' Idas cupped his hands around his mouth. 'We'll lose the surprise.'

It looked to me like there was no Keftui to surprise. I signalled to my scribe to hurry as I wanted him with me.

'It looks like there will be no attack from the enemy, so you can all get back to work.'

'Theseus sends a message, Callias,' Idas said as we clambered down the rope ladder. 'Kill a few priests for him. Save him the trouble. But watch out. This could be a trap.'

The Spartan prince's breastplate sparkled in the sun. Red plumes from his helmet fluttered in the light breeze. This made him look a lot taller than he actually was. The handle of his new, number two, xiphos poked from his left arm pit and an inlaid gold dagger hung from his belt. I wore my white Greek toga, the peacemaker. I had a small dagger hidden under the folds in case of an emergency. Beads of sweat dripped from our noses. I carried a bronze cylinder, containing the surrender terms, over my shoulder.

My scribe hitched up his loincloth and hurriedly tried to unfold our white flag. His oiled, shoulder length hair, was held in place by a red bandanna. 'I'd rather be carrying a sword,' he said as he sat down next to me.

'If we aren't back by four suns, Theseus is going to land,' Idas said. 'If we are all dead, he will tear the place apart.'

'There'll be no need,' I replied. 'I know these people. They'll listen to reason.'

'Come on. Let's go ashore,' Idas said as the slaves pulled on the oars.

'Which beach?' the other prince asked.

'Malia beach. That is the second palace after Knossos and the royal family spend a lot of time there,' I suggested.

'Malia it is, then,' Idas acknowledged.

The oars splashed in unison as we drew toward Malia beach. No dolphins raced alongside. The place was deathly quiet. We peered up at the palace; I didn't recognise it. The two top floors had collapsed. Blocks of stone lay piled in a jumbled mass. Some of the larger blocks had tumbled down the outer walls and rolled toward the beach. Brown clay tiles from the roof lay smashed and broken in the debris. The skiff slid to a halt on the wet sand and we sprang over the bow. There was no welcoming party armed with spear and sword. I glanced at Idas and just shrugged as we cautiously jogged up the beach towards the smashed walls.

'Hold that flag up, this could be a trap,' I said to the scribe.

The two Spartan princes drew their swords.

'Put the swords away,' I growled. Still no-one.

I jumped over a large piece of broken masonry and headed towards the central court. The Snake Mother sanctuary was just as I had left it, burnt and black. The bodies were gone. A putrefying hand stuck out of a pile of mortar.

The complete floor where my room had been, had collapsed onto a lower floor. I stumbled through the rubble to the archive rooms. Pithos jars and tablets lay scattered across the tiles. The other three members of our landing party poked about in the ruins. This wasn't a trap. There was no life left here.

I called the others across to the temple. The half-burnt Snake Mother still lay on her back and her faience eyes gazed lifelessly at the sky. Her two clay feet were baked hard by the fire. They were strangely welded to the floor where she used to stand. Her legs had broken away from the feet when she fell backwards. Idas drew his sword and with one quick blow, severed her head from the neck.

'That's the end of that goddess. She won't be needing our blood any longer,' he grinned.

I watched with a kind of sick satisfaction as the faience head rolled away. 'It's hard to kill a religion after so many years, Idas. She may come back, re-incarnated as something else.'

'Let's hope not,' he said.

'I have to make a visit to Iraklion. Will you three keep looking about here for anything of interest, anything which may indicate where these people have gone. See if you can find some fresh water which our warriors can use when they come ashore. Take our boat around the point to Iraklion. I will meet you there in two suns. Oh, and on your way, have a look at Amnisos and see if the wind funnel is smashed.'

'Will we smash it, if it is not damaged?' the younger Spartan asked.

'No, you idiot! I want to use it.'

My scribe and I set off at a fast pace along the track that I knew so well; the track to Imira. *Dark memories of that night long ago; the gaping wound in Alexandros's throat; the screaming priestesses trying to escape from me.*

I would be glad to see Imira's smiling face again. The password – *Passing the night away*? It didn't matter now, did it? We thought it was a joke.

We were still several stadion from Iraklion when we caught the smell. We slowed to a fast walk and held our scarves over our noses. This was worse than Malia. Body parts of dead horses stuck through the rubble.

Strange, Imira had told us Iraklion had not been hit. This must have happened after I left for Agia Triada. We gingerly stepped over some bloated pigs. A woman's mutilated head protruded from the doorway of a stone hut. My scribe looked at me and held his nose.

'I'm feeling sick,' he mumbled through his scarf.

We made our way through the devastation to Imira's taverna. Someone, surely, had been spared. There had to be a survivor somewhere. I pushed my way through a half-burnt curtain into the bar which I knew so well. Two corpses lay on the floor. My heart sank. The largest of the bloated corpses lay face up with flies buzzing around a dark patch on its stomach; it was the portly serving girl.

A younger woman lay across one of the rough timber stools where I had sat several times. The blood had set in a pool on the floor. I recognised Imira's skirt. I sank to my knees and buried my face in my hands. There would be no more passwords. No more jokes at the palace.

Theseus and his big mouth, everyone had heard how angry his wife was that Imira would be returning from Iraklion and now – she was dead – murdered. *We must have a spy amongst us.*

'Do you know these women?' my scribe asked.

'Better than you would ever know,' I cried.

'Prince Idas is sailing in, Your Highness,' my scribe pointed to our skiff in the distance.

'I am not leaving until I have sent her to the gods,' I said quietly. 'Help me get her off that stool.'

We laid Imira on the floor. Her grey skin was stretched tight over her stiffened frame. She would be frolicking, joking with Persephone by now, as she had done in real life.

'Help me build a fire,' I sobbed.

'Lord, we haven't got time,' the scribe said. 'Idas is coming.'

'He can wait. Tell those two warriors to come up here and help us,' I ordered.

'The Spartan princes will not like this,' the scribe said.

'Just do it,' I ordered.

I started to pull Imira into the open, where we could build a funeral pyre.

The stiff fingers on her right hand were clenched around something. I prised the fingers open. A small gold button, with a bull's head stamped into the top, clinked onto the pavement.

I knelt beside her. 'Goodbye, Imira, my favourite lady-in-waiting. When you see Alexandros, tell him I'm sorry. I should never have left him behind, and Theseus should never have left you behind. I know you'll be happy in Elysium. We will find the sentina who did this.'

I dropped the button into a pocket in my filthy toga then pushed a glowing piece of railing into the pyre.

* * * *

The dead port of Iraklion faded into the distance as our little boat skipped across the waves. I looked back at the last plume of smoke – Imira's funeral pyre. Theseus should award her the green garland for bravery.

I pulled myself together and turned to look out to sea. The lead ships were almost on Malia beach.

The Spartan princes complained. 'Five suns have passed. If we hadn't wasted all that time …'

I was growing tired of Idas.

'Imira has been a loyal servant to Theseus. When he finds out you helped me to send her safely to the gods, you will be suitably rewarded,' I answered.

Theseus's triantaconter flew the royal flag of Mycenaea, the Golden Lion. His ship had just beached and marines were piling out onto the sand.

'Theseus,' I yelled from the bow of the skiff. 'Theseus, stop!' He didn't hear.

The last hoplite turned around just before he leapt off the warship. We waved and yelled when we saw him.

'Callias is here. Stop!' the hoplite yelled at the other warriors. Theseus was out in front. Theseus held his hands up, for everyone to stop. Half the invasion force had landed. Six hundred invaders stopped. The small beach was a mass of heavily armed warriors, their helmets dulled by the fading light. They were ready for a fight.

'All of you – stop running! Stay on the beach!' Theseus yelled.

The warriors looked around at each other. 'We'll be massacred here!' a Mycenaean said.

'Look behind you! Callias and Idas are alive!' Theseus yelled.

We kept waving as our skiff slid up onto the sand.

'Theseus. There are no people left here. There are no javelins and no swords waiting for us!' I yelled.

'Where have you been, brother?' he asked.

'I'll tell you later,' I said.

'Callias ordered us to build a funeral pyre for a woman. That is where we have been,' one Spartan prince complained.

'A woman?' the king asked.

'I'll tell you later,' I said. 'The entire population has gone,' I went on.

Theseus held his hands up for his army to stop muttering. 'There is no enemy. Stay where you are until we decide what to do next.'

A groan went up from the troops. They wanted blood and gold. Some started to gather driftwood to make fires. Others sat down on the sand and started to chew dried goat's meat from their rations. Some of the larger ships, which were still coming in, dropped their oars to slow them down. Others, which were still out at sea dropped anchor when the captains saw what was happening. I walked up to my brother and shook his hand. I hadn't seen him since Piraeus. He was taken aback.

'Good to see you. I told you that I would save a lot of lives,' I said.

'By the look of that palace, I'd say that an earthquake has done the job for you, Callias,' he replied.

'Yes, this side of the island is devastated. We couldn't find a living soul,' I went on.

'Where have the survivors gone?' he asked.

'I found this at the west court,' Idas said. He handed Theseus an arrow. Theseus glanced at it and handed it to me. 'What do you make of this?'

It had a razor sharp bronze tip and multi-coloured fletching. 'It is not one of the Minoans, at least not the palace guard. It could belong to the natives or … does anyone know what type of arrows the Sea Scum use?' Everyone shook their heads.

'If the Sea Scum have beaten us, they would hardly bury all their victims,' Theseus went on.

I handed the arrow back to Idas. 'Keep this. Ask around the troops. See if anyone recognises who might have made it.'

The shadows were getting longer and some arguments had broken out amongst the troops. They were bored with sitting on wet sand. The invasion ships listed on their sides as the tide went out.

'Right,' Theseus said. 'We walk in and make ourselves at home. We take over the palaces and the towns and try and get the place moving again.'

'Malia palace is built over a spring, but it will have to be shovelled out. The well looks like liquid mud at the moment,' a Mycenaean prince said.

'Organise that, Prince. Take a few of your men and start straight away,' Theseus was in control mode.

'Callias, call all the officers together and get the men to clean up these towns. Make sure they post guards at every entrance in case someone returns. We need a prisoner. Break

out the rations from your ship. See what food you can scav-
enge from the farms. I'll leave this part of the island in your
hands.'

'Theseus, I found Im ...' I started to say.

'I am returning to the fleet sitting at anchor out there.
I need to know what is happening at the rest of these towns
– Palaikastro, Kato Zakro, Agia Triada and Phaistos. I'll be
away for a few moons. Send your ship back to Athens for more
supplies.' The orders flew thick and fast.

'Theseus, I found Imira murdered,' I managed to get it
out. He didn't realise what I had said for a few moments.

'Who?' he asked. His mind was away with a thousand
other things.

'Imira,' I said again.

'Oh. No. Are you sure?'

'Yes. Imira and the girl from the taverna – both murdered.'

He shook his head. 'Not Imira. I begged her not to go
back, after the argument with Helen.'

'I'm sorry, Theseus. It looks like we have a spy amongst
us. Your remark at the war council,' I said.

'Imira.' He held his hand over his eyes. 'I am responsible
for this.'

'That is why we were late. The Spartan and I sent her to
Elysia.'

'Where, where did you ...?' he asked.

'Outside the taverna,' I said. He nodded. He knew which
one.

'Ask those Spartan princes who were with you, to come
back for a moment,' he said. 'We will remember them on her
mortuary.' He turned to the captain of the fleet. 'Captain, we
are returning to the ships. But first I need to sail around to
Iraklion to collect someone's ashes.'

'Theseus, before you go, I found this in her hand.' I opened my palm.

He picked up the gold button, and looked closely at the engraving.

'The owner of this is a dead man,' he said.

* * * *

I rowed back to my merchantman. The class of scribes stood around their tablets; they looked as if they had all swallowed poppy juice.

'We have the answers!' one junior exclaimed.

'I hope they are right, or you will have a hungry army chasing you around this island for a long time,' I jested.

* * * *

Hypnos was not kind to me as I tossed and turned on my goat-skin hammock. My brain decided not to switch off and visions of Imira's pyre burnt behind my eyes. Limbs of dead horses flew in and out of the fire. Persephone appeared, dancing with Imira, as a stray arrow flew overhead. They weren't going to let me rest. The first rays of Helios burst through the square timber window which served as a porthole. As I tried to shake the image of our goddess from my eyes, I promised her that I would sacrifice a piglet as soon as I could. The captain burst into the cabin and asked if I wanted to go ashore with the first load of supplies.

'Yes, yes, coming right away,' I snapped.

'Hurry up, Lord, they are ready to leave,' he mumbled, slamming the door on his way out. Our bow wave reached out to ships on either side of us. The smoke from several palace camp fires meandered into the sky. Faint echoes of the officers' voices rolled across the water in the still morning air. A few early risers swam out to meet us and I quickly ordered them to help carry the supplies up to the magazine rooms. My feet made no impression on the wet sand as I sprang over the bow. My three apprentices pushed each other and fooled about a few steps behind, but I was not in the mood for frolicking.

Theseus had made me the new Prince of Keftui and I had a thousand and one other things on my mind. *Where had the population gone? Would we face another quake? If we were attacked while Theseus was away, we would be an easy target. What did I need to do to get these towns back on their feet? Who would live in this ruined place?*

'Stop fooling about, you lot. Grab something to eat and come back to the magazine rooms. I have a job for you all,' I said as I looked behind me.

'We worked out the total kabs of wine, last night, Lord,' one yelled back.

'Don't worry about that now,' I said. 'I want to know what happened to these people. You may find some clues in the archives.'

'Leave it to us. We are experts at finding clues,' the junior joked.

'You haven't seen any Keftui hieroglyphs yet, so don't be so sure of yourselves,' I replied.

'We are the masters, Prince. Just point us in the right direction,' one boasted.

They were a cheerful bunch.

I could do without the responsibility of rebuilding the island just now. How I longed to be alone with Kitane for a few moons. Demeter or Aphrodite would know where she was.

'Where do you want us to start?' the junior scribe asked. My daydream was broken.

'Junior, I want you to find those two Spartan princes and ask them to meet me in the throne room. The rest of you, the archive room used to be over there, under that rubble. So start digging.'

'We need slaves for …' my assistant started to say.

'Just get on with it,' I ordered.

I stepped over piles of broken blocks. Puffs of ancient dust rose from the floor with every step. The throne room was unrecognisable. Minos's stone chair had toppled over and the colourful murals of the griffins looked like a giant puzzle with the missing pieces lying all over the floor.

'Prince Callias, we meet again,' Idas said from the collapsed doorway. 'No more funerals, I hope!'

'No. No more funeral pyres. The king was very pleased with what you did that day,' I replied.

'Who was the girl?' he asked.

'One of his ladies-in-waiting.'

'We'll leave it at that then,' he grinned. 'About this arrow which was found in the west court,' he handed it back to me.

'What did you find out?' I asked.

'One of my men showed it around the ranks. One of my warriors, who came over here with Pirithios, recognised the fletchings. He says that the local natives decorate their arrows with similar feathers,' the Spartan said.

'Gadeirus told me about these tribesmen, but I have never seen them,' I claimed.

'They live up on the Lesithi plateau and melt into the forest as soon as anyone from the lowlands appears,' the Spartan explained.

'I wonder, did they come here to help everyone?' I asked.

'Possibly,' the Spartan replied.

The younger prince said, 'A whole population would hardly escape to the plateau?'

'Hardly. And where's Pirithios? I haven't seen him since we set up the furnace at Zakro,' I wondered out loud.

'I have no idea,' Idas said.

'Why don't we send a scouting party to Lisithi to see what we can find,' the younger prince suggested.

'Yes,' I agreed. 'Send that warrior of yours, the one who identified the arrow, and two others. They are to melt into the forest like the tribesmen and they mustn't be caught under any circumstances.'

'I'll see to it,' he said.

'Now about food and water for the troops,' I said to Idas.

'Before, we look at that,' he interrupted, 'when you lived here, did you have any idea where old Minos hid his treasury?'

I had a suspicion that it was guarded by the Minotaur.

'No. No idea. Minos never confided in me. If we ever find Gadeirus, he would know,' I replied.

'Where was that snake pit?' Idas asked, an evil smile on his face.

'Gadeirus is a friend of mine. Do not lay a finger on him,' I looked him straight in the eye. I didn't finish the threat.

'Or else?' Idas asked.

The Spartans were a ruthless race. I would have to watch my back.

'The king has left me to run this island while he is away. If you try to do things differently, you will have to deal with me first, and then my brother when he gets back,' I said calmly, noting his displeasure.

'My men, how will they be getting paid?' he scowled.

'We have our own store of silver pieces. They will all be paid as agreed, before they return home,' I said.

'Yes, that is their basic reward, but they also want a share of the spoils,' Idas kept it up.

'I don't know where Minos's kept his vaults. You will not be torturing Gadeirus, if we ever find him. But, once you have all made camp here, you can plunder Iraklion and share anything of value that you find there. Find out what is required to repair the docks and start the ships moving again. Leave a detachment there to tidy the place up,' I ordered.

'Now about the rations, we have brought thirty days supply ashore with us. I have sent our merchant back to Tiryns for more supplies. See if you can find any livestock which we could slaughter, but leave them alive until we need them for food. Scout the farms around the palaces. You may find some fruit, grain or stored oil. Leave half the men here to help me with Knossos and Malia. We have a good supply of fresh water from the well which you cleaned out. I am relying on you, Idas, as my right hand man. Now, do you have any more complaints or questions?' I said quietly.

'Yes, if we find the treasury in Iraklion, do we get to share it with the troops?' he asked.

'No,' I was becoming exasperated now. 'The treasury remains the property of King Theseus and all Mycenaeans. His advisors will decide. We do have an empire to run. Anything else you find in Iraklion, can be shared amongst your men.'

'We'll leave it at that then,' he mumbled, looking defiantly at me.

'Take your fellow prince with you and report back here in seven moons. Our scouts should have returned by then.'

Without a word to me, he turned on his heel and barked at his aide, 'Well, you heard the Athenian. Get the men together!'

I started to wonder how long it would be until Idas meant trouble.

CHAPTER XII

Keftui – 1190 BC

The wind funnel at Amnisos was a mess. I looked down on the broken snake from the top of the cliff face. Half its body had collapsed. The holes through its backbone looked like it had been mauled by the dragon from Colchis. I could hear the wind howling out of the first few bites.

As Pirithios was missing in action, I had appointed a new bodyguard, Meriones. He was born and bred in Athens, so I knew I could trust him with my life. He stood, shaking his head.

'What in the name of the gods is THAT?' he said pointing to the smashed monster.

'That, my good man, is a wind tunnel. Well, it used to be a wind tunnel!'

He obviously had not been to Pylos. Meriones was from my village of Artemida, near Athens. 'The tunnel is used to make that xiphos you are carrying.'

'When we get back to Malia, you will put some slaves onto rebuilding the frame of the snake as soon as you can. There is a stockpile of the necessary red earth over there. We need to get this going again.'

'Show me that xiphos under your arm,' I requested.

He pulled the short sword from its scabbard and handed it over to me.

'See those two vertical marks on the hilt,' I pointed.

'They look like a flaw in the metal,' he said.

'No. When we made the new swords at Pylos, we marked each of them. The two lines tell us which particular batch of metal was used to make that weapon.' I explained.

'Which batch did I get?' he asked.

'You got the same as Prince Idas, lucky number two.'

'Was that the best mix?'

'We don't know yet. If there had been a fight here, we would have found out.'

'If I am fighting the Sea People, I hope to the gods that I have a trusty weapon that will kill the enemy!'

'They will all kill with equal capability, but some may last longer than others,' I tried to reassure him.

We turned our back on Amnisos and Boreas blew into Malia. A fine day it would have been for making aforinium today. I would need to transfer one of those alchemists from Pylos after we had repaired the snake. I wanted all our men equipped with the new swords if the Peleset and their Sea Scum friends decided to attack.

The shadows grew longer as we walked along the track towards the palace. Meriones chatted about his wife back in Attica, and how they still didn't have any children after being together for a great year. I suggested that he was never home long enough to father a child but apparently that wasn't the reason.

When she was a girl, his wife had worked in the palace attending to my mother. As teenage boys, we were both in the games at Olympia, long after Androgeus had died. We had a great laugh about the girl from Sparta who tried to compete in the hoplitodromus, where we had to compete in full battle gear. She almost made the starting line-up, until the archon made her strip off. I had just started telling him a story about a goat which had escaped the altar at Zeus's Temple, when my scribe came running up the track towards us.

'Your Highness, the spies from Lesithi are back,' he gasped. 'They arrived at the palace before the sun went down.'

I looked at him. 'Just catch your breath, man. How many are there?'

'Two of them ran in about half-a-sun ago.'

'Did you talk to them?'

No, Prince. I came straight here to tell you.'

'Don't you realise, we sent three of them?'

'I, I … didn't know, Your Highness,' he spluttered.

'You better take us straight to them.'

The three of us trotted the rest of the way into the palace and the scribe led us into the half-restored throne room. The two scouts were gulping water from bamboo cups. Their bodies were being sponged down by slaves who had been on my ship. As soon as we jumped through the collapsed doorway, they stood at attention.

'At ease,' I said. 'Sit.'

'Where is the other scout?' I asked.

'He has been captured by the natives, Lord.'

'I gave strict instructions that you were not to be seen, let alone captured.'

'Yes Lord, but he was caught while we were spying on the Dikteon Cave,' one explained.

'Ah. The birthplace of Zeus, an ideal place for someone to hide. Where is the scout now?'

'The natives have him,' he replied.

'Well, they will certainly know that we are here, now.'

'Yes, they will, Lord, but I don't think it will matter,' the other scout said.

'Why is that?' I asked.

'We only saw Pasiphae and Phaedra and a few palace staff living there,' he replied. 'They were not hiding. The queen and her daughter wandered outside to gather food.'

'Where is their army then?'

'We did not see any palace guards or any sign of Minos's soldiers,' the first scout replied.

'Did the natives kill our other scout?'

'We don't know, Lord. We saw the natives leading him to the cave, with his elbows tied over his head. We decided to head back here quickly before he opened his mouth.'

'Well, Pasiphae will know that we are here. Phaedra is too empty headed to work out what is going on,' I said. 'Minos and Gadeirus must be away fighting. They may not even know about the devastation here.'

'I don't think the natives will attack without some instructions from Minos,' Meriones said.

'I don't trust them.' I said. 'Make sure you double the guard tonight. You and I and a small detachment will pay Pasiphae a visit tomorrow.'

* * * *

The birdlife in the dense forest chattered wildly as the first rays of sun filtered through the leaves. We spaced ourselves at long intervals on the padded track so that we had a better chance of escape if we were ambushed. The scout from yesterday's patrol was out in front and his partner brought up the rear. Meriones and I, plus four other guards, walked quietly along between the two of them. The forward scout thought he heard something in the undergrowth and held his hand up for us all to stop. He sprang onto the limbs of a low hanging tree, for a better view, and gave the all clear.

The hot Aegean sun soon moved above the tree tops and I took a couple of gulps of water from my goatskin bladder. We had let our guard down slightly as the morning wore on. I could see the track opening up into a cleared patch in the forest. The front scout was just through the clearing when I heard the whoosh of an arrow thud into the tree beside me. We hit the ground. I looked around to see if anyone had been hit. Meriones crawled up to me on his belly.

'Anyone hurt?' I whispered

'No-one has been hit,' he said quietly.

'We would all be dead by now, if they wanted us dead,' I said.

The forward scout did not see the arrow and kept creeping along the track.

'I think we should all very gently, show ourselves,' Meriones said quietly. 'No sudden movements. Put our hands up.'

'Yes, I think that's the smartest move,' I said.

We held our hands high and gingerly rose to our feet. A ring of Lesithi warriors, wearing nose rings and green palm leaves, materialised from the forest.

'Careful,' Meriones said quietly, as the nearest native came towards us. The warrior didn't say a word. He raised his right hand and gestured with his index finger for us all to follow. Our forward scout had now stopped and fell in with us as we trooped past.

'Can you speak their tongue?' Meriones asked our scout.

'No. Just sign language,' he said.

'Where are they taking us?' I asked the scout.

Our escort marched silently in front of and behind us, the sharp end of their spears urging us along. The whole exercise was planned. They knew that we would soon return. *How could I have not seen it? We weren't dead yet so they must have instructions from higher up.*

'Is this the track to their camp or the cave?' I said quietly to the scout.

'The track to the cave,' he whispered.

I looked at Meriones. 'It looks as if Pasiphae wants to see us.'

'Looks like it.'

I took another gulp from my goatskin bag, as we started on the steep climb up to the cave. As I walked along, I thought about Cronos, the leader of the Titan gods. Why would he eat his children? Rhea had escaped her cannibal husband and given birth to Zeus in the Dikteon cave. Cronos searched all of Keftui, but never found the cave. I was beginning to know how he felt. The track from Knossos wound up the side of the ridge like an endless coiled snake. We were strung out over several stadia and could have escaped at any time, but I needed to see Pasiphae. *What sort of reception would she have in store? The reception could be more than cool. Would she tell us where Minos and Gadeirus were? She had good reason not to say anything. And what happened to Kitane?*

As we rounded the last bend, I could see a well-worn cart track coming from the direction of Palaikastro. Several local farmers were leading animals into an opening in the cliff face. The priests of Zeus locked the animals into a small pen, ready for sacrifice. These were the first Keftuins we had seen on the island since we had landed.

An old wooden cart rattled over the cobblestones on its way to the east coast with a load of empty barrels. Other locals carried small kraters of wine and oil for the priests. The tranquillity of the scene was hard to believe.

The Lesithi tribesmen led us down into the depths of the cave. Down and down a series of winding steps cut into the cave face. Flickering oil lamps reflected off the cool waters of an underground spring. Long limestone columns hung down from the ceiling and met short thick columns growing up from the floor. Rhea could easily have hidden Zeus in here. A huge shaft of limestone hung down over the small lake; the legendary Mantle of Zeus. I had heard a lot about this place. The oil lamps flicked over Zeus's golden image, as he stared at the prostrated worshippers before him.

The head Lesithi tribesman held up his hand for us all to stop, turned to me and growled in our own tongue, 'Wait here!'

'He can speak our language,' I was astonished.

'Yes, luckily we haven't said anything,' said Meriones.

After a few moments, the warrior emerged from a large room cut into the cave wall. His nose and ear rings glinted in the firelight.

'Her Highness will see you now, Callias. You may take your bodyguard with you,' he said in perfect Mycenaean.

'The rest of you, do not try and leave, and do not speak!' I ordered. The Lesithi natives had not budged and stood guard over the only exit. Meriones and I followed the guard into the stone room.

'Prince Callias and his bodyguard, Your Highness,' the guard announced.

We could just see three figures by the flickering light. The old queen sat on a stone throne at the back of the room. On her left side, *was that Phaedra*? I looked twice. She had grown a lot since I had seen her last. Her breasts had filled out and her long, coiled, black hair was decorated with white crocus flowers. On the right of the queen sat a girl in the shadows. She turned her face to look at the queen. It was … Kitane.

'Hello, Callias, we meet again,' Kitane smiled.

My heart thumped so loudly, I'm sure she must have heard it. I opened my mouth to say something. Nothing came out.

'You have turned your back on Keftui, Callias,' the queen said. 'I should throw you to the snakes.'

'I ... I ... Kitane ...' I tried to pull myself together. I had planned to control this meeting. It wasn't working out.

'After all that Minos and I did for you, Callias. We freed your hostages, we entrusted you with Kitane and the search for the new metal. We gave you control of the wind tunnels and let you into our secret archives. This is how you repay us.'

'I ... I ... can expl ...' Kitane had thrown me.

'You murdered our chief priestess, betrayed our trust and sailed to Athens to organise an attack,' she ranted.

'Your malaka of a brother captured five of our ships and killed all the crew!' Her old face wrinkled up even further. Her black curls had long ago turned grey and her voice cracked now and again as she kept up the tirade.

'I know you have eyes for Kitane, but you can forget any ideas you have for her,' the old queen gnashed. 'You are a traitor! You are not one of us!'

This wasn't going to plan.

'Your Highness. S ... seeing Kitane beside you gave me a shock. I know we are your prisoners in this sanctuary but we have many warriors camped at Malia. If we do not return by nightfall, they have orders to destroy what is left of this island and take you and your daughters as slaves,' I said.

'Your many Achaeans will be no match for thousands of loyal tribesmen who guard us here,' she went on.

Phaedra, who had not said a word until now, looked at me. 'When father and Gadeirus return from Alasiya and Ugarit, they will sink your ships.'

The queen glared at her youngest daughter. 'Be quiet,' she said.

Now I knew where the king and the prince had gone. *When would they get back?*

'You are not in a position to argue, Queen Pasiphae. My warriors far outnumber your antiquated tribesmen, and our weapons are far deadlier. If you agree to a merger of our two great nations, you will remain queen and your daughters will remain princesses. You will save a lot of lives if you agree. Once we have rebuilt Knossos you can live there with us. You will do as Theseus directs, but otherwise you can live your own lives. We do not intend to execute Minos and Gadeirus. I don't know whether they are still alive, but they will be placed under house arrest if they do return. We would rather see Keftui and Achaea form one great alliance so that we can live and fight together.'

I finally got my speech out. I had rehearsed it in my mind many times over.

'I cannot speak for my husband. He will not like being a puppet to you people. He has ruled us for many moons. Gadeirus will do as I say, and Ariadne has a mind of her own.'

'Mother, when he has rebuilt Knossos, I want to return to the palace,' Phaedra interrupted.

The queen glared at her again. 'Silence!'

I looked longingly at Kitane. She must have known what I was thinking. 'I am a barren princess, of no use to Hittite kings,' she said.

'Kitane, you are of no use to Athenian princes either. Now both of you, hold your tongues. We have far more important matters to discuss,' the queen growled.

'If I agree with your terms, Callias, will you guarantee that none of my people will be killed or sold as slaves?'

'If they do not rise against us, I have no reason to kill them. Your remaining soldiers are free to join us. The farmers and artisans will be free to carry on as before. None of your people will be enslaved,' I promised.

'We would welcome any additions to our ranks,' Meriones said. 'The people from the north will take some stopping.'

'Mother, you can't speak for all the warriors who have sailed with Father. And what about all those who have joined the pharaoh?' Kitane asked.

The girls had let me know, inadvertently, exactly what I had come for. Minos must have some of the army with him, but many had fled the earthquakes and gone to fight for Ramesses. The only defence the island could muster at present comprised a few thousand primitive tribesmen with stone axes and ancient bows and arrows.

'Callias, the Sea People have attacked Alasiya, Ugarit and Amurru. Kitane's ex-husband and Ramesses sent emissaries here asking for help. Most of our fleet sailed for Alasiya and many of our warriors continued across the narrow channel from Alasiya to fight at Amurru,' the queen's voice faltered.

'We have been tricked by you and the Sea People into leaving Keftui undefended. Our palaces are in ruins, our navy is many stadia away and our soldiers are fighting in foreign lands. I don't know whether my husband and son are still alive but my daughters have given me strength to carry on.'

'I can assure you that we have tricked no-one. You may think I am a traitor, but Minos angered our people by taking our finest youths and maidens as hostages. I came to Keftui to find out what you had done with them – it looks as though they have all been sacrificed.'

'We have killed your wretched Snake Goddess in retaliation and I think we should call a truce. You can help us re-build the island,' I offered.

'Are you a heartless mercenary, Callias, or have you been sent by the gods to rescue us?' she asked. 'You have betrayed us many times. How do I know that you won't do it again?'

'I will make an offering to Zeus and swear to the King of the Gods, that we will do what we can to rebuild your island and defend it from all invaders. I will have my scribe draw up suitable laws for us to follow from now on. If there are any disputes between us both, we can then refer to what has been written,' I said.

'We have much to consider, Callias. My husband is far away. You are asking me to hand over the rule of this land to Mycenaea and Athens. How can I trust you, Callias? Return here at the same time tomorrow, and I will give you my answer,' she said quietly. 'Let them go,' she said as she waved us away.

The natives and Zeus worshippers cleared a path for us as we made our way to the stairs. They had been listening intently at the doorway and let us pass.

'We will not be fighting for you filthy Greeks,' the chief said as I walked past.

'Then I count on you not fighting against us,' I replied.

'We will see,' he said in perfect Mycenaean.

We reached the top of the stairway and I made my way over to the pen of sacrificial animals. I picked out a fat kid and paid the priest in silver pieces.

'I wish to make an offering to the King of the Gods,' I said to him. 'I promised on the oath of Zeus that we would rebuild your island, not harm a single Keftuin, nor take any of you into slavery. The offering must be in front of all these people to bind my oath,' I went on. 'If the queen disagrees, my oath is worthless.'

'Very well. The smell of Zeus's personal incense, gum ammoniac, wafted through the cave. I washed and dried myself as the priest had directed, using the lustral water from the lake. I tidied my hair and gave my sword to Meriones.

An apprentice priest led the kid to the sacrificial altar. The chief priest held a basket of barley, which concealed the sacrificial knife. He placed the basket of grain on the altar and the kid nuzzled its nose in the fresh grain. It munched on a mouthful of grain while the priest sprinkled some red wine on its head. The animal's head nodded up and down and approved the sacrifice. The apprentice held the kid's horns while the head priest plunged the knife into its neck. It gave a gurgle and sunk to its knees. Hot blood spurted from the wound as the head priest held the libation bowl. I took the basket of barley and sprinkled it around the shrine. Zeus smiled down on me as I poured the hot blood over the shrine.

I recited a hymn with my hands held out in front of me:

'Oh mighty *di-wo Zeu*, King of the Gods
Consort of the mighty Hera
Father of Persephone and Athena
I give you the blood of Amalthea
I, Callias of Attica, have honoured you greatly at Olympus and Athens
I have made libations for you at Pylos and Corinth
The people of Keftui I will treat as my own
I offer you this barley and blood in return for your sanction.'

I was bound. I nodded for the warriors to bang their spears against their shields, so that Cronos would not hear the baby Zeus's cry. I sprinkled the hot Amalthea blood around the shrine and stared silently at the god. The smell of roasting goat flesh wafted past my nose and I knew that Zeus would rise up from Erebus and give us his blessing. The warriors in the cave lined up for some tasty morsels. The aroma from the leg bones and entrails brought a smile to Zeus's face.

'I have read Amalthea's liver and all the signs are with you,' the temple augur said.

I thought back to our voyage from Piraeus. The albatross was right. The signs in the goat's liver agreed with the albatross. I had saved many thousands of lives so far. But how long would the gods smile down on me?

* * * *

We camped in the pilgrims' bark shelters that night. Uranus held the stars in the heavens, and Zeus and Hera asked their children to sparkle at us from far above. My men had a satisfied look on their faces as they sat around the fire eating roasted goat flesh and drinking fresh wine from Palaikastro. Meriones told some extraordinary stories about fighting for the pharaoh in Gaza and one of the Lesithi warriors showed us how to flake stone axes. The first watch sat quietly holding his spear, looking at the heavens. Hypnos was kind to me as I drifted off thinking about how I could get Kitane away from her mother.

As Helios's rays bounded into our native hut, we rubbed the sleep from our eyes and walked along the well-padded path to Pasiphae's chambers.

'I watched your sacrifice to Zeus last night, Callias, and we have decided to accept your offer,' the queen announced.

'We want our agreement recorded by your scribes and ours, and if you do not keep any of your promises, the tablets will record the actions to be taken to remedy the situation. We are at your mercy at present, but that may not always be so. We don't know if any of our soldiers or sailors will return, and we can't afford to be conquered by the People from the Sea. If you betray us again, Callias, my native warriors will drive you from the island.'

I swallowed all this with a grain of salt. *How would a tribe of hunter gatherers drive us back to the Peloponnese?* There would be no betrayal.

'You have made the right decision, Your Highness. I'm sure Minos would have agreed with you. I need you by my side, to rebuild your great nation. When we have rebuilt your rooms at Knossos, I will send for you,' I said.

'I am not convinced that I am doing the right thing, Callias. You have yet to prove yourself,' she went on.

'It will be slow going as we have no gold and no slaves but we can make a start today,' I replied.

'I would like Ariadne to return from Akrotiri. I am too old for this, Callias. You will work with her,' the queen instructed.

'Could we appoint Kitane as my assistant?'

'Most definitely not. I have other plans for her. You are to stay away from her,' the old queen snarled.

Other plans for Kitane? Surely not another arranged marriage?

'I will work with Ariadne as you require. But she is very strong willed.'

'Those are my terms,' she grumbled.

'Then, I accept. Before I go, do you have news of an old bodyguard of mine, Pirithios?' I asked.

'Pirithios, Pirithios, the Athenian who trained our warriors?'

'Yes, that's him. He came with me to Alasiya,' I said.

'Minos took him back there when the fat Hittite asked for help,' she said. 'He was in command of the foot soldiers,' she replied.

A commander now! Pirithios had come up in the world. He could be in Alasiya, Amurru or the Elysian Fields. It would be good to see him again, but hopefully not with the gods.

'We have a nation to run. I will report back every full moon and send a runner to tell Phaedra when her room is finished!' I smiled. There was no sign of the princesses.

CHAPTER XIII

Malia – 1180 BC

The small specks on the horizon gradually grew into Greek biremes. I started to count from left to right as they came into view. Fifteen, sixteen, seventeen … I waited for half-a-sun. Some sea birds, looking for scraps, flew out to the ships. Gannets and petrels plunged, like Persian arrows, into a shoal of bait fish. The royal dolphin bodyguards cut through the waterline with our navy. Sixteen, seventeen … I couldn't get past nineteen ships.

Theseus had sailed with twenty ships. The noise from the masons and carpenters ruined my concentration. I grabbed Meriones.

'We must go and welcome them home. There is one missing,' I said.

We made our way through the rubble on the second floor, down the cleared stairwell and out on to the sand dunes. The first skiff from the lead ship slid onto the sand and one of the captains sprang over the bow.

'Welcome back,' I said as I shook his hand. 'Where is Theseus?'

'I have some bad news, Lord. As we were sailing back from Agia Triada we came across some ships from Alasiya.

We thought they were King Mutallu's ships. We thought they were sailing home,' he said.

'Yes, yes. What happened?' I said.

'We were deceived. Theseus sailed over to them to speak to the captains. When he pulled alongside, many Sea People warriors sprung from the holds. A monster emerged. He looked like Cerebus, the two headed dog, with a fearsome black beard and wore a gold armband. They made our crew kneel and then started cutting throats and throwing corpses overboard,' the captain cried. 'The ships were the same as ours, the same ships which you took to Alasiya.'

'Did they kill Theseus?' I asked.

'The monster tied a prisoner to the main mast, and several of them were using him for knife throwing practice. It couldn't tell who it was. May the ferryman be kind to him.'

'Was it Theseus?' My anxiety was rising.

'I'm not sure,' he replied. 'They were a long way off.'

'So, Theseus has been taken hostage?'

'Yes, it is possible,' the captain went on.

'A fine ransom he'll bring, if they realise who he is,' I said.

'A faint hope,' the captain added.

'Why didn't you attack them?' I demanded, trying to control my anger.

'A large fleet of warships waited just below the horizon. Many had the duck bill prow. It was a trap,' he explained.

I lost it. I grabbed him by the cuirass and pulled his face next to mine. 'You made no attempt to rescue the king, you gutless vlaka. You had nineteen warships! You are relieved of your post.'

He shook himself free.

Visions of Theseus lying in Minotaur manure at Knossos crossed before me. He was all that I had. Now the Sea Scum may have done what the Minotaur could not do.

I turned to Meriones. 'Warn the palace that the Sea People are on the way.'

I asked Demeter to watch over my brother. If Theseus had gone to the gods, I was now in command – or should I say, Ariadne and I were now in command.

'Captain,' I calmed down. 'Stay at your post. Any news of Minos and Gadeirus?'

'One of the sailors at Zakro told us that the king and prince had taken their ships to Alasiya. None of them had returned.'

'Yes, yes, I know that much. They may have sailed for Amurru to help the pharaoh,' I said.

'Maybe we should send someone to Salamis to find out what has happened?' the captain suggested.

'Yes, you are right. The Sea Scum seem to be everywhere, like the gods,' I said. 'Now Captain, what of the freemen left behind at the Keftui ports. Do they object to being over-run by us?'

'Word travels quickly here, Lord. They have a well organised network of tracks and messengers. At nearly every port, the locals knew we had landed at Malia. Some had already received your scrolls. They shrug their shoulders and say, "We put up with you! You are better than the cursed Danaoi,"' the captain replied.

'We are better masters than an army of Sea Scum,' I replied.

'The only people who hated us were a tribe of natives near Kydonia. They shook their shields and spears at us, as we sailed close to shore,' the old seaman said.

'Yes, they were hostile at Dikteon too. They refuse to join us.'

'What were you doing at Zeus's cave, Lord?'

'While you were at sea, I found Pasiphae, Kitane and Phaedra hiding there. They told me about Minos and Gadeirus.'

'I thought Kitane was married to Mutallu?' he replied.

'I haven't finished that story yet,' I said.

'Captain, re-provision all your ships and make sure your crews are on full alert. Make sure that no Keftui ships sail for Aegyptus. Post a watch at all the ports. Pasiphae has agreed to join us, but I don't trust her as far as the dead can jump.'

The midday sun bounced off his leathery skin and his long grey hair whipped in the breeze.

'I need you personally to sail home and tell Queen Helen what has happened – that Theseus may be dead. I will give you a scroll for Ariadne. You are to stop at Thira on your way back and deliver it to her. You will bring her back with you, is that clear?'

'Yes, Lord. Will I tie her up if she won't come?'

'Yes, but make sure her slave doesn't give her a black eye!' I said.

He gave me a strange look.

* * * *

The small wrens chatted to each other the next morning as I walked back to the archive rooms. After all their complaining yesterday, the scribes had almost finished the peace treaty and the request for Ariadne to return.

'Take that scroll for Ariadne to the captain, so that he can sail to Athens,' I said to no one in particular.

'Prince Callias, I was hoping to ride to Lesithi with you, today. I want to see Phaedra for myself,' the youngest said.

'Phaedra will be moving back here soon, so you will see her shortly. She is probably promised to an Egyptian pharaoh, so she won't be looking twice at a poor scribe. She is spoilt rotten; she wouldn't suit you at all.'

The young scribe groaned. 'I like girls who know their own mind and I could spoil her rotten,' he smiled as he jumped over a pile of rubble at the doorway carrying the scrolls.

'I want that treaty finished in two suns, so get a move on,' I said to the others.

Just as I turned to leave, my assistant walked over and held something out.

'We have been digging through the smashed tablets here, trying to piece them together. Most of them are only records of sheep, cattle and grain and the names of the people who grew the crops or raised the livestock. But what do you make of this?' he asked.

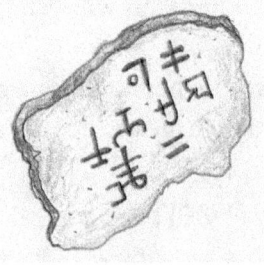

He was looking at a blackened piece of clay with a few obscure inscriptions. 'This is their old writing. But I can't understand any of it.'

'I think you have it upside down.'

He flipped it around.

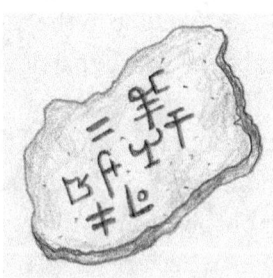

'This looks better,' I laughed. 'This lazy scribe did not bother with an "X" to mark the beginning. It's another one of your livestock records,' I said.

'Two straight lines at the top and the crossed stick say: "twenty bulls".

'And then the next lines say: "o ... u ... ru ... to ... pa ... ra ..." So we have: "twenty bulls plus ... o ... u ... ru ...to ... pa ... ra ...", or "twenty bulls look over ancient ... what?"' he asked.

'There is something missing after the last square with the circle,' I said. 'More records of livestock. Put it with those other pieces in the jar. Now come on. We need to get up to Lesithi before it gets too late.'

* * * *

A string of worshippers padded into the sanctuary at Dikteon. Some carried small bags of grain, some carried goat bladders full of wine, some carried small amphora of olive oil. The wealthier worshippers pulled a fat lamb or a squealing pig to the pens.

The priests were not sacrificing today, but all animals were gratefully accepted. The priests would wait for the middle day of the forthcoming games to Zeus and sacrifice them all at once. The entrails would then be offered to the wide-mouthed one – the King of the Gods – and the worshippers would have a mighty feast.

I was not a great believer in Zeus. He was renowned for his love affairs with many of the female gods and he made his wife, Hera, very jealous. Once again, my scribe and I made our way carefully down the rock stairs into the lower sanctuary of Zeus. Pasiphae's native guard announced our arrival and motioned us into her chambers. The ageing queen sat motionless on her granite chair. Phaedra sat on the queen's right-hand side, fiddling with an Egyptian sistrum – the sign of the Egyptian goddess, Isis. There was no Kitane.

'Kalispera, Prince. What news have you brought?' she said.

'We have brought the peace treaty. The scroll says under the oath of Zeus that we would rebuild your island, not harm a single Keftuin nor take any of you into slavery.'

'And what is to become of me and my family?' she asked.

'You may all return to Knossos and take up your old positions in the palace. We have finished rebuilding your rooms,' I replied.

'Oh mother, when can we go?' Phaedra said happily.

'Soon, soon. We have a lot to consider,' Pasiphae said. 'What will become of Minos and Gadeirus if they should return?'

Before I could answer, the crowd parted and a messenger from Kato Zakro came running into the room. His dark skin glistened with sweat and his long hair was tied into many knots.

'Your Highness, please excuse me, but the Princess Kitane has returned,' he gasped.

'Where is she?' the queen asked.

'Her … her ship landed at Kato Zakro a few suns ago, Your Highness. She should be here very soon,' he panted.

'Efcharisto,' the queen said. 'You may go now.'

'We will soon learn the fate of my husband and son and your friend, Pirithios.

'I sent Kitane and my bodyguard back to Alasiya; she knows the island better than any of us. I hoped her wretched husband had sailed for Hatti. A barren wife, hmmph! I know who was the barren one, and it wasn't my daughter! '

It sounded like the crushed acacia tree bark and date juice had been a success. King Mutallu had sent her home. Home to a ruined palace; home to no father or brother; home to a cave in the hills. Sending her back to Alasiya was a very risky idea.

Phaedra jumped off her stone chair and ran after the messenger.

'Wait, wait,' she yelled. 'How far away is she?'

'Follow me, Princess. I'll take you to her,' the runner replied.

The cool spring water from the underground stream gurgled along as it ran into Zeus's lake. The candle below his shrine flickered on the rough, hewn walls. I could hear the excited chattering of the crowd as Phaedra and the runner climbed the stairs.

It wasn't long before we heard the cheering from the natives as Kitane came into view. Phaedra ran up to her and grabbed her by the hand. Her small sister tried to fit an ocean of news into a few heartbeats, as they came down the stairway. Kitane was not paying attention.

'Phaedra, do you mind?' Pasiphae growled at her youngest. 'Your sister has important news for us.'

Kitane hardly recognised me as she passed.

'You are safe and sound. I couldn't bear to lose another child,' Pasiphae said as she hugged her daughter. 'What have you found?'

'Mother. We sailed to Salamis without striking any Sea People and found that King Suppiluliuma had replaced my cowardly husband. Mutallu had fled to Hattusa at the first sign of trouble.'

The cave went quiet. Someone dropped a bronze bowl on the floor and the sound rang around the walls.

'Suppiluliuma showed me a clay tablet which he had just received from his ally, Ammurapi, at Ugarit,' she went on. 'I copied down what it said. Maybe Callias can read it.'

I glanced down at the script. It was in Hittite so I could only read the odd word here and there:

............., *the enemy's ships came...; my cities were burned, and they did evil things in my country. Do you know......... my troops and .... are in the land of Hatti and all my ships are in the Land of Lukka? ...... the country is abandoned .... May you know it; the seven ships of the enemy came here and inflicted much damage upon us.[1]*

'Ammurapi was in a lot of trouble. Suppiluliuma asked father and Gadeirus if they would sail to Ugarit to help. Father agreed to help and sailed off to that far land. None of them were ever seen again.' Kitane started to sob. Pasiphae rushed over and gently stroked her daughter's long black hair.

'It doesn't mean that they are dead,' Pasiphae said quietly. 'They could be hostages or they may have swum to a beach in Canaan.'

'Mother, I think we better accept that they are gone, so that we can move on,' Kitane sniffed. 'Callias will look after us.'

'He won't be looking after me,' Phaedra cried. 'I'd rather have a hyena for a minder.'

Handling distraught women is not one of my major strengths. Nevertheless, I plunged on.

'Theseus is also missing. We will need to be careful that we are not next on the Sea Scum's list. Kitane, your mother and I have made a treaty. My warriors will protect the island in the event of an invasion, but we are only so many. We won't be able to protect the whole empire. I suggest that you all return to the palace at Knossos. I have sent for Ariadne to help run this island and between the two of us, we will do what we can to protect you all.'

'I am not having Ariadne tell me what do,' Phaedra sobbed. 'I thought we had got rid of her to Thira.'

---

1 *The Ugarit Letters, Ras Shamra, RS.18.147, Syria, 1190BC*

'You will do what you always wanted to do, as usual.' Pasiphae struggled with a smile.

'Kitane … will you all come back to Knossos?' I pleaded.

She stopped sobbing into her mother's shoulder and her bloodshot eyes looked straight at me.

'As long as we can build a memorial to Father and Gadeirus,' she said. 'I hate this cave.'

'They won't be forgotten,' I said. 'We will hold a great festival in memory of them both.'

The crowd in the cave turned solemnly and began to file out, up the stairs and into the daylight. The chattering had stopped and the smiles for Kitane had stopped.

I knew then that I had to take command. My hands weren't sweating and the only reason my heart was racing … well you know why. Aphrodite had control of my heart. I had seen Kitane again, but I was the last person on her mind.

I had calmed the three royals – well, maybe not Phaedra – and convinced them to return to Knossos. I would ask them to try and restore some order to Malia and Kato Zakro palaces as well, to keep them occupied.

'Pasiphae, I will leave the move back to Knossos in your hands. We have almost finished your rooms,' I said.

'What choice do I have?' she asked weakly.

I turned to my scribe and was about to make my way up the stairs.

'Callias, wait a moment,' Kitane said. My heart started thumping again. 'Before you go … while I was at Alasiya, a vizier from Ramesses sailed into the harbour. When he found out that Minos was missing and that I was his daughter, he made a request.'

'What was it?' I asked, disappointed that her report was not about us.

'He told me that the Sea People had burnt Amurru to the ground and that they were now planning an attack on Djahy. The vizier begged that Keftui and Athens send ships and warriors to help the pharaoh.'

A great year went by while we rebuilt Keftui, but the situation with the Sea Scum only worsened.

CHAPTER XIV

Malia – 1179 BC

I stared down at the wind tunnel that Pirithios and I had designed at Kato Zakros. The smoke from the furnaces swirled endlessly around the thatched huts. The landscape was devoid of grass and trees, and any rainwater that fell, had cut deep furrows in the streets. The birds had long since left the town, searching for clean air. Meriones had started the fires again and I wondered what proportions of aforinium and charcoal the alchemists were using.

Our troubles certainly came in batches. Theseus, Minos and Gadeirus were still missing. The Sea Scum had attacked Alasiya, Hattusa, Ugarit and Amurru and now the pharaoh wanted us to help fight on his border at Djahy.

His wars would soon become our wars. We couldn't defend our own land if all our troops were in Egypt.

A lesson could be learnt from Amurappi's plea. He had sent all his forces to Hatti and left his own city undefended.

'We decided to use the number two mixture,' the chief alchemist from Pylos said, as if reading my mind.

'Why?' I asked.

'The xiphos made from number two have a stronger blade and hold their edge for much longer,' he replied.

'Are they easier to sharpen?'

'No, they take much longer to sharpen, but stay sharp for a long time,' he answered.

'We will soon get a chance to try them out,' I said. 'The pharaoh has asked us for help.'

'We are smelting as much ore as we can. One of my men has found an aforinium mine near Sparta, so we don't need to ship the ore from Alasiya any longer,' he said.

'That is good news. Which batches are you using at Amnisos?' I asked.

'We are using number one at Amnisos, and number two, here,' he replied. 'I have kept a record of which units are armed with which blades, so I will soon know of any faults.'

'Well, speed up production as much as you can. We will soon need every sword you can produce. I will send more slaves to help cut firewood.'

I turned to my scribe. 'Did you note that down? They are using Spartan ore here and mixture number two,' I dictated. 'They are producing number one swords at Amnisos.'

'Yes, master, I have all that,' he said. 'I don't need reminding all the time.'

We ran down to the wharves where one of our ships had just finished loading some copper ingots. It took four slaves to carry each heavy ingot by the handles. The captain was surprised to see my scribe and I helping the slaves. He was happy to have some company on the trip back to Amnisos.

It was a slow trip back to the harbour near Malia. We hung heavy in the water as the ingots pulled the bow down low to the waterline. The wind gods were not very kind to us and sweat ran in rivers from the slaves as they tried to keep us moving. As we sailed into the harbour, I could see that the wind snakes were mended but the fires were not burning. At least we had plenty of wind at Kato Zakro, so some ore was being produced today.

A surprise greeted us as we stepped onto the dock – Ariadne.

'Callias, you malaka. We trusted you with our lives and this is how you repay us! You invade our land, take over our palaces and farms and send my family to a cave in the hills!' she shouted. 'Then you send your soldiers to Thira to kidnap me! This is the second time!'

I had heard it all before.

'I wish we had never saved you and your brother from the Minotaur.'

Did I say Ariadne would not give me any trouble? I wish Theseus were here. He would know how to handle her.

'Ariadne!' I smiled.

'I can't believe what you have done to us. Where is your brother? At least he is not a traitor!' she ranted on.

'Your words sting me, Ariadne. But your facts are wrong.' I adopted my best voice.

'Theseus is missing at sea. I didn't send your mother and sisters to Zeus's cave, and I didn't send my soldiers to kidnap you.'

'You lie, you kopria! When you and your traitorous army landed, my family were so afraid that you would take them as slaves, they ran for the hills!' she shouted.

'You are talking nonsense, Ariadne.' I said. I walked over to her and tried to put my hands on her arms. Her curly black hair hung down to her waist. Her face was starting to turn from a lovely shade of olive to deep red.

'Don't touch me, Callias,' she shrugged herself away from me. 'You have a lot of explaining to do.'

She turned quickly on her heel and walked back to Malia. I had to admit, when Ariadne was wild, she was almost as attractive as her sister, but with a far worse temper.

I followed her along the beach, as the soldier crabs scuttled out of the way. My scribe looked on in amusement. 'Will I note this down?' he laughed.

'Ariadne, the original Snake Goddess,' I said. 'I will need an offering to calm her down! What do you suggest?'

'Maybe, your brother,' the scribe jested.

'Now there's an idea, if we only knew where he was!' I chuckled.

Later on, I found her sitting with her ladies-in-waiting in the ruined shrine. The vapour from their herbal tea rose in small puffs as they calmly chatted to each other. By now, a calmer demeanour had passed over Ariadne.

'Ariadne, did you read my scroll?' I said.

She didn't reply.

'It's no good trying to get at my sister through me, you know Callias. You and your brother have betrayed me before,' she kept on.

I didn't want to get into a slanging match.

'Ariadne, I need you to help me re-build this island. Your mother is too frail to help. Can you forget all that's happened in the past?' I pleaded.

'How can I forget? You have shown us your true colours. You had access to all our records, you dined at our table and drank our wine. We even let you escort my sister to Alasiya. Her slave tells me that you did more than just escort her on that ship. We trusted you with Kitane as well. Now you expect me to work with you!'

'Ariadne, it is all in the past. There was no-one left alive here when we landed. Your mother and sisters had already left for Lesithi after the earthquake struck. We never had any intentions of enslaving them. In fact, we have rebuilt your rooms at Knossos and want you to help us rebuild the other palaces. I have signed a treaty with your mother. We will help rebuild the island and use our warriors to defend you from the Sea People. Your mother has nominated you to help me rule here. What do you say?' I said.

'My mother has nominated me, has she? Where are my father and brother? Why can't you work with them?' she asked.

'This is sad news for you, Ariadne, but they are missing in Hatti,' I replied.

'How do you know all this?' she asked.

'Kitane has just returned from Alasiya. She has the news first hand from King Suppiluliuma.' 'How does she know they are dead? They could be taken hostage or even have escaped to Aegyptus.'

'Yes, that is possible, but if they were fighting at Ugarit, there were no survivors,' I said. 'Kitane wants us to build a memorial for them.'

'I am not building a memorial until I know for sure that they have gone to the gods.'

She didn't even shed a tear.

'We will make an offering to the Snake Mother for their safe return.'

'You must speak with Pasiphae and Kitane and decide,' I said. I didn't say that Meriones had killed their wretched goddess. Maybe Zeus would listen to her. But, this was a good sign. She was beginning to sound like a queen.

'We should include Theseus in our sacrifice, as well,' I said.

'Theseus will not be dead. He can't be,' she went on.

'He is still married to the Queen of Boetia,' I said.

'Yes, I know,' she said. 'That kuna warned me to keep away from him.'

'Ariadne, I don't have time to discuss the loves of your life. I need help here. You will know how to handle your subjects far better than I would.'

'I will work with you under two conditions, Callias. Condition one – my decisions will have to be discussed with my family first,' she said.

'Agreed,' I said. 'What is the other?'

'If I find that you have broken your word in any way, I will no longer co-operate with you. I cannot ask you to step down as you are in control, but I will make life very difficult,' she threatened.

I had a laugh to myself. *I will make life very difficult* was the understatement of the great year. I needed her to rule this island if I was called to Egypt. If I wanted to get rid of her, I would just need to break my word.

'And last of all. I want you to find Theseus,' she said.

I thought she hated Theseus?

'I have already started looking for my brother,' I replied

'Good then. When do we start?' she asked.

'Tomorrow. Come to the central court tomorrow. We have something important to discuss. Your mother and sisters should be back in Knossos by now. I am sure Phaedra will give you all the news,' I said.

I detected a faint smile. 'I'm sure,' she said.

* * * *

The masons chipped away at raw sandstone, moulding one block with another. The sounds of hammers and chisels rang around the walls. Ropes and pulleys were strung tight as carved blocks were slung into place. The overseers barked orders to the stoneworkers. Malia palace began to take shape again.

I was shuffling stools around getting organised for my meeting with Ariadne, when the chief mason from Knossos struggled up the stairs.

'Kalimera, Lord. I see your masons are way ahead of ours. You must send some of them over to Knossos, I will send my lazy vlakas back to the quarry.'

'I will come over and spark some life into them,' I offered.

'I don't think the Persian army could spark any life into them.'

'Your Highness, there are some old signs scratched into the labyrinth wall, near where Minos locked up the Minotaur,' he said.

'Signs?' I asked.

'A couple of bull's heads with marks underneath. I know that you may be able to read them.' 'I have some important matters to discuss here before the sun is overhead. I will pay a visit when I have finished here.'

The old mason turned to leave and almost knocked over Idas, the Spartan.

'Watch where you are going you old fool,' the prince barked.

'Sorry, Your Highness. I didn't hear you behind me,' the mason apologised.

'Off you go then.' The Spartan waved him away.

They might be the best warriors in the empire, but no-one had ever taught them any manners.

'That "old fool" is in charge of rebuilding these palaces. I hope that you never want your quarters rebuilt, as you will be doing it yourself,' I glared at him.

'We can cut blocks if we have to, Callias. Why have you dragged me here today?' he scowled.

'Idas, take a seat and wait for the others to arrive. I am not going over everything twice.'

'Before they come, Callias, there is one matter which we need to discuss. We are not taking orders from Meriones any longer. He is not a zeugitai and the only other person who can instruct us is your king,' the Spartan complained.

His attitude riled me. 'Idas, Theseus is no longer with us. I am ruling this island with Ariadne. If you are not prepared to take orders from us or my bodyguard, you had better return to Sparta.' I was furious underneath but kept as calm as I could.

'I don't know why we decided to invade Keftui with you. We have found nothing except saffron flowers and olive oil. We have taken no slaves and not even seen a fight. My men need some action and some gold. So far we have had neither,' the Spartan criticised. 'And where has old Minos hidden his treasury?'

'I've explained to you before. The treasury belongs to us all. We need money to run this empire. If there is a treasury, we haven't found it yet,' I said.

'If you do find anything, you will be keeping it to yourself, that is obvious,' he said.

'Idas. I think it best for all of us if you muster your troops and return to Sparta. There is no treasury, there are no women and no slaves. Find another war.'

'That suits me fine,' he growled and stormed off.

I breathed a sigh of relief. The Spartans would have been useful but they were more trouble than they were worth.

'Kalimera, Callias,' a female voice called from behind.

'Ariadne, it's good to see you. And I mean it this time,' I said.

'What did you say to that Spartan. He looked as if he had swallowed two snakes,' she joked.

'We had a difference of opinion. The Spartans won't be helping us any longer,' I replied.

'That is a shame. One of their hoplites is worth ten of ours,' she said.

'Wait here. My men will show up soon,' I said. 'By the way Ariadne,' I said. The Spartan had lit a spark. 'Do you know where your father kept his treasury? We need gold and silver badly, to pay for this palace.'

'It would be a rich reward for you to take back to Athens.'

She still didn't trust me. She was glowing this morning. Her galena eyes gave her an almost ethereal look. The white make up on her cheeks reflected the sunlight, and her hair hung in long coils over her dark nipples. She could wind men around her little finger if she wanted.

'Ariadne, we have to work together on this. If you do know anything, we would both be using the treasury to rebuild Keftui,' I said.

'All I know is that Father would disappear to the lower levels of the labyrinth and sometimes return with a valuable object to give to a foreign king or prince,' she replied.

The lower levels of Knossos. At least, now I had some idea. It would not all be hidden at Knossos. I was about to ask her more when Meriones walked in with the Keftui warrior chief and my weather-beaten sea captain.

'Kalimera, sit down,' I politely gestured. 'I am sure you all know Minos's eldest daughter, Princess Ariadne.'

They all nodded and smiled at her.

'Ariadne and I will be ruling this island until we have finished rebuilding.'

'With Theseus, Minos and Gadeirus missing, you are the best we have,' the old captain commented.

'I'm afraid the Spartans will be leaving us soon. There is nothing here for them,' I said.

The three men breathed a communal sigh of relief.

'We won't have to watch our backs any longer, then,' Meriones relaxed.

'They were the best hoplites we had,' Ariadne said.

'Some of my Thracians are just as good,' Meriones replied.

'They will soon have a chance to prove it,' I said.

'Why is that?' the Keftui chief asked.

I looked at them all.

'Princess Kitane has just returned from a trip to Alasiya to find her father and brother. King Suppiluliuma told her that Minos and Gadeirus had volunteered to help Amurappi at Ugarit. The remainder of our ships and the king and prince have not been seen since. Princess Kitane brought back a copy of a letter from Amurappi to Suppiluliuma, asking for help. The Sea People had already overrun Ras Shamra and their warriors were trying to turn them back,' I said.

'Yes, they were scouting Keftui when we ran into them at Agia Triada. That is how we lost Theseus,' the captain said.

'Did you actually see them killing Theseus?' Ariadne asked.

'No, we were too far away,' he said.

'So, Theseus could be still alive?' Ariadne asked.

'Yes, Your Highness. That is possible. But if they kidnapped him, we would have received a ransom demand by now, don't you think?' the captain asked.

I tried to steer the conversation in another direction.

'Like Minos and Gadeirus, he could still be alive or at the bottom of the ocean. We have to carry on without them. Now, another important matter, while Kitane was in Salamis, the Aegyptus vizier sailed into the harbour. When he found out who she was, he asked if we could help the pharaoh fight the Sea Scum at Djahy. They are gathering there, ready to invade Aegyptus,' I explained.

The clang of the bronze chisels bounced off the walls around us. The shadows in the courtyard were gradually disappearing and the heat shimmered off the pavement. A slave brought in some cool water in bamboo mugs.

'Do you think the Sea People would attack us?' I asked.

The young warrior chief looked thoughtful. 'From what the captain tells us, they have already checked whether this island would be of any use to them. I have spoken to several captives. They are looking for a new homeland – rich land which has plenty of fertile soil and water – somewhere like the Great River, not somewhere like Keftui.'

'Yes, Ugarit had plenty of grain stored underground. That will feed their people for a very long time,' Ariadne said.

'Keftui could be a staging post for them, halfway between Sparta and Libya. They could use our harbours to anchor many ships,' the captain said.

'They have overrun Ugarit and Amarru, so it would look as if they have bypassed us,' I said.

'Yes, Your Highness. They look with envy at the Great River,' the warrior chief said.

'I don't think we should leave this island undefended. Look what happened at Ugarit,' the captain rasped.

'Yes, that leads me to the next question. Should we help the pharaoh and if so, how much help should we send?' I asked.

I looked at Meriones. 'What do you think?'

'I think the pharaoh's war will become our war if the Sea People conquer Aegyptus. The pharaoh has been our ally for many great years. If we do not help him in his hour of need, we can't expect him to help us,' the general said.

'What do you think, Ariadne?' I asked the princess.

'I'll tell you what I think, Callias. We already have our hands full, trying to rebuild Keftui and feed our own people. Why take on another war? Many of our young warriors will die with no advantage to us. What if the Sea People are luring you away to Djahy, so they can walk in here with no resistance? Who will stop them?' she said.

201

'I say we help the pharaoh. We will need him if the Sea People attack us. It would be safer to leave some of our forces here just in case, and send our best ships to Aegyptus,' the old salt suggested.

'We need to keep all our ships here,' Ariadne objected.

Meriones said, 'I'm with the captain. We need to help the pharaoh, but not with everything we have.'

'Do you agree with the captain's plan?' I asked, looking at the warrior chief.

'Yes, I think it's a good plan. We need to talk to the pharaoh first, to make sure all our warriors will not be slaughtered,' he replied.

'That makes it four to one, Ariadne,' I said.

'I will have to discuss this with my mother before we allow any Keftui warriors to sail with your ships,' the princess argued.

'The rest of us will start making preparations to sail to Canaan. We will leave half our force here and the other half will help Ramesses,' I said.

'Who will be leading us?' Meriones asked.

'I will be,' I announced.

* * * *

The dust from many moons of rubble rose in a cloud above the labyrinth. I had come to have a look at these old messages that had been scratched into the wall near the Minotaur's cage. The very place where I had jumped in to help Theseus with the Minotaur was nothing but broken blocks. The ashlar ceilings had collapsed into the passageways and the spot where my brother had dropped the first xiphos now lay under a cubit of rubble. The old stone mason had started excavating the passageways near the beast's cage. The great bronze door, which had held the beast in, was a twisted wreck. The slaves shovelled dust and rock into large wicker baskets and then passed them to other slaves in a chain up the stairs. 'What was it that you wanted to show me?' I yelled at the mason.

When he saw me, he dismissed the slaves and the dust gradually settled.

'Follow me.'

I was intrigued now. We walked down the stairwell, through an archway where a heavy stone door used to swing. A twisted metal gate poked through layers of broken blocks. I remembered Minos yelling to his slaves to raise the gate at the bull leaping festival. It seemed like a lifetime ago. The light shone on a patch on the wall where the mason had cleaned the rock face.

'I was working in here a few moons ago. I thought this would make a good wine storage room, it is so cold and dank,' the mason said.

'Or a good prison!' I replied.

'Yes, that too. Anyway, I scraped some filth off these walls and if you look here, someone has chipped these inscriptions into the rock.' He pointed to the light patch he had scraped clean.

I looked closely, trying to make out the marks. The putrid smell of the unwashed Minotaur still lingered in the cage.

Half the signs were filled with black Minotaur grease.

I brushed the dust off some of the signs. 'The two drawings at the top look like bull's heads. Under the heads, I think it says: "o … ú … ru … to … pa … ra … jo – two bulls watch over old memories".'

I thought for a while. And then Helios lit a spark in my mind. The burnt piece of clay back in the records room. The piece my scribe had held upside down. But it had said "twenty bulls look over ancient …?" In the Keftui old language the two straight lines meant "two" not "twenty"'. *Was Minos trying to tell us something?* This inscription was more than a coincidence. I pretended not to know anything further.

'Two bulls owned by an elder of the tribe, probably held here at some time,' I said out loud.

'Just another list of livestock, by the look of it,' the mason observed. 'Nothing of any importance then.'

'No. But, don't plaster over them yet,' I said. 'I may need to come back.'

'With my vlakas, no chance of that for a long time,' the mason smiled.

CHAPTER XV

The Anemoi had deserted us for several moons. The calm water lapped at the bows of our fighting ships and the warriors and seamen grew restless waiting for Zephyrus. We sacrificed a horse to the wind god of the west, but it made no difference. The augur saw a gannet flying towards Eurus just after we offered the horse blood to Zephyrus. The bird flapped its right wing very high as it flew past. We knew that this bad omen could not be ignored. I sent my army back to shore. The pharaoh would have to wait. Zephyrus at best was only a breeze but he would halve the sailing time to Alasiya.

We had built the latest bronze rams into the nose of the biremes. The master had mustered another twelve monoremes from Piraeus. Six merchantmen were loaded with supplies and foot soldiers. Each warship was equipped with the latest grappling hooks and boarding ramps. The dolphin mastheads were painted bright blue. The evil eyes on the bows were ready. The ships which Theseus had captured from Minos were sleek and fast but they were not equipped with battering rams. They would be our eyes and ears.

The alchemist had issued half the warriors with the new xiphos. These valued weapons soon became the prize if a warrior won a bet. None of us knew if they were any good, but the shiny new metal was very attractive. The whetstone-sharpened blades could shave the hairs from a man's arm and were only half the weight of the old bronze weapons.

Many of the old boar's tusk helmets had been pulled to pieces and the tusks threaded on leather thongs. These necklaces were a warning to evil spirits. Hundreds of new bronze helmets glinted in the sun. Wealthier tribal leaders had custom-made bronze cuirasses, but the lower ranks wore polished leather "fish scale" body armour. The archers were bare compared to their swordsmen brothers. The oak longbows hung over their shoulders and arrows were packed in a leather quiver hanging from their waist. The slingers had practised until they could hit a cock at fifty paces. The whistle of the stones was the last noise many enemy soldiers ever heard.

Yes, except for Zephyrus, we were ready.

The water lapped gently along Amnisos beach and the flames from the campfires danced in the warm night air. The Anemoi still did not stir and the echo of a dirty Laconian war song drifted over the waves. I watched the flames dancing a slow rhythm from the front of my ox hide tent. The horse offering was ignored. Maybe a Minoan bull would be more acceptable. The augur had not sighted a Eurus bound gannet for a long time now. I was becoming mesmerised by the orange dancing flames when some high sparks started to fly toward Alasiya. I blinked to make sure I was not imagining things. The flames started to bend. I shook the captain.

'Wake up. Wake up. The wind gods have heard us!' I yelled at him. 'Look at those flames.'

It felt so good to be on the open sea again. Cool Zephyrus billowed the sails toward the enemy. My long hair blew back out of my eyes and I could see the Keftui monoremes out in front. They hadn't heeded my orders to stay within one stadia of the fleet, but they were keen. Pasiphae had disagreed with Ariadne's plan, and had ordered half the Keftui warriors to fight alongside us.

My officers tried and tried to drill them in our new fighting techniques, but their old habits were hard to break. We wouldn't be fighting in dense forest like they were used to. We would be out in the open, probably running over sand dunes.

As the cool waters splashed off our bows, I began to wonder about my brother. Where would I start to look? If we could take some prisoners at Alasiya or Djahy, we may be lucky to find a Sea Scum who was there when he was captured.

Did I really want him back? I cursed myself for even thinking this. I was starting to get used to this feeling of being in command but, unlike Theseus, I learnt as I went along. The school of life was my teacher. *Did I really want to find him?* It was my duty to find him, not just to please Ariadne. He would do the same for me.

Our royal companions splashed happily alongside us. It didn't matter how hard Zephyrus blew, they could always match our speed. Maybe they took it in turns, but I suspect the leader of the pack was allowed to stay in front.

After two moons of good sailing, the lead monoreme spotted gannets diving for fish several stadia ahead. Alasiya wasn't far away. I was anxious to find out what had happened there. Since my visit with Pirithios, when Salamis was a hive of activity, it looked as if the place had become like a large mausoleum.

I signalled the captain to anchor offshore and we rowed into the harbour.

Nothing moved except a few half-starved dogs pulling entrails from corpses, long dead.

This reminded me of the day we invaded Malia, with the smell of rotting flesh added. The remains of the warehouses, where I had threatened the king, were nothing but black ash. There was no smoke. The port had been pillaged many moons ago. Meriones and I sprang over the bow and signalled for twenty hoplites to follow.

The tops of broken masts poked above the water line, like some bizarre burnt forest. Headless Hittite warriors bobbed up and down against the pylons. I held my scarf over my nose and signalled the men to follow me to the palace. As we jogged along, I noticed that there were no women and children amongst the dead. There were no cattle, sheep or goats in the pens or fields.

The Sea Scum would herd the livestock along behind their army for fresh meat.

Every hut had been ransacked – stripped of anything of value. It was clear evidence that Chief Lydus had been here. His marauders did not have a supply line; they lived off conquered land as they went. Lydus made sure that no one else could use the land, either.

A dog yelped in pain as one of my men kicked it off a corpse.

'This is a Tartarus on earth,' I said to Meriones. 'We even have the dogs guarding the corpses of the dead.'

'Cerberus would feel at home here,' he replied. He quickly pushed his scarf back over his nose.

As we approached the palace, Meriones pointed to four dark objects stuck in the ground in front of the gates. As we drew nearer, we could hardly believe the sight in front of us. Four blackened corpses hung from the top of four poles. They had been impaled.

One of the bodies had decomposed and hung limply in the hot sun. The corpse used to be very fat. I looked away when I realised who it was. My stomach began to churn. I couldn't control myself. Warm vomit came racing up my throat. I fell on my hands and knees on the burnt grass and emptied my last meal on the grass. Two of the men broke ranks and retched beside me. I felt a hand on my back.

'Let's get out of here, Lord,' Meriones said through his scarf. 'There's nothing we can do here. We won't forget this.'

I tried to pull myself together in front of the men.

'I thought Mutallu ... Kitane said her husband had escaped to Hattusa. The Sea People must have captured him somewhere. He was a coward. Still, he didn't deserve this.'

I rinsed my mouth out with some fresh water and took a gulp.

'No, we aren't going yet. Check the palace. Get those men down,' I yelled at several hoplites. 'The largest corpse is King Mutallu. He was Princess Kitane's husband. Bury him under those trees over there and place a new sword beside his body. Without him, there would be no aforinium swords.'

My men groaned as they walked across to the victims. Some started to dig a shallow grave and the others heaved the stakes out of the ground.

'You two,' I said to my fellow weak stomachs, 'clean yourselves up and come with me.'

We walked quickly through the main gate into Mutallu's throne room. The luxurious Persian carpets were covered in smashed amphora and broken furniture. A fine, white cotton veil, soaked in blood, lay in a pile near the king's chair. As we walked in, I heard a scratching noise coming from the concubine's room.

'Listen. Check that out,' I said to Meriones. He drew his sword and quietly stepped through the doorway. A large rat scurried for cover.

'Just vermin,' he said.

The other two hoplites started to sift through the debris. One of them had turned white and I told him sit on Mutallu's broken throne.

'What do you make of this, Your Highness?' The other hoplite held up a leather helmet stitched around with red and blue feathers.

'That is from the Peleset ... I know who ...' I heard a crash from the concubine's room. Meriones looked at me and ran back through the door. We heard a scuffle and the three of us ran after him. The bodyguard emerged from behind a blood spattered Persian tapestry dragging a filthy boy by the ear.

'Look what I found hiding in the harem! Another filthy rat!' he grinned.

The boy's dark eyes went wild. They darted from side to side when he saw the rest of us in full armour, with our swords drawn. His long black hair was knotted and covered in cobwebs. Some wounds on his legs oozed pus. He could have been seven or eight sun years.

'Stand still,' I said. 'We aren't going to hurt you. If we let you go, do you promise not to run away? Do you understand?'

He nodded his head. His mother must have known our tongue. I remembered that Mutallu had many Keftui slaves and concubines.

'Let him go,' I said.

The boy rubbed his red ear. 'Ow! That hurts,' he cried. Tears cut a track down his filthy face.

'Now stop crying. We will not harm you. What is your name?' I asked.

'K ... K ... Katuzili,' he said as he looked at the floor.

'Where is your mother?'

'The, the ... soldiers took her away with the other mothers,' he cried.

'Why didn't they take you?' I asked.

'I hid over there.' He pointed to the blood spattered tapestry.

'Where did they take all the mothers and your playmates?'

'Th ... they ... put them in the ships down there.' He pointed towards the wharves.

'Did you see them sail away?'

'Mmmmm ... yes.' His chest heaved up and down as he tried to stop crying.

'You have been very brave, Katuzili. Now, can you remember which way they sailed?'

He just pointed this time. He pointed over the hills towards Canaan.

'Where is your father, Katuzili?' Meriones asked.

His bottom lip started to tremble again. 'On that pole out there. He was very fat. He screamed and screamed and took a long time to die,' he said.

'Did you see who killed him?' the bodyguard asked.

'A b ... beast with a black beard and a gold armband,' he stammered.

I looked at Meriones. 'Our old friend.'

'Don't worry, Katuzili, We will find your mother,' Meriones said. Only the gods would know what this poor child had seen. It would take him many moons to recover.

'We will also find that beast for you, Katuzili. You can come with us now and live on our ship. We will show you how to be a sailor. Would you like that?'

This suggestion seemed to take his mind off the ordeal for a short while.

'Oh, yes sir, I would. When can we start?'

'Take him back to our ship. Get the slaves to give him a good soak and cut his hair. Tell the pharmacea to dress those wounds and give him a good meal. We have ourselves a royal cabin boy,' I said to the hoplite sitting in Mutallu's chair.

Lydus. He was a few moons ahead of us but he left a trail of blood.

* * * *

The copper mines at Mt Troodos were mines no longer. The tunnels were caved in, the smelters smashed and, like the rest of Alasiya, the odour of death floated on the breeze. I couldn't understand why the barbarians would smash these huge smelters. Maybe they didn't want anyone using them after they had gone. They weren't planning to come back.

We sailed over to Amathous, where we had first seen the Alasiyans making aforinium swords. Not one green leaf could be seen on the hills. The town had suffered the same fate as Mt Troodos. A few dazed mine workers picked through the burnt rubble of the ancient huts. The giant wind funnel looked like some grotesque crippled lizard. The alchemist's huts were burnt to the ground and the round grinding wheels had been used for some childish game of skittles.

I said to Meriones, 'This is where Pirithios and I spied on the sword makers.'

'Why were you spying?' he asked.

'The Alasiyans didn't want to show us everything. Have a look on the hilt of your xiphos, what marks does it have?' I asked.

He pulled his sword from under his shoulder. 'It has one mark near the handle.'

'Well it is made from a mixture which we are testing,' I said. 'You have a lucky number.' 'This is the place where this information came from. Without Mutallu, we would still be using bronze.'

'Why would these scum destroy all this?' he said.

'I don't know,' I replied. 'They mustn't have known what was going on here.'

I gazed out across the beach where I had smelt the grilled fish all that time ago. It was now littered with coloured flotsam from the smashed boats. A few corpses washed back and forth with the tide. *The barbarians must not have the formulae for these new swords, or they would have used all this to make their own weapons.*

Our monoreme bobbed patiently in the harbour waiting for us to return.

'We should try and rebuild all this, one day,' Meriones said.

'Yes, we have a long list. That son of Mutallu's – what was his name?' I asked.

'Katuzili,'

'Yes, Katuzili. When the boy pointed to Apeliotes, where do you think Lydus was heading?'

'If the pharaoh said the barbarians were going to attack Djahy, they would need a base near the pharaoh's border,' Meriones thought as he scratched his head.

'Somewhere like Amurru.'

'Yes, Lord. Somewhere like Amurru, but he would have to pillage the Hatti settlers there first,' the bodyguard observed.

'We'll follow his trail of blood, then, and see where it leads us.'

Chapter XVI

Amurru (Hatti) – 1178 BC

The foreign countries made a conspiracy in their lands. All at once the lands were removed and scattered in the fray. No land could stand before their arms: from Hatti, Qode, Carchamesh, Arzawa, and Alashiya on, being cut off at one time. A camp was set up in Amurru. They desolated its people, and its land was like that which has never come into being. They were coming forward toward Egypt, while the flame was prepared before them. Their confederation was the Peleset, Tjekker, Shekelesh, Denyen and Weshesh lands united. They laid their hands upon the land as far as the circuit of the earth, their hearts confident and trusting: Our plans will succeed!

– Ramesses III mortuary stele, Medinet Habu, Thebes

* * * *

We were too late. The Amorites were decimated. Rivulets of sweat made small tracks down the grime on our chests. I was last in the climb. All that time spent in the archive rooms had made me soft. I needed a few more rounds with my old Spartan sword master to toughen me up. All I could see was Meriones' rear end way ahead of me, as we climbed the mountains near

Gebal. I stopped to catch my breath and gazed back out to sea. I could just make out the tops of the main masts of two or three of our ships. The captain had anchored the fleet just below the horizon. We were in dangerous waters and had been fortunate so far, not to have been spotted by the enemy.

'Wait!' I gasped to my bodyguard and he turned around.

'Get a move on, Callias, you are holding us back,' he teased.

The scouts were by now, lying on their stomachs, under a cedar tree, at the top of the ridge. Something had their attention. Their tanned bodies and camouflage made them almost invisible against the Amurru hills.

A startled pheasant suddenly flew up in front of me and an annoyed scout looked around and held a finger to his lips. When he saw that it was me causing the commotion he said quietly, 'Oh, sorry, Your Highness, I hope none of them saw that bird. You better take a look at this.'

He nodded at the scene unfolding in the valley below.

The old Hatti trading town was alight. Thatched rooves exploded in the sun and sent clouds of black smoke swirling up to the clouds. Women and children ran screaming from their huts, but they were soon rounded up by warriors wearing feathered headdresses, and pushed into a large group in the town square. Men, young and old, were being systematically slaughtered. As soon as they were flushed out of their hiding places, they were speared or caught with a well-aimed arrow. Hundreds of mutilated Hatti corpses lay scattered about the village. Sea Scum warriors went from door to door looking for more victims. They were after more than blood. Many of them carried pithos jars back to a huge dump near the women and children. Most unusual of all, a long, winding line of wagons carrying their own women and children trailed off into the distance. The line had stopped moving as the battle raged on ahead. Sea Scum women in coloured shawls walked along beside old and battered wagons; small children with their grandmothers rode on the seats; young boys with thin sticks herded flocks of goats behind the wagons; and the old men rode along on stolen mules and donkeys. I had never seen anything like it. A mass migration of an entire race of people; but where were they going?

A woman's scream echoed up the hills as a tall warrior with a gold arm band walked up to a village chief, who was kneeling in the middle of the village square. Two feathered warriors grabbed the woman by the arms. She screamed again as the executioner swung his long sword. A flash of sunlight glinted off the polished blade as it swished through the air. The victim's head left his shoulders and rolled in the hot sand to stop at her feet. The warriors let her go and she fell forward and grasped the warm head. The screams from the captured women and children were so loud, they could have woken Zeus. The warriors picked her up again and threw her into the crowd of wailing women.

There was nothing we could do. Not now. We won't forget. Meriones pushed one of the young scouts in the back as he retreated down the slope.

Several of the Peleset and Danaoi women left the wagon train and started to load the plundered food and clothing onto donkeys. I wondered if our cabin boy's mother was among those women. We were all stunned into silence and crawled silently away. Now, we knew what we were up against. We were no match for these thousands of nomads. We had to find the pharaoh.

CHAPTER XVII

Zahi (Djahy), Southern Levant – 1178 BC

'Dust storm!' our lookout yelled from the crow's nest. We turned to where he was pointing and could see clouds of dust billowing into the clear morning sky.

'Dust storms early in the morning. I don't believe it,' Meriones said.

After the destruction at Amarru, Arpactias billowed our sails towards the land of the pharaoh. We kept the fleet together during the night, sailing as close to the coast as we could. The lookouts could see several large campfires amongst the sand dunes, but we couldn't tell if they were friend or foe. The relentless Arabian sun was just poking over the horizon.

'What did you say?' I asked my bodyguard.

'A dust storm at daylight. In all my travels, I have found that these dust storms only start when the sand has heated up,' he explained. 'And that is usually not at daylight.'

I yelled through cupped hands up to the lookout. 'What else can you see?'

'It's not a dust storm. Looks like an army. Thousands of chariots.'

'Do they belong to the pharaoh?'

'I can't tell from up here. We are too far away, Your Highness.'

'Meriones, signal one of the monoremes to come alongside and go and investigate. Hoist our red flag in case it is the enemy,' I ordered.

Meriones rowed off with twenty slaves and ten of Pasiphae's warriors. We polished our armour and sharpened our weapons while we waited for him to return.

Three or four suns passed when we saw his monoreme push off from the shoreline. Meriones sprang back on board with a smile that lit up the ship.

'We have found the pharaoh!' he exclaimed.

'Did you speak to him,' I asked.

'No, he was busy with his troops, but the vizier saw us rowing in and gave us a warm welcome,' the bodyguard said.

'What is the latest on the enemy?'

'They have overrun Amurru and are preparing to invade Canaan. They are forming up on the border,' Meriones went on. 'Ramesses has personally taken command of the army.'

'Did you tell him that we are here to help?'

'Yes, the vizier was very pleased to see us. Ramesses is planning to attack at daybreak. He wants us to form up on the beach before the sun comes up.'

We had sailed a long way to stop these animals. If I found Lydus, we could cut the head off the snake and maybe the body would die.

As we disembarked in the early morning light, more plumes of dust billowed up inland from us. The hoplites were pleased to have their feet back on Mother Earth. As they piled off our galleys, I thought, *Now we will see if these new weapons are any good.*

I pulled mine from under my shoulder to remind me of the alchemist's mark. Two marks, near the hilt. The rows of new bronze helmets of my small army glimmered in the morning sun. The polished leather cuirasses made them look invincible. I assembled the first five hundred or so hoplites on the beach and our column snaked its way inland to Zahi.

We had only marched a few stadia when, from the distance, out of the cloud of dust, came a gold chariot being pulled by two magnificent grey stallions. Two Aegyptus warriors stood on the deck. The driver had a high, cream, leather crown on his head and the second warrior had a strangely shaped bow slung over his shoulder.

As the chariot grew nearer, I could see that it bore the cartouche of Ramesses on both sides. He looked like Helios himself, flying out of the morning mist, to kidnap Persephone. But, no, it was the living god – Usimare Ramesses III – Beloved of Amun, Born of Ra, Ruler of Heliopolis.

They knew how to give themselves some great titles, these Aegyptus pharaohs. The stallions skidded to a halt in front of our column, their nostrils flaring.

'Is Prince Callias among you?' Ramesses called.

'You are looking at him.'

'Welcome to our land, Prince. My vizier tells me that you are here to help. The princess at Alasiya – I forget her name – gave you my message,' the pharaoh said.

'Her name is Kitane, Great Pharaoh. She was betrothed to the Hittite, Murappu but he has been butchered by the enemy.'

'Yes, my men told me that Murappu had been impaled. If we catch Lydus, he will meet the same fate. Your great king Minos sailed to help us at Ugarit. What has happened to him?' he asked.

'Our king and Prince Gadeirus are missing.'

'If we capture Lydus, he will tell us the fate of my old friend Minos before we are finished with him. But for the barbarians, their journey to Aegyptus stops here,' the pharaoh said.

'Join our foot soldiers on the left and take command of all those men. Callias, it's up to you to make sure the invaders do not outflank us.'

Memories of my father saying it was up to me to save Athens came flooding back.

'It will be my honour, Great Pharaoh. We have about two thousand hoplites and one hundred cavalry. We could not load any more onto our ships. Our strength is at sea, in our galleys. They are waiting offshore should any of the foreigners try to make a run for it,' I replied.

'Very good tactics, Prince. We won't forget this.'

He glanced down at my front row of hoplites with their flashing xiphos and scalloped shields.

'What are those strange swords that you carry? They are very different to our khopesh,' the pharaoh asked.

'They are called "xiphos" and are made from aforinium,' I said. 'We haven't tried them in battle yet.'

'Let's hope they serve you well, my friend.'

Looking skywards, the pharaoh continued. 'My father, the Mighty Ra is with us, today.'

I leant across from my saddle and shook his hand. His grey stallions had recovered and stood flicking their tails at the buzzing flies. Again, I noticed his driver had a strange bow slung over his shoulder. It was shaped like a soaring eagle – nothing like our long bows.

Ramesses flicked the reins before I could ask anything, and the chariot disappeared like a golden ghost, back into the shrouding dust.

* * * *

The charioteers were warriors ... and all good officers, ready of hand. Their horses were quivering in their every limb, ready to crush the foreign countries under their feet ...

– Rameses III Mortuary stele, Medinet Habu, Karnak

Row upon row of warriors faced each other over the horizon. The Sea Scum were riding a mixture of captured Hatti, Amorite and Ugarit chariots with no two alike.

The pharaoh's chariots were like peas in a pod. Their handrails glistened; the headdresses of the drivers sparkled white as the first rays of the sun stroked their bare skin. The pharaoh's chariots were manned by two men: a driver and a bowman. The Sea People machines had only one horse and just a driver.

I could see the Great Pharaoh himself, galloping up and down in his golden chariot in front of his troops. The sand spat skyward as he lurched into a turn and ran back down in the opposite direction. His well-disciplined, professional army didn't need any motivation. I could see that they had trained for this day for many moons. Row upon row of bronze shields and highly-polished khopesh flashed in the sun.

On the other hand, the Sea People were from every walk of life. Some were captured slaves forced to fight alongside their Dorian masters. Some were mercenaries paid to fight for Lydus with stolen gold. Some were young men given the choice of fighting for the cause or being executed. Some were Canaanites willing to avenge their tribes which were overrun by the pharaoh.

In the centre stood Lydus's crack troops, the Sherden, with their strange two horned helmets. On the right flank, I could see the cavalry of the Tjekker in front of the dark Weshesh tribesmen. On our flank, I recognised the Peleset with their bright plumed headdress.

I caught a flash of light from an armband on a tall Lukkan horseman. He cantered up and down in front of his men with a highly polished sword held high in his right hand. I was a long way away, but it looked very like the one I had given Theseus many moons ago.

'Keep your eye on that sentina,' I said to Meriones. 'I want him taken alive.'

'The gold armband from Salamis and Amurru – how could I forget,' he said.

I signalled to the Companions, my personal bodyguards. 'Stay with me. I want that Lukkan sentina alive.'

The pharaoh's chariots trotted toward the enemy lines in disciplined orderliness. Our hoplites could learn a lot from the Aegyptus.

His foot soldiers followed closely behind the rows and rows of churning wheels.

A few Sea Scum arrows began to land harmlessly, half-a-stadia away from the front ranks.

Suddenly, the chariots halted a stadia or so away from the Sherden and Ramesses dropped his hand. His archers pointed high in the sky and a thousand arrows almost blotted out the sun.

The strange weapon which Ramesses's bowman had carried was a super bow.

A few enemy arrows landed harmlessly in front of our chariots while the pharaoh's archers rained death from above. The super bows had twice the height and twice the range.

Row upon row of Sherden front ranks toppled over. Wounded horses bolted back through their troops, causing chaos, charging over foot soldiers and other chariots.

Ramesses dropped his hand again and a wall of swirling wheels raced towards Lydus's front line. The two-man chariots carved a swathe through the one-man machines. The drivers' reins flicked up and down, one machine behind another, at full gallop. A chariot archer fired off three or four shots in rapid succession and I watched in amazement as wounded Sea Scum horses and drivers nosedived into the sand. A Dorian driver catapulted backwards, off his wheels, as an arrow caught him in the throat.

This new warfare was something my men would have to learn. I was so engrossed in the efficiency of Ramesses killing machines, I hadn't noticed a troop of Lydus's cavalry galloping around our left flank.

Out of the mayhem, several Lukkan horsemen raced out of the haze, straight for me. A blade whistled over my head. I hauled on my horse's reigns and spun in the loose sand. 'Look out!' I screamed.

I slashed with my xiphos as he swung again. It struck the Lukkan's blade with a loud clang of metal and my sword broke in half. Horrified, I stared at the useless handle in my right hand.

Fearing a fatal blow from the brutal Lukkan, I quickly resigned myself to a gruesome fate and prepared to meet the gods.

As I raised my arms to form a useless shield against the Lukkan – strangely – the Sea Scum rolled forward in the saddle, an arrow sunk deep in his back. I sprang down and grabbed his old bronze sword.

Away in the distance, Ramesses' trumpet sounded a general charge.

I whirled and yelled, 'Open up!'

Responding to the order, the ranks of hoplites instantly parted, leaving a gap in our centre. The tactic for capturing cavalry was a drill learnt in the wars with Corinth and Thebes.

The enemy cavalry charged in, their long slashing blades whistling from side to side. A hoplite crashed down, holding his face, as a blade caught him square in the front of his helmet.

Where was the gold armband? Desperately, I scanned the mayhem as the enemy cavalry became snared in our trap.

'Circle around them!' I yelled but no one heard.

'Where is the gold armband?' I yelled.

Another horseman flew out of the haze and charged straight at Meriones.

'Behind you!' I screamed.

The blade flashed – it hit him high up in the right arm. A river of blood ran down his curiass, leaving his right arm hanging useless by his side. Small spurts of blood sprayed over his saddle, before I grabbed him as he reeled over. I pushed him back into his saddle and he slumped on the pommel. Snorting and rearing, the frightened barbarian horses had nowhere to go and added to the chaos.

A Lukkan foot soldier swung his heavy bronze weapon at one of my Companions. My guard swung wildly and blocked the bronze blade with his new xiphos. The two swords clanged loudly as metal bit into metal. To my horror, the xiphos bent in two.

I reefed at my bridle and spun my horse as the Lukkan took aim at the guard. I flashed past and the tip of my old bronze sword caught the Sea Scum's hand. His fingers flew off into the air, still clinging to his weapon.

'Grab his sword!' I yelled at the hoplite. 'It won't bend.'

Meriones looked like death was upon him. I pulled him from his horse, tore off my scarf and pulled it tight around his butchered arm.

'Leave me be, Callias. The pharaoh needs you,' he murmured.

224

'Never,' I said. I threw his good arm over my shoulder and dragged him to the rear.

I grabbed the nearest pharmacea. 'If he dies, I will hold you personally responsible,' I yelled. The pharaoh's army battled their way up the dunes. The foot soldiers with their khopesh and super bows slaughtered thousands of nomads.

The enemy finally beat a hasty retreat back to Amurru. The Great Pharaoh encircled the Sea People's army and took thousands of prisoners.

They would be recruited into his ranks and made to fight their own brothers. The pharaoh's officers had roped large numbers of Peleset together around the neck. Their arms were tied by their elbows behind their backs and above their heads.

I wondered which was a better fate for them: to be forced to fight for Ramesses or spend a life of wandering with Lydus.

* * * *

I turned back to where I had left Meriones. My small army had fought well. Several Messenians wandered through the battlefield, finishing off wounded Sea People and despatching bleeding horses. A troop of Pasiphae's warriors herded the remnants of the enemy with Ramesses prisoners, their dejected faces hidden under helmets and headdresses.

I pulled my mount to a halt where my sword had snapped in half and pulled it from the hot sand.

'Those new swords are skata. They could have got us killed!' a voice behind me shouted.

I turned to see the Athenian I had rescued earlier.

'You saved my life, Lord, but I'll be using the old bronze swords in future,' he growled, shaking his old blood stained weapon in the air. All around, a rowdy bunch joined in, voicing their displeasure.

Guilt and self-doubt flooded over me. *How could I have been so foolish, to put so many men at risk in battle with untested weapons? Why didn't I remain where I belonged – as a scribe? Oh how I wished I had Theseus's ability to make good decisions. But without Theseus, I had no option but to appear strong in front of the men.*

Displaying a confidence I did not feel, I addressed the men.

'The new swords may have failed us today, but they are light and sharp. They can still cut a man's head off in a single blow. Our old bronze swords cannot do that! I will go back to the alchemist and make stronger ones. We will keep making them stronger, and stronger, until we have swords so strong that no Sea Scum will ever dare attack us!'

I was met with a mixed response. Some men responded enthusiastically, shouting praise for me, others cried out with threats.

Shaking from my exaggerated bravery, I turned my broken blade over. It had two marks on the hilt. I had killed several men with it, but it was totally useless in a sword fight.

'My xiphos worked perfectly,' yelled someone from the crowd. 'I fought off many Sherden with it. It slashed throats and held strong against the bronze weapons.'

I felt a brief wave of relief. 'Bring it here,' I demanded.

It was a xiphos with one mark on the blade. This was a good sign; I would keep experimenting with the formula. I held the xiphos high above my head. 'This is a fine example of a xiphos! I will not stop until every man has such a sword to protect himself!'

As the men disbanded, I went to check on Meriones. He was as pale as a white linen cape and had been laid on a soft goatskin mattress in an Aegyptus tent, along with the wounded. I stopped and spoke some encouraging words to the other wounded as I found his bed. The pharmacea was busy bandaging and administering doses of poppy seed elixir to other moaning patients. I looked down at Meriones, gently touching his good arm. His eyes flicked open.

'Prince,' he whispered. 'Did we t ... t ... teach them a lesson?'

'They are on the run back to Amurru. The pharaoh has taken many thousands of prisoners,' I said.

A faint smile lit his lips.

'Any sign of the golden arm band?' he asked quietly.

'No. He has slipped the net I'm afraid. But we will get him. How's the arm?'

'The head pharmacea says the arm will have to come off. My fighting arm,' he groaned. His eyes fluttered and closed, yielding to a good dose of poppy elixir.

'You will soon learn to fight with your left arm,' I said, but he didn't respond.

The head pharmacea walked quietly up beside me.

'Let him sleep, Lord. The wound has cut all the major blood tubes in his right arm. He has lost a lot of blood. I don't know whether he will survive an operation.'

'Make sure that he lives,' I said sternly. 'If he should die ...'

The pharmacea held his hands up in a gesture of doubt.

'I will make a sacrifice to Asclepius,' I said.

* * * *

Row upon row of unharnessed chariots formed the perimeter of the pharaoh's camp. The horse handlers fed out choice green hay and dozens of slaves tipped water into long troughs in the horses' enclosure. The animal skin tents were arranged in rows inside the chariots. Squads of bare chested Aegyptus warriors drilled on the hard sand around the camp. Their white linen skirts swung in unison as the officers barked orders at them.

I marvelled at the well-oiled military machine which Ramesses had assembled. His father had reigned over Aegyptus for eight great years – more than a lifetime for most of us. I could see where the current Ramesses had learnt all that he knew. We had much to learn from them.

'I congratulate you and your fine army from Keftui,' the pharaoh gestured as I walked into his command post. 'Your cavalry fought bravely against the invaders and your hoplites used a shield wall. We could use that.'

'The Lukkans took us by surprise and I lost quite a few men. I'm afraid Lydus escaped our clutches,' I replied.

'The barbarian realised he was doomed early in the battle and escaped back to Amurru,' the pharaoh said. 'But we taught the sentina a lesson they won't forget for a long time. I now have an extra ten thousand prisoners which will swell our ranks.

'What of these new weapons of yours?' he went on.

I thought for a moment. *How would I handle this?*

'They are made from a new metal called aforinium, which comes from Alasiya. The swords are light and sharp, but some of them failed us in the battle – my warriors are not pleased.'

'We need to know about them, as soon as possible,' the pharaoh said. 'We are running out of copper and already have to bring tin from Hatti.'

An officer's voice barked through the tent and he stopped for a moment. 'We have plenty of food and water which the Sea People desperately need. We also have plenty of gold and silver which is useless for making weapons.'

I thought for a moment. *Maybe we could do a trade.*

'Great Pharaoh, I saw your magnificent bows in action. They slaughtered many barbarians long before they could get near us.'

'Yes, they were designed by our Hyksos brothers. They are made from horn, spruce and sinew, glued together in layers. They are so strong that we need two men to string them,' he explained. 'My father used them at Kadesh. But, they cannot be used in wet weather.'

'I like them. They have twice the range of our old timber bows. I say from here on in, we share our weapons. With your bows and our swords, no one will be able to defeat us! ' I said.

'Agreed, Callias. We have been allies for many great years. As long as you give us the correct formula for the swords. Now, you must sail down to the Great River and meet us at Heliopolis. You will be our guests until we are sure these invaders have left our shores.'

* * * *

The pharmacea could not look me in the eye when I returned to the tent of the wounded.

'I regret Your Highness, your bodyguard did not survive the operation very well,' he offered.

'Very well? What do you mean "very well?"'

'He is still alive but only clings to life by a thread.'

My trusted companion lay unconscious, his eyes closed. His colour had changed from pale white to a pallid shade of grey. His right arm was gone, the stump wrapped in blood soaked linen. I pulled the fly screen aside and said quietly, 'We're going to Heliopolis, Meriones, to the land of milk and honey. Many eastern beauties await you there. Ramesses wants you to train his warriors.'

His eyes fluttered open. 'You go, my Lord. Hermes is waiting for me,' he whispered.

'The pharaoh needs you, Meriones.'

He held out his only hand to me. I grasped it and squeezed it gently. It was cold.

'Please tell my mother that I died a hero, Callias. I died saving the new king of Keftui. I will soon be with Demeter,' he gasped.

I had to lean down to hear his last few words. He gave a short choking cough and his mouth dropped open. He was gone. He had waited for me. I gently closed his eyelids. My great general was gone. Thanatos had taken his spirit but his great deeds would live on.

I looked at his earthly remains. 'We will build you a great pyre. The gods will remember you, Meriones. I will carry your ashes back to Attica and your mother will build you a mausoleum. You will always be with us.'

The pharmacea pulled the linen shroud over his head.

'Make the preparations,' I said. 'We send him to the gods before we sail.'

'Yes, Lord. I will see to it,' he said.

'Your punishment for losing my trusted friend and general will be to supply two oxen for sacrifice,' I ordered.

'Asclepius did not listen, Lord,' he said quietly.

'Meriones called you "the new king of Keftui". Are you our new king?'

'No. Minos and Gadeirus may still be alive. I am still a mere prince from Athens.' I replied.

One of Pasiphae's delirious tribesmen let out a piercing yell and the blood spattered pharmacea hurried off.

* * * *

The smoke from the funeral pyre rose to the Titans. It reminded me of father's funeral pyre at Athens. The flames licked around Meriones shrouded corpse. Sparks leapt into the sky as several Elysian priests intoned the ferryman. The cedar logs crashed down and sent waves of scented air through the ranks of warriors.

The sacrificial oxen were led in. The high priest cut several strands of hair from their heads. He sung a hymn to Persephone and threw the hair into the fire. He sprinkled some barley on the ground and the beasts nuzzled into the welcome grain. Their heads went down, and he sprinkled some votive wine between their ears. The beasts shook their heads and gave their approval to be sacrificed. The priests thrust their sacred knives deep into the animal's throats and the oxen slumped to the ground.

Other attendants rushed in to collect the animals' blood and started butchering the carcasses. The sacred offal was placed on a large bronze grille and the scented smoke wafted up to the gods. The animals were cut into their sacred portions and my army feasted on roast oxen until well into the small moons. The campfires gradually flickered out, and it wasn't long before the first rays of the merciless sun rose over the desert.

I watched a priest carefully sift through the ashes and tip Merione's remains into a marble urn. The priest shuffled over to me and said, 'You will know what to do with these, Lord, when someday you return to Attica.'

Chapter XVIII

Heliopolis, Great River Delta, Aegyptus – 1176 BC

As for those who reached my frontier, their seed is not, their heart and their sole are finished forever and ever. As for those who came forward together on the sea, the full flame was in front of them at the Nile mouth, while a stockade of lances surrounded them on the shore, prostrated on the beach, slain, and made into heaps from head to tail.

– Battle of the Nile Delta, Ramesses III Mortuary Temple, Thebes, 1176 BC

We had left the shores of Keftui two sun years ago. My troops were longing to see their womenfolk. The young children had forgotten what their fathers looked like. I was hearing rumblings of discontent from some quarters, especially Pasiphae's tribesmen.

They had wanted me to release them from their service and supply three ships to take them home.

I was furious. They would stay with the hoplites and cavalry until the pharaoh no longer needed us. If anyone left their ranks, they would be regarded as deserters. They knew the penalty for desertion.

To keep them occupied, I set them the task of learning how to make the new horned bows. It was the kind of work that the natives had a gift for, and they soon learnt the necessary skills from Ramesses' craftsmen.

Since our battle at Djahy, the Sea Scum had mounted small raiding parties along the pharaoh's coast. Ramesses could not rest. He did not have a strong navy. Most of his sailors were accustomed to cruising in calm waters up and down the Great River.

On the other hand, the Sea People were excellent sailors, and since they had made a peace treaty with the Phoenicians, they ruled the waves.

Ramesses' secret weapon was his well-trained army. His father had turned an unruly bunch of farm labourers and assorted tradesmen into a fearful fighting force. Many of Ramesses' troops were now permanent soldiers who spent their working life protecting the realm.

I spread our hoplites and natives amongst the pharaoh's men so that they could learn each other's fighting techniques. There had been a clash of cultures to start with, and fights had broken out. I bashed a few heads together and now there was an uneasy peace in the ranks. Fortunately, the men had accepted that I was their leader.

The pharaoh's men were now resigned to the fact that their women were attracted to the strange, long haired, dark men from the north and that our gods were different to theirs.

The canals around the pharaoh's capital city buzzed with traders from all over the world. The small, wooden dhows, which plied goods as far as Karnak, jostled for positions at the wharf. There didn't seem to be any regulations, and arguments broke out regularly. Lines of slaves wove their way in and out amongst the merchants. The slaves glistened with sweat, but they were well fed and healthy. The Phoenicians sailed the largest galleys, and they carried linen, grain and spice to all points of the oceans.

One of my captains had learned that the barbarians had agreed not to attack any Phoenician ports or ships in return for being able to use their ports as a safe harbour. This information could help us to finally capture Lydus.

The huge temple of Re-Atum, which Sesostris had built an eternity ago, towered over Heliopolis. Two massive granite obelisks, at least forty cubits high, stood at the entrance. The inscriptions sang the praises of the great pharaoh and showed his intimate relationship with Atum, the Sun God.

Pharaoh Thutmose, not to be out done by his ancestor, filled the streets with more obelisks, singing his own praises.

I was impressed with the memorials that they left behind. We had only built a small mausoleum for my father on his death, and some of our largest temples to Zeus would fit many times over in the Temple of the Sun.

After we had re-grouped from the battle at Djahy, the pharaoh asked again about our new swords. I had to tell him the truth, and admit that some of them were not satisfactory. Some of the troops found the swords totally useless; others said they were extremely good. The swords with the two marks were sharp like a razor and were very brittle, but they were still better than the ones with no marks.

The weapons with one mark were the strongest and could withstand anything, but the weapons with no mark were too soft. They bent easily when hit with a bronze weapon.

I called my commanders together to discuss the matter.

'What does it all mean?' one sergeant asked.

I was not an alchemist, but I had been at Pylos when we decided on this experiment.

'The quality of your new swords depends on how they were made. It depends on the mixture of the metal in the blade and the heat treatment,' I said, keeping my explanation as vague as possible. Not only was I not too sure about all this, but someone in the vicinity may have big ears.

'What will we do with the new weapons you have issued us?' a Mycenean asked.

'Those who have one mark on their blade, keep them for battle. Those who have no mark or two marks, hand them in to the armourer. They will be melted down and reused to make stronger swords. In the meantime, you will use your old bronze weapons.'

I would get a message to Kato Zakro and Pylos that two out of three of the new weapons were useless. I was determined to keep my promise to the men that they would have swords so strong, no one would dare attack them.

* * * *

I carried on with the meeting.

'The pharaoh's men have been battling small groups of Sea Scum ever since we sailed down here from Djahy.

'We know that these wretched barbarians will never say die and Ramesses suspects that they are planning something big. He knows we have good knowledge of the sea and good tactics of defeating enemy ships and wants us to stay.

'You all long to see your families, but I say we must stay for one last effort to help Ramesses. We cannot let the heathens invade our doorstep and take over to rule us all! We need to help the pharaoh.

'We will be armed with the same mighty horned bows that the pharaoh used at Djahy. We will have new and better swords. Together with the pharaoh, we will be a powerful army and we will defeat the Sea Scum!'

* * * *

'You sent for me, Ramesses?' I said.

'Come, take a seat next to me Prince. You are not one of my subjects.' He indicated a cushioned seat with gold armrests.

'Callias, I have news of our mutual enemy: the Sherden, Peleset and Tjekker. It appears that they have not learnt their lesson at Djahy.'

Two dark slaves walked in and started fanning us with huge palm fronds. Their pearly white teeth flashed against their jet black skin.

'We did not cut the head off the snake,' I said. 'He slithered away to fight another day?'

'Yes, he has attacked Acre and Gaza. We have a prisoner from his raid on Gaza. The prisoner was in possession of a Phoenician papyrus detailing large numbers of weapons recently delivered to Amurru. He could not read the Phoenician tongue, but was told to deliver it to Lydus.'

'So, the snake is still with us,' I said.

'They are planning another assault. Unfortunately, my men were a little too enthusiastic and our prisoner died before we could extract any more information from him. I am sure Lydus would not be so stupid as to attack Djahy again,' the pharaoh said.

'They have a large navy, Pharaoh. Many pirated ships from my country and the land of the Hatti.'

'That is why I have asked you here, Callias. You have the best naval power of our alliance. I ask that you send spies to each major port on the west coast of our land and report back to me any unusual ship movements. They may attack from the sea this time.'

'We will be waiting.'

'How many of the new swords do you have?' he asked.

'The Sea Scum have destroyed all the aforinium mines at Alasiya, but our alchemist has discovered more of the ore under our noses at Sparta.'

'We too have discovered a mine in Canaan. But we know nothing about making the new metal,' he said

'My alchemists used three different mixtures of ore and charcoal at Pylos to make our new xiphos. However, at the battle of Djahy, only one of the mixtures proved successful. Two out of three of the new weapons failed us.'

'I thank Ra that we can share these burdens. Together we are a formidable force, but separately we may be conquered,' he said.

'I saw a good omen this morning. An albatross flying from Boreas to Zephyrus,' I said.

'Your omens are no good in the land of Ra,' he said. 'I shall consult the augurs at Re-Atum.'

* * * *

Time in the Great Eastern Land dragged on as we waited for word from our coastal spies. The tribesmen became expert at mastering the new horned bows. They had a natural instinct for the bow and arrow, born into them from fighting each other since time began. The Mycenaean and Messenian hoplites were much more at home with shield, spear and sword. Many of them were happy to fight for the pharaoh, now that they knew their weapons would not break in half or bend.

I gazed out from my room at the palace, watching the hive of activity unfolding each day before me. Ramesses' scribes and philosophers, in their pure white robes, debated each other on the morning trek to the centre of learning in the Temple. Wagon loads of grain, from their vast irrigated fields, wound their way to the underground granaries. Platoons of army recruits and mercenaries jogged in unison around the temple square. Some of the pharaoh's unbroken horses objected to being tied to a chariot. They reared and pawed at the air as their handlers tried to calm them. New groups of black slaves, recently arrived from Punt, were being auctioned off to the highest bidder.

I wished Kitane could be here with me to experience all this. *I will bring her back here one day. Someday, maybe, Knossos and Malia could be like this again.*

The local olive skinned women were looking more and more attractive as each moon went by. The vizier had offered me any number of female companions, but some of my men had described in vivid detail the weeks of suffering they had gone through after being with these companions.

Pasiphae's tribal chief had agreed to show me the new archery skills of his troops this morning. I was waiting for news on the xiphos formula when I heard a sharp rap at the door.

'Prince Callias, let me in. It's me, your sergeant.'

I lifted the heavy wooden latch and pushed the door open. His eyes were bloodshot and his long hair was twisted and knotted.

'What news have you?'

'I've been on the coast watch at Acre. You must contact the pharaoh urgently,' he gasped. 'I've been riding all night.'

'What is happening?'

'The barbarians are on the move again. We saw a vast flotilla of enemy ships sail past just before sundown.'

'How many? Did you count how many ships?'

'We counted two hundred and forty before the sun dropped below the horizon.'

'There could be a lot more, then.'

'I couldn't say, Lord.'

I dropped everything. 'Get a fresh horse and ride to Gaza,' I shouted. 'Find out what they have seen this morning and get back here urgently. I will go straight to Ramesses.'

'Yes, Lord!' he yelled as he bolted out the door.

* * * *

I knocked over a couple of Sun Gods as I raced up the stone stairway of the Temple. A couple of elders from a nearby village were asking the Great Man for some more slaves to help with the harvest. I brushed past them and they threw their hands in the air. I didn't have time to apologise.

'Ramesses, it's time!' I yelled. 'The Sea Scum are on their way!'

'Leave us now,' the pharaoh said to the old chieftains, but they wouldn't budge. They were all ears.

'The foreigners – my coastguard spotted over two hundred ships just off Gaza before sundown. They are sailing towards the delta.'

The elders stood, mouths agape, glued to the floor.

'The sentina don't know when they are beaten. When did he spot them, again?' the pharaoh asked.

'Before sundown, last night,' I gasped, trying to get my breath back.

'I hope your albatross was right, Callias. They will be halfway down the coast by now,' the pharaoh rubbed his brow.

'Find the vizier!' he yelled.

His retinue waited behind a thin curtain, ready to jump at each command.

'Coming, Great Pharoah,' the vizier said.

Ramesses was a fighting king. He pushed the Nubian fan bearers out of the way as he paced up and down the floor.

'Vizier, the time has come. Callias's men have seen over two hundred of the barbarians' ships sailing for the delta. We have prepared for this battle for a long time,' Ramesses said, deep in thought.

'We put into effect our first plan immediately. We should still have time. Send our decoy ships urgently out to the Pelusium main tributary. We must lure the enemy in to the delta. Send the fastest we have, so that they arrive there first. Some of our ships must pretend to be crippled. Break a few masts. Tear some sails. They must be easy pickings. The invaders must follow them in to the Great River at that point. This is crucial. The Sea Scum must not be allowed to land.'

Ramesses was thinking on the run. 'We will be waiting for them. Now get going.'

The vizier scurried off, a thousand things to do.

'Callias, you remember what we discussed for your ships. Wait here while I find my admiral. It will be best if you talk to him.'

'I'll wait.'

The Great Man hurried off into his centre of learning.

'Where is that admiral of the fleet?' I heard him yelling.

A long time later, the admiral came pounding up the staircase, gasping for breath.

'Admiral, the Sea Scum are nearly upon us. I have sent the vizier to get our decoys moving. You know what we discussed. We lay in wait, in the side channels, remember?' Ramesses said.

'We set the trap, Lord. Once we have lured them in, we attack,' the admiral had his breath back by now.

'We must get them all the way into Pelusium before you make a move,' the pharaoh said.

One of the scribes had found Ramesses' general by now. He ran in from the library and stood next to us.

'Admiral, plant some crippled ships a few stadia inside the mouth of the delta. Make them look like a storm has hit us. Make sure all the barbarians are inside the trap before you close the trap door. The trap door is you, Callias. Sail in behind them. Close the trap. Make sure no one escapes – not like Djahy. Ram them from behind.

'Admiral, use your grappling hooks to reel them in. Send our warriors across to kill them in their ships. General, you recall our plan for your troops?' the Pharaoh asked.

'We will line the banks of the Great River with our archers and spear men. I will get the Keftui warriors to help the archers. Our new bows can reach well out into the water. If any barbarians manage to swim ashore, we will butcher them on the banks. No barbarian will survive,' the admiral boasted.

'My hoplites, where will I send them?' I asked.

'Your hoplites will help the admiral board their ships. Do they all have good swords now?'

'Yes.'

'Any further questions?' he said.

'Any prisoners?' the admiral asked.

'If an enemy captain surrenders his ship before starting a fight, we will take his men and his ship. We will not take prisoners if they don't surrender.'

'Any that swim ashore – will we take them prisoner?' the general asked.

'No. They are all to be killed. None of the filth is to soil our land. I am depending on you all to save us from this scourge. If they should land, we will have to battle them here at Heliopolis and Memphis. This is our chance to get rid of them forever.'

'Admiral, I will be sailing on your galley. I am looking forward to this,' the Great Pharaoh said.

'The head of the snake – I want him alive,' I said.

241

'Yes. Lydus is to be taken alive,' the pharaoh ordered. 'I have a special finale for him. Ra is with us today. The augurs have read the goat entrails. Now get moving!'

* * * *

Unlike the tempest which was about to explode, I listened to the calm lapping of the Great River as we peered over the dunes. My monoremes were hidden in an estuary near the river mouth. They were fast, twenty rowers per side and had a small battering ram below the waterline. About fifty hoplites could crouch on the centre deck, ready to spring across a boarding plank.

Remember Salamis, remember Amurru, I had told them. Show no mercy.

Their fiercely decorated hoplons along each side formed a barrier from enemy arrows. Rows and rows of pointed bronze helmets winked in the sun. Each warrior had a one mark xiphos or a heavy bronze weapon and a short dori with a leaf blade. The officers looked invincible in their muscled cuirass.

My sergeant had ridden all day from Pelusium. The observation posts there had counted nearly three hundred enemy ships. I sent a courier straight to the pharaoh. It was more than we expected.

I told the troops to stop their nervous chattering as the captain and I crawled, lizard like, up the highest dune. The sand burnt into us as we lay in wait.

I could see the admiral's decoys bobbing in the distance. He had done a realistic job. Some dhows had torn sails, some had broken masts. He had even started a highly visible smoke fire aboard one of the merchantmen. They were easy prey.

But where were the vizier's sail boats? We waited. We waited and finally one of them limped into view on the horizon. Its torn mainsail flapped in the breeze and only half the slaves appeared to be rowing. A stadia behind them, I could just make out the lead scout of the Sea People's armada. He was rapidly catching up.

'Here they come, Captain,' I whispered unnecessarily. 'It looks as if the rest of the vizier's decoys have been sunk.'

'I hope the gods are with us, Callias. If that scout does not see this smoke from out there, our plan is doomed.'

The pharaoh must have had some observation posts on the far bank. The enemy's forward scout then caught sight of the vizier's decoys. Magically, the volume of smoke from the crippled dhows in the river mouth doubled.

'They have to see that from out there.'

The last of the wounded decoys out at sea gradually sunk below the waves. I wondered how many of the pharaoh's men had been lost. The lead barbarian scout lingered agonisingly in the one spot, watching the pharaoh's dhow go down.

'They must see the smoke,' the captain murmured.

'A burning merchantman. An attractive prize for a hungry Sherden,' I wished.

'I think we've got him, Lord. He's heading in,' the captain whispered.

'Where're the rest of them?' I asked.

Then, about twenty enemy ships appeared over the horizon behind the scout. Their white sails looked like white specs on a vast blue landscape. The rest of the flotilla was below the horizon. The lead scout was almost parallel with us by now. The lookout's gaze was fixed on our burning decoy. They sailed straight into the trap. The other twenty galleys trailed along several stadia behind. I prayed to Athena that the pharaoh would not make a move just yet. I could just see several of Ramesses' sailors running about on the burning deck with buckets of water. The other crippled dhows wallowed helplessly alongside.

We watched as the Sea Scum on the leading galleys lev-
elled their bows and fired into the pharaoh's crew. Several
white kilted sailors splashed into the river. Some escaped over
the side and swam to the opposite bank. The Sherden from
the lead barbarian ship sprang onto the burning deck and
soon had the fire under control.

Ramesses waited.

'They are pillaging our ships,' the captain smiled. The
Sherden had cracked open a barrel of wine and were drinking
from their helmets. The general had thought of everything.
One of our flags was hauled down and thrown into the water.
The Peleset, with their plumed helmets, boarded another
crippled dhow, and threw rolls of linen overboard.

But, where in Hades was Lydus?

Ramesses waited.

We watched as the lead scout, finally satisfied that there
was no danger, hauled up a green flag. The last of the twenty
galleys was almost opposite us by now. It followed suit. I
didn't need to say another word. The captain looked at me
and smiled. We had them. A flotilla of duck billed prows now
appeared on the horizon. The Anemoi were on our side today,
as the barbarians were not using oars. Their single, square
woollen rigs pulled them into our ambush.

The pharaoh waited. We waited. The sun burnt into our
backs.

'Get back and prepare the men,' I said to the captain. 'I
will wait until the last of the ships are in the trap.'

The captain slithered down the dune as the last of our
ships was turning around in the narrow estuary. I had lost
count of the number of enemy ships which sailed past. The
river mouth was rapidly filling with enemy ships. Some were
heading for the south bank so that their infantry would not
have to cross any water to march on Bubastis.

Then Ramesses attacked.

I remembered his words – *none of the filth are to soil our land*.

An army of the pharaoh's archers appeared out of the sand. Row upon row lined the south bank. More appeared from behind the dunes on the north bank. A vast cloud of arrows whistled into the sky. The first onslaught caught the lead ships by surprise. Hundreds of invaders died where they stood, without firing a single shot.

But they were prepared for death from above. They quickly hauled heavy woollen covers over their infantry and our arrows stuck fast in the wool. Enemy lookouts yelled instructions from their crow's nests as each volley came in. The last of the enemy ships had seen what was happening in front of them and changed course. They were turning quickly, trying to escape the trap.

I half ran, half rolled down the dune, sand spraying left and right, and jumped onto our ship. 'Quickly, captain. Some of them are escaping back out to sea. Take five of our fastest ships and catch them before they out run us. I will close the trap door.'

My captain caught the first of the tail-enders and threw out his grappling hooks. The rest of us rowed in behind the enemy and closed the trap. We lined up the nearest galley and called the slaves to ramming speed. One … two … one … two … the drum beats got faster and faster. And then an almighty crash!

There was no better sound than the crash of splintering wood as we drove a hole into the enemy's bows. The hoplites dropped their boarding plank and ran across the narrow gap. One-on-one the assaults began. The Peleset were well protected with their fish scale body armour, small round shields and heavy swords. Large numbers of them just kept coming and coming even though their long bronze swords were not suited to close fighting

A Sherden arrow from another ship whipped past and hit one of my guards in the neck. He went spinning overboard. Tell-tale bubbles broke the surface as his heavy armour pulled him down.

Ramesses saw us closing the trap door; then he unleashed his ships. The enemy did not have time to draw their oars and couldn't manoeuvre in the mayhem. A grappling hook flew through the air and wrapped high around a barbarian mast.

A group of the pharaoh's sailors hauled on the rope and a ship load of Peleset warriors splashed into the water as their ship capsized.

The pharaoh's archers now sent a hail of death into the other ships. I ducked as one of the pharaoh's arrows hit a Peleset slingman in the throat. The force of the new bow was so great that the shaft emerged on the other side of his neck and sent him spinning into the water.

The lion headed prows of the pharaoh smashed into the Sea People up and down the river. Several enemy ships were burning in the water from fire arrows – their crews leaping into the water and swimming for the shore.

A worse fate awaited them there. The general's men cut them up as they struggled up the banks. The shallows along the banks turned pale red with enemy blood. Body parts washed in and out with the swell.

A burning sail leapt into the sky and drifted across to one of my ships. The sparks showered down and started a fire amongst a pile of rope. By the time I saw it, the fire had well and truly taken hold.

Some Mycenaeans struggled out of their gear and dived into the wreckage strewn water where the Sherden warriors fired upon them relentlessly.

'Help those men before they all die!' I yelled. I spotted Ramesses himself firing a horned bow into a group of Tjekker militia.

Like Theseus, he led from the front. An army of minders surrounded him, ready to die for their living god. Several of the pharaoh's ships were by now, laden with prisoners. They headed for the south bank.

They were the lucky ones. They flew the white flag. Many of their other ships had capsized from the grappling hooks and started to drift out to sea as the tide turned.

But where was Lydus, the head of the snake? Did he lead from the rear?

I said a silent prayer to Athena. Lydus was the only one who knew the fate of Minos and Theseus.

We tried to pull ourselves out after our battering ram had sunk into the enemy's bows. The last of the Sherden were thrown over the side. I was ducking arrows: the enemy's and our own. We were totally absorbed into separating the two ships when a duck-billed prow smashed into our stern. With my hoplon attached to my left arm, I grabbed an abandoned spear off the deck. More Sherden leapt onto our deck. The first man slipped on the wet timber and he went down in front of me. I drove the spear into his stomach.

The second came in swinging his sword. I feinted the spear to his groin, but the sentina caught me as he twisted past, his blade scraping my left shoulder. I didn't feel anything. I twisted and ducked low under his second swing. My weapon sliced through the tendon on the back of his leg as the Spartan had taught me. He dropped his weapon, grabbed his leg and tried to jump overboard. I wrestled him from behind and pushed him to the deck.

'I will let you live if you tell me where your chief is hiding,' I yelled.

By now, the rest of my crew were up on deck.

'Lydus, where is the sentina?' I yelled again.

The Sherden shook his head. A small river of his blood began to run across the deck.

'One last chance. Your chief. Where is he?' I shook him with my good arm.

'The I ... I ... I ...' he murmured. He slumped underneath me, all his blood pumped out on deck.

Useless scum, I thought as I rolled him into the water.

Some of my men were writhing in pain, but the rest of the crew were still killing.

The pharmacea ran across to patch me up. 'Don't worry about me, fix the men up first!'

The timbers groaned as the captain and crew continued to lever the enemy ship off our bows. One of the warriors hacked at the enemy hull with his old axe to make sure it followed its crew to the bottom of the river.

The pharmacea ran back to attend to my flesh wound. He cleaned the dried blood away and applied some egg white and honey. I gritted my teeth as he stitched the wound together. 'That Sherden was saying, "The I ... I ... I", what did you make of that?'

'Yes, Lord, I heard you yelling,' the healer said.

'Was he trying to say "I ... I ... don't know," do you think?' I asked.

'Maybe he didn't mean "I" as in "you and I". Maybe he meant an "eye",' the healer pointed to his eye. 'Hold still, Prince, I'm just tying off,' Asclepios's servant said.

'A "seeing eye", not an "I" as in "you and I"?' I mumbled.

The battle raged on in the bloodied waters between our blockade and Ramesses ambush. The barnacles on the underside of many capsized enemy galleys showed that they hadn't been cleaned for many moons. More of them floated towards us as the tide turned.

The pharaoh was gaining the upper hand. Some barbarians threw down their weapons and surrendered.

The Sea People had captured a boat load of the pharaoh's archers. Because of the devastation they had wrought with their new bows, they started to behead their own prisoners, one by one. I was horrified as the headless corpses, like lifeless rag dolls, splashed into the water.

Averting my gaze from the dreadful sight, I noticed that the enemy galley had something painted on the bow – an eye, the same as our "evil eye".

'That's it!' I pointed across the waves. 'A duck bill with an evil eye painted on the bow.'

'It's one of ours,' the captain squinted against the sun.

'We wouldn't be executing our own soldiers, you blind old dog. That's it. The snake's ship. Break ranks, captain. Get us over there, fast!' I yelled.

'But we were instructed to blockade the river mouth,' the captain argued.

'Don't argue! Get the slaves going; head for that ship before he executes them all.'

I struggled to see through the smoke and carnage. The pharaoh's own vessel was hot on the heels of another barbarian galley.

The Sea Snake's vessel had now finished executing prisoners, and it turned to escape.

'Captain!' I screamed. 'Get those slaves up to ramming speed. I want that ram aimed directly at that ship with the evil eye. Don't miss, or we are finished. Lydus is on board. We want him alive. Signal our sister ship to follow.'

The duck-billed prow with the blue and red eye was aiming directly at us. They didn't have a ram, but we already had a hole in the stern from our previous collision. We were in danger of being sunk.

The coxswain's call went up a notch. 'One … two … One … two.'

We had lost slaves and it took us longer to gain speed. The Sea Snake's galley was a slug in the water compared to the monoreme, but they were heavily built, giving them an advantage.

'One! Two! One! Two!' The coxswains call went up two notches. The enemy ship was only half-a-stadia away now. I could see a tall, bearded barbarian wearing a feathered head-dress standing at the bow. He wore a golden armband. Several heads rolled off his deck and floated along in his wake. I could see now, head on, he would reef on his tiller at the last moment and he would go speeding past.

'Cut him off!' I screamed.

We were at full speed now. The slaves could only keep this up for a short time. We were almost alongside. The snake's steerage master reefed on his tiller but was a moment to slow. Our ram ripped into his stern. Again, I heard that wonderful sound of splintering wood. Several cedar planks from their galley flew through the air and landed on our foredeck.

Both vessels jolted to a dead stop.

Lydus was thrown down amongst the heads and several of his bodyguards flew into the water. Our grappling hook wound high around his mast but I yelled, 'Don't pull them over, I want him alive!'

I sprang across on the boarding plank to confront the snake.

'I've been waiting a long time for you, Callias,' he snarled. 'I thought I had rid the world of you Achaean kunas. You trod on us for many centuries. Prepare to meet your pathetic gods.'

He held his sword high. The sun glinted off the blade – it was *Blood Seeker* – Theseus's sword! It had killed the Minotaur and murdered our hostages. The fox's ears twitched in the sunlight.

'Where is Theseus, you worthless skata? Where did you get that sword?' We circled each other in a deadly game.

'I sunk him and his ship long ago. He was foolish and fell into my trap. Taking his sword was easy. And I will enjoy killing you with it,' he growled. *Blood Seeker* smiled.

He lunged at me viciously. I blocked with my shield, but with a stitched arm, I was slowing down. He drove *Blood Seeker* hard at me again as I went for his back leg. The deck began to tilt at a precarious angle. I went down on my haunches and slipped on wet blood. Gloating, the snake pounced on me, thrusting the mystical sword at my throat.

'Where did that dim-witted old Minos keep his gold? We couldn't get it out of him!' he menaced. 'You will live, Callias, if you tell me now.'

He pushed on the point of *Blood Seeker* a bit harder. 'The old vlaka was cooked alive by my stupid Sicilian friends before they could get him to talk. But now you'll tell me.'

He pushed the point in further, warm blood oozed from my neck. The galley gave another lurch.

'Never in a thousand moons,' I cursed.

I twisted sideways, kicked upwards and scrambled up the sloping deck. I watched in slow motion as he drove *Blood Seeker* into my lower leg.

Lydus scrambled after me, ready for the final strike. The galley lurched again as the water rose further up the deck. Severed heads floated up around us. *Was I already in Hades?* I heard a thud and, like something out of the War of the Titans, one of Ramesses' arrows cut straight through the barbarian's chest. The point stuck, grotesquely, out of his back. Lydus crashed back into the water of the sinking galley.

'No!' I screamed. 'Where are Gadeirus and Pirithios?'

But he was gone. He slid down. His sandalled feet went under, his red and blue kilt floated up around his chest, and then his feathered head gurgled down. His hand was locked around my brother's sword. It was the last thing I saw as it slid beneath the surface. The blade was still straight and true.

Water was lapping my feet now and I clawed at the deck trying to gain a foothold. My old bronze weapon slid under the surface. Then, a couple of strong, leather clad arms – archer's arms – dragged me back over broken bodies and broken masts. Each time my leg hit a corpse, I screamed in pain.

Then I blacked out.

At last, I was with Hades. Free from the torment. I saw Theseus and Meriones. I saw old Minos directing the dead. I saw my father, Aegeus, sitting on his orichalcum chair.

Sometime later, the sound of foggy voices forced my eyes to blink open.

I shook my head. Several blurred images waited near the doorway of my cabin. They gradually merged into two blood-ied warriors: Ramesses and his vizier. Ramesses had lost his crown and the vizier's sweaty galena cut tracks down his dark cheeks.

'You will need to take more lessons from your Spartan teacher,' the pharaoh said. 'The snake had you that time.'

Everything was still a blur. 'I thought I was in Hades,' I said to them. 'Zeus was ready for me.'

'You broke the line, Callias. When I saw you heading for that evil eye, I had no idea Lydus was on board. We owe you for finding the head of the snake.'

'You owe me nothing, Ramesses. But, why did you kill him? You said that you had a special death waiting for him.'

'Yes. I thought a taste of what he did to King Mutallu would be a suitable. He was about to send you to the ferry-man. Would you rather be dead?' he asked.

'No, Great Pharaoh, I thank you for saving my life. I now know that Theseus and Minos are dead. '

'Now that you have returned from the gods, I think we can assume that you will soon be king of Keftui. I lost many of my people at Amurru. We will never know their fate either,' Ramesses replied.

He continued on: 'After today, the heart and soul of the Sea People are finished forever, but their seed is not. The flame went up before them and the survivors were prostrated on the beaches. Pelusium will remember this day as long as the Atum shines. Our children and our children's children will tell of the day when Ramesses and Callias rid the world of the scourge of the sea at the Great River Delta. Ra be with you.'

The two turned and seemed to melt away in a haze, like that day in the sandstorm at Djahy.

EPOCH IV

'I settled them in strongholds, bound in my name. Numerous were their classes like hundred-thousands. I taxed them all, in clothing and grain from the storehouses and granaries each year.'

Rameses III, Papyrus Harris, in Breasted, J.H., Ancient Records of Egypt, 4.201, 1906.

Chapter XIX

Iraklion Crete, The Aegean Sea – 1175 BC

'Please King Callias, sit still while I try and dress this leg,' the pharmacea ordered. The pain in my leg was getting worse. The last blow from the snake had hit bone and the poppy elixir was not working.

'I think the swelling has gone down slightly,' he said as he applied some more honey, 'but it will take a long time to heal. I'll see if we can make a crutch for you.'

'That potion you gave me, can you make it stronger?' I asked.

'Goodness, no!' he said. 'Any stronger and you will be singing with the gods.'

'Singing with the gods would be better than this.'

'I'm afraid, it's out of the question, my Lord,' he went on. 'If you stop hopping around all day on one leg, it wouldn't throb so much. Sit down. Rest the damaged leg on something and you will find it will ease the pain. You have an empire to run.'

The fleet stretched over the horizon behind us. As usual, our royal escorts kept pace with the wind and their glossy black skins sparkled in the waves. The fleet was in high spirits as we headed for home. We had lost only a few ships at the

Delta and the families of the dead could be proud that their sons had died heroes.

We had been away for many moons and only the gods would know what awaited us on our return. I had sent a skiff ahead to let Pasiphae and Ariadne know that we were a few days away and to tell them nothing. I wanted to personally tell our story exactly as it happened. I did not want another black sail day.

My slave rigged me a comfortable goat skin chair with a linen sling to rest my damaged leg. It was an opportunity to take the pharmacea's advice. I had posted lookouts to watch for strange ships as I wasn't sure whether the Sea Scum had been totally destroyed.

Before we left Aegyptus, Ramesses had asked me to attend a meeting with those who had surrendered. What to do with them? Several thousand had surrendered, along with their women and children.

Ramesses did not want the burden of them in his country, draining food supplies or begging in the streets of his cities. Some of the young bloods volunteered to join the pharaoh's army, but the women and children and older men were a problem. After much discussion, Ramesses agreed to resettle many of the Peleset in Canaan. They could build their own cities and farm their own land. This would reduce the drain on the pharaoh's resources greatly. These people had finally found a land they could call their own.

Some survivors of the Delta were disarmed and had filtered back to their homelands. Of all the cities the Sea People had conquered, of all the lives that had been lost, they had not settled any of their conquered land. They only had eyes for Aegyptus. Ramesses had given them a small part of Canaan. I wondered about their years of struggle and their grand plan.

They had no reading or writing, so their history was lost forever.

I had lost my brother and my bodyguards and Keftui had lost Minos. Many families had lost far more than I. If Gadeirus was with Minos, he had probably suffered the same fate as his father. I drifted off again, the pharmacea's elixir taking over in the warm sun.

As I dreamt, the smoke from Imira's funeral pyre floated into the sky. The gold button in her stiff fingers winked up at me. My warriors were already calling me "King" but I still had Pasiphae and her daughters to cope with. Like her father, Ariadne could be difficult. Sadly, her beautiful sister had been unfriendly towards me since she returned from Alasiya. I dreamt of that one brief moment aboard the galley with her.

The pain in the leg now only resembled one bout with Cerberus.

I dreamt of that day back in the labyrinth. I saw Ariadne run down to Theseus with the thread. *Why would she give Theseus a thread? She had no idea who we were.* The flash of light from Kitane's mirror temporarily blinded me as I dazed on. No, it must be a beam of sunlight shining through a torn sail. *And then, why had they let us use the new xiphos?* Strangely, after we had killed the Minotaur, they both clapped and Ariadne said to her sister, 'Thank the Mother Goddess, Kitane, that was close!'

They were glad to be rid of their badly deformed brother – that was obvious. *Was that reason enough to set us up?*

And poor old Minos, boiled alive by the Sicilians. The snake's sword was digging into my leg, again.

We hit a trough and I jolted awake. The dream was still fresh in my mind, and my leg started to throb. The Minoan treasury – Minos died rather than reveal its whereabouts. I wonder if Ariadne knew where it was. I had already told

Ariadne that we needed gold to run the empire, but she told me that she only saw her father walk downstairs should a gift be required. A likely story!

Then, it slowly dawned on me. The Minotaur must have been guarding the vaults. The sisters knew. The inscriptions in the beast's cage that the mason had shown me; they weren't records of livestock.

"o … u … ru … to … pa … ra … jo – two bulls watch over old things," it had said. The "old things" – according to the Keftui scribes – are a reference to "gold".

That day in the archives when I was trying to inject some enthusiasm into my scribes to finish the treaty, I remember it started off: "o … u … ru …"

The chief scribe had shown me the same marks on a broken tablet. *How could I have not seen it?* I was wide awake now. *The sliding door to let the beast in and out of his cage; Minos would let the Minotaur out when he wanted something from the vault. The girls must have known about this.*

'Can't we speed this slug along?' I yelled at the captain. 'Put up some more sail!'

'No, Your Majesty. Notos is not kind to us today,' he replied.

The thread and the mirror? They wanted their half-brother, the Minotaur, dead. Ariadne had already been promised to the fat king from Alasiya. That was an arrangement she was never going to like. At the last moment, Minos had substituted Kitane. The sisters must have decided that day, during the bull leaping tournament, that they weren't going to be exchanged for shipments of ore or marriages to foreign princes who they detested. No, they wanted the King's gold and riches for themselves so they could live in freedom.

And who should conveniently appear? Two young hostages from Athens.

Theseus played right into Ariadne's hands by kidnapping her. Kitane had me wrapped around her little finger. And we liked it. They gambled on us taking command. They were right.

I wonder if there was anything left of the treasury, if there ever was one? They had plenty of time to shift it all while we had been fighting for the pharaoh.

I needed to get home quickly.

If I was right about the vaults, we could rebuild the empire, build Cyclopean walls around all our cities, build bigger and faster warships, make thousands of weapons using the "one mark" swords and the new horned bows from Aegyptus. Now that we owned the island, we could rebuild the wind funnels at Alasiya and turn Salamis into the biggest port of call in the Aegean.

It all depended on Minos's daughters.

* * * *

The bow of our warship made a deep furrow in the wet sand as it slid ashore. The captain grabbed my good arm and eased me over the side. I wanted to do this by myself. I splashed through the shallows using the crude wooden crutch the sailors had made. But it was not to be. The poppy elixir had not quite worn off and the end of the crutch sunk into a soft spot in the sand. I splashed down awkwardly onto my face.

As I raised myself onto my elbows, the warm, salt water dripped from my nose. Nobody laughed, as soon I would be King of Keftui.

Several officers sprang over the bow to help me onto my feet. The salt water stung my eyes but I could see a welcoming committee on the beach.

A blurry figure with black, bouncing, curly locks left the group and came splashing toward me. The figure's long white linen skirt was soon wet to the knees. Her dark breasts caught the sun as the salt water sprayed over her skin.

Trying to show some dignity, I shook free the two officers who hauled me to my feet.

'Kitane?' I wanted to reach out to her but didn't have enough hands.

She threw her arms around me and the memories of that day on the trip to Alasiya came flooding back. I was in Elysian Fields with a live Persephone hugging me. She smiled, threw the crutch in the water, and dragged my good arm over her shoulder. I was home.

'Callias,' she said. 'We thought Zeus had taken you.'

'Yes, Kitane. I saw him a couple of times but Cerberus let me go.'

An army of soldier crabs scuttled out of the way as we hobbled up the beach.

Pasiphae and her other daughters, along with Theseus's queen, were waiting at the water's edge. *Of course,* I thought, *they all wanted news of their family.* They anxiously gathered around us.

'Where are Minos and Theseus?' was the first question Helen asked.

I noticed she was wearing a woven jacket with several gold buttons lining the front. Most of the buttons were engraved with a bull's head but dulled with age. One of the buttons was new and caught a ray of sunlight. It had no engraving. It was then I realised the price of love, and that Imira had paid the price. I would not trust Helen again.

'Come up to the palace,' Kitane said as she tugged on my good arm. 'You can give us all your news up there.'

The new orichalcum columns, shining marble walls and terracotta tiles threw a large shadow over us as we shuffled up the pathway between the dunes. We were almost at the main portico when I heard the captain yelling from the beach.

'*Och ochi, no!*' He was pointing towards Boreas. A ship with a duck billed prow had just appeared over the horizon. It was heading this way.

'I'm sorry Kitane. My story will have to wait.'

'Quickly, get our ships back out to sea,' I yelled at the captain. 'Send our fastest ship back to Ramesses. We are in trouble.'

'Yes, King Callias. It looks like we've been followed all the way.'

EPILOGUE

The Aegyptus (Egyptians)

Ramesses III was the last great pharaoh of Egypt. In 1175 BC, he defeated the invading Sea People at the mouth of the Nile Delta. The location of this first ever recorded naval battle has never been found. After this battle, the power and strength of Egypt began to decline. The period 1100 BC to 30 BC, saw Egypt reduced to a minor player on the world stage. In 8th century BC, Egypt was overrun by their southern neighbours, the Nubians. In 7th century BC, the Assyrians conquered the Nubian pharaohs and ruled the Delta from 672–664 BC. After the Nubians, the Persians ruled the land for nearly two hundred years, but Egypt was still not free from foreign invaders. In 332 BC, the country was freed from Persian rule by Alexander the Great. The Egyptians welcomed him as their saviour and Alexander proclaimed himself as pharaoh in the same year. For three hundred years, the land was then virtually a vassal state of Greece, ruled by Greek-speaking pharaohs, including the Ptolemys and Cleopatras. When Cleopatra VII died in 30 BC, Egypt was "annexed" by the Romans.

The Sea People

Historians and archaeologists have discovered negligible evidence of the fate of the Sea People. These invaders left no records of their offensives and they destroyed most of the records kept by their enemies. Fortunately, they never conquered the Egyptians and the late New Kingdom pharaohs recorded some of their major victories over these "foreigners" on papyrus scrolls and mortuary stele. The Harris Papyrus, which was found in a tomb at Medinet Habu, relates how the Peleset were brought in captivity to Egypt and were settled in "fortresses" after the Battle of the Delta. Ramesses III settled some captives in Egypt and the rest of the Peleset were settled in the five coastal fortress cities of Ashdod, Ekron, Ashkelon, Gath, one unknown. These people came to be known as the Philistines in the Old Testament. They became lifelong enemies of the Israelites as portrayed in *1.Samuel.17, David and Goliath*. Some archaeological evidence from southern Palestine shows the destruction of a Canaanite culture of the late Bronze Age and its replacement with a culture of Aegean origin. Mycenaean pottery from the area was identified by archaeologists as Sea People pottery or "foreign" pottery. These are very tentative links and no record of the wholesale re-settlement of the Sea People exists in ancient texts.

The Achaeans

Unlike Egypt, after the Dark Ages, Greece blossomed into a major power of military strength, culture and democracy. The Greeks set an example for the Western world to follow. As the novel outlines, Keftui (Crete) was annexed by the Mycenaeans in the late Bronze Age. After many civil wars with neighbouring city states in the first millennium BC, the Greeks formed alliances and became the ancient world's academic leaders. Principal among these advanced city states were Athens, Sparta, Thebes, Corinth, Mycenae and later on, Macedonia. During the Archaic Period, Homer led the way with his oral poetic traditions of *The Iliad and The Odyssey* from 800 to 700 BC. Recurring themes of the Greek heroes, Achilles, Hector, Patroclus, Menelaus, Priam and Helen can be found throughout Classical and Hellenistic Greece in poetry, literature and art. The Hellenistic period (323 BC to 146 BC) was the pinnacle of Greek power after Alexander conquered Persia and Egypt. As in Egypt, the Romans ruled Greece after the Battle of Corinth in 146 BC.

Ancient Greek Writing Systems

The Bronze Age people of Crete were among the first Europeans to use a formal writing system. Cretan hieroglyphs have been dated back to ca. 2100 BC. These early pictograms and ideograms resemble Egyptian hieroglyphs and Anatolian Luwain glyphs. The original Cretan hieroglyphs have not been deciphered and the ideograms on the Phaistos disk still remain a mystery. The motifs on the xiphos in this story (the boar's snout and foxes ears) were Cretan hieroglyphs found on a sacrificial knife at Anemospilia in 1979. The ancient Cretans used these hieroglyphs, in conjunction with linear A, from ca. 2100 BC to ca. 1450 BC. The Mycenaeans modified linear A into their own writing system, linear B, from ca. 1450 BC to the time of the Greek Dark Ages. Even though approximately 80% of the linear A symbols correspond with linear B, linear A has still not been fully deciphered. The linear B inscriptions used in this story are symbols used by Mycenaean scribes over 3200 years ago. The linear B writing system, seems to have been lost in the Dark Ages. Homer's scribes used a completely different writing system for *The Iliad and The Odyssey*.

Early Iron Age

Early metallurgists must have wondered why they had chosen such a useless metal as iron to make weapons. The search for hard steel is the theme of this novel; I have imagined the trials and tribulations those early alchemists must have endured to find a metal that would work. Early weapons were soft and made of copper. By adding varying amounts of tin (10% to 20%) to the copper, the resulting bronze alloy could be made at varying degrees of hardness. When copper and tin ran out, those early alchemists turned to iron ore to make weapons. Bronze swords were cast and iron weapons were forged. The first iron produced was relatively impure low carbon "bloom" iron as used in the Roman gladius. This "bloom" iron can then be forged with a hammer. The earliest "bloomer" smelting of iron was found at Tell Hammeh, Jordan dated to ca 930 BC. In a "bloomer" the temperature is kept low enough, at ca.1250 °C so that the iron does not melt. This was still far hotter than that required for melting copper ca.900 °C–1000 °C.

This, of course, leads us to the question, 'How did those early alchemists raise the temperature to 1250 °C when they only used wood as a fuel?'. G.Julef (1996) describes in *Nature* magazine (379.3): "An Ancient Wind Powered Iron Smelting Technology in Sri Lanka." This article details an ancient, monsoon powered Sri Lankan wind furnace capable of producing high-carbon steel. The novel details how the ancient Alasiyans (Cypriots) discovered this technology by building wind funnels where sea breezes were consistently high, thus producing "blue or crimson" coloured fire.

The next complex question in iron metallurgy regards that of carbon content of the alloy. During the Iron Age, the best weapons were those which contained between 0.30% carbon and 1.2% carbon by weight. Steel with a carbon content below this level will be of low hardness and bend in battle.

Alloys with a carbon content above this level will be brittle and cannot be annealed or tempered. The higher the smelting temperature, the more carbon the iron ore will absorb, up to levels of 2.1%. Early metallurgists, such as those in the novel, used charcoal to harden their iron. One can only imagine how many experiments, successes and failures, they must have experienced before the correct ratios were found.

Orichalcum and Aforinium

We have no idea what the early metallurgists used for the name "iron". I had considered a few possibilities: "ferrum", "orichalcum" and "aforinium". I discovered on reading Plato's *Timaeus*, he describes a compound used on buildings on Atlantis: *Something more than a name, orichalcum, was dug out of the earth in many places of the island, and, with the exception of gold, was esteemed the most precious of metals among the men of those days. The entire circuit of the wall which encompassed the citadel, flashed with the red light of orichalcum.*

To this day, no metallurgist has discovered a sample of orichalcum. From Plato's description, scientists believe that orichalcum may have been an alloy of gold and copper. This would make it far too valuable (and soft) to use to make weapons. Ferrum is the relatively recent Latin name for iron so the Alasiyan alchemists had no option but to call this new metal aforinium.

GLOSSARY

Achaeans	Ancient Greeks (as in Homer's Iliad)
Adonis	Greek male god of beauty
Aegyptus	Bronze Age term for Egypt
Aeolus	God of the Winds
aforinium	Used as fictitious name for iron, iron ore, steel (in novel)
Agamemnon	King of Mycenaea in Homer's Iliad
Agia Triada	Ancient Minoan trading port on south coast of Crete
agora	Central part of Athens. A meeting place for the population
Akrotiri	Minoan settlement on Southern Thira
Alasiya	Ancient Cyprus
Albion	Island of Albion. Ancient name for Great Britain. Source of tin mines
Amathous	Bronze Age town on Alasiya (Cyprus)
Amnisos	Bronze Age port city of northern Crete. Sea port for ancient Knossos and Malia
Amorites	Biblical name for Semitic tribe living in northern Syria (Canaan)
amphora	Large clay storage jar with pointed base
Amurru	Kingdom of the Amorites in Northern Syria

Anatolia	Ancient Turkey
Anemoi	Ancient Greek wind gods (collective name for all the wind gods)
Anemospilia	Temple dedicated to the Snake Mother, Crete
Anthesteria	Ancient Greek festival in honour of Dionysis, God of wine. February – March.
Anthesterion	Months of February and March in ancient Greek calendar
Aparctias	Northern wind god; sometimes called Boreas
Apeliotes	South eastern wind god
apothecary	Bronze Age pharmacist
archon	King of the ruling tribe in Athens. Elected by the nobles. Ruled for one year only.
Artemida	Town near Athens
Asclepius	Ancient Greek god of healing
ashlar	Carved masonry
Athena	Greek goddess of war, wisdom, courage, law and justice. Parthenon goddess.
Attica	Ancient land of Attica surrounding Athens
Atum	The most important Egyptian god. The first Egyptian god.
augur	One who practices divination (reads signs and animal entrails)
augury	The practice of divination
auroch	Ancient cattle (Lascaux cave paintings, France)
baldrick	Scabbard for sword. Worn under arm.
Basellinna	Ceremonial wife of the archon – king during Anthesteria (festival of Dionysis)
bastardos	Bastard

272

bireme	Large galley – two banks of rowers per side. Used by Caesar in invasion of Britain
Boreas	Northerly wind god. Sometimes called Aparctias.
boukolion	Small house in the agora. Ancient official residence of the archon
boule	Greek senate. Council of 400.
Bubastis	Capital of the eighteenth nome of Lower Egypt; located in the Nile delta.
Carthaginians	Ancient race of seafarers from Carthage (present day Libya)
Cerebus	Three headed dog, guarding the entrance to Hades
Charon	The Ferryman rows the dead over the Styx River to Hades
Choes	Second day of Anthesteria
Chrysokamino	Ancient copper mines on Crete
clay tablet	A tablet could be a multi-shaped piece of clay to record ancient writing
Colchis	Ancient region on east coast of Black Sea. Destination of the Argonauts
Companions	Greek bodyguards
cow hide ingots	Ancient copper ingots; flat shaped with a handle on each corner
crucible	Small clay vessel for heating ore
cubit	44.5 centimetres (17.5 inches)
cuirass	Ancient body armour; could be made of leather or bronze.
Cyclopean walls	High battlements made with huge stones shifted by Cyclops (Mycenae)
Daedalus	Greek architect who designed Knossos palace and labyrinth

Danaoi	Dorians. Race of Sea People who overran Greece in late Bronze Age
Demeter	Greek goddess of agriculture and seasons. Cult of Demeter.
dhow	Egyptian boat designed for sailing the Nile
Dikteon	Large cave on Lesithi plateau, Crete. Legendary birthplace of Zeus
Dionysis	Greek god of festivals and wine
dori	Spear. Main weapon of the hoplites
Dorians	Ancient race of Sea People
Duck-billed prow	The Sea People used warships with a high prow in the shape of a duck's head
durum	Native wheat
efcharisto	'Thank you' (modern Greek)
Erebus	Hades, Greek underworld ruled by Zeus
Erigone	Daughter of Icarius of Athens. Dionysis taught her to make good wine
Eurus	Easterly wind god
faience	Man-made Egyptian substance resembling coloured glass
ferryman	Charon, the ferryman, rows the dead in Hades. Must be paid with a coin.
Gadeirus	Minos's eldest son
galena	Dark mineral used for eye make up
galley	Ancient warship rowed by slaves
Gebal	Byblos in the Levant
Great River	The Nile
great year	Seven sun years (as per ancient Greek legends. See 'sun year')
Greater Mysteries	Unknown rituals of the cult of Demeter

greaves	Bronze leg armour
Hatti	Anatolia (present day Turkey) Land of the Hittites, Land of Hatti
Hekatombaion	Ancient Greek New Year. Attic calendar. Began July 9th
Helios	Ancient Greek god of the sun
helots	Spartan slaves from Messenia
Hera	Chief goddess of Greek Olympian family. Wife of Zeus. Goddess of childbirth
Hera's Scorpion	Hera uses scorpions to sting other wives and children of Zeus
Hercules	Heracles (Greek) Son of Zeus. Incredible strength. Twelve labours of Hercules.
Hermes	Fleet of foot. Zeus's messengers
hermoioi	Spartan upper class
hoplite	Ancient Greek warrior. Originally 'Spartan' hoplite. Named after 'hoplon' shield
hoplitodromus	Ancient foot race with competitors in full hoplite battledress
hoplons	Hoplite shields
horned bows	Very powerful Egyptian composite bows introduced by Ramesses II
horned sword	A horned sword has metal hand guards between handle and blade
Horus	Egyptian falcon-headed god. Son of Isis and Osiris
Hyksos	Warrior race of Northern warriors. Ruled Egypt during 15th dynasty 1650 –1550 BC
Hypnos	Greek god of sleep
Immortals	Unlimited supply of bodyguards to a Persian king, when in battle
Ionian	Originating in Spain

Iraklion	Present day Heraklion (capitol of Crete)
kab	One kab = 1.2 litres
Kadesh	Battle of Kadesh between Ramses II and the Hittite Muwatalli II 1274 BC
kalimera	'Good morning' (modern Greek)
kalimera kyrie	'Good morning, sir' (modern Greek)
kalispera	'Good evening' (modern Greek)
kantharos	Ancient Greek drinking cup with two distinct handles
kantheros	Clay bowl to receive votive offerings
Kato Zakro	Minoan Palace and settlement; eastern coast of Crete
Keftui	Ancient Egyptian word for Crete. See also 'Caphtor' (Biblical name)
Keres/Ceres	Female death spirits. Greek mythology. Daughters of Erebus (Hades)
kernos stone	Circular vessel containing bowls for offerings found at Malia
khopesh	Curved Egyptian sword
kikeon	Alcoholic drink used in the cult of Demeter
klaretoi	Freed Cretan slave
komos	Ritualistic drunken procession as part of Anthesteria festival of Dionysis
kopria	Dung
kopros	Manure, dung, muck
Kore	Roman name for Persephone, daughter of Demeter
kouloures	Underground grain store at Malia
krater	Two-handled drinking vessel
kylix	Two-handled drinking vessel

Labu	Race of dark-skinned Sea People from western Libya
Laconia	Southernmost region of Peloponnese Peninsula
lapis lazuli	Precious stone from Egypt
Lesser Mysteries	Known rituals of the cult of Demeter
libation	A sacred fluid offering to a god. May be wine, olive oil, blood or listral water
linear A	Early Minoan writing system from ancient Crete. Replaced by linear B
linear B	One of the earliest writing systems introduced to Crete by the Mycenaeans
lion's-head prow	Pharaoh's warships were adorned with a lion's head on the prow
Lukkan	Resident of province of Lukka on W coast of Hatti (Anatolia, Persia, Turkey)
lustral water	Holy water used by priests as thanksgiving to the gods
Lycia	Ancient Greek settlements west coast of Hatti (Anatolia, Turkey)
magazine room	Narrow storage rooms at Malia and Knossos
malaka	Jerk, arsehole
Medinet Habu	Mortuary temples of the pharaohs at Karnak
Medon	Archon of Athens
merchantman	Ancient ship carrying commercial freight
Messenia	Ancient Greek polis in the Peloponnese near Sparta
mina	One mina = 570 grams
Minos	Ancient king of Minoa (named by Sir Arthur Evans)

Mitilene	Ancient capital of Lesbos. Founded in 11th century BC
monoreme	Fast, single decked ship powered by single row of rowers and one sail
murex	Snail found in the waters off Crete and the Levant. Excretes a prized purple dye
neodamodeis	Freed Spartan slave
Nestor's Palace	The palace of Pylos in the Peloponnese
Notos	Southerly wind god
nykteri	Sweet Thiran wine
one moon	One day from sundown to sundown (as per ancient Greeks writing)
one sun	One sun = one hour
orichalcum	Ancient metal described by Plato in 'Timaeus'. Composition unknown.
Palaikastro	Minoan settlement on far E coast of Crete, just north of Kato Zakro
Peleset	Race of Sea People depicted wearing short, feathered headdress
Peloponnese	Southernmost peninsula of mainland Greece
Pelusium	Ancient port city located on the eastern bank of the most eastern Nile tributary
penteconter	Fast, dual purpose Ancient Greek ship with twenty five rowers per side and sails
petrels	Sea bird
Phaistos	Ancient Minoan palace located in south central Crete
pharmacea	Ancient Greek medicine or name for a healer
Phoenicia	Ancient land of Phoenicia (Western Syria, the Levant, Canaan)

Pithoigia	First day of feast of Anthesteria. Pithoigia, Choes and Chytroi. Three days of feasting
pithos jar	Large clay storage jars
plakous	Greek bread
Poseideon	Sixth month of the Attic calendar. December – January
Poseidon	Ancient Greek god of the sea. Neptune (Roman). Earth shaker.
Posidae	Dionysian festival of Posidae was held in December – January
Pudahepa	Ancient Hittite queen. 13th Century BC. Friend of Queen Nefertari of Egypt
Punt	Unknown land visited often by the pharaohs to obtain slaves and gold
Ras Shamra	Ancient port city of Ugarit in North Syria. See Ugarit Letters
Re-Atum	Egyptian god of Creation. The first Egyptian god. Major temple at Heliopolis.
rhyton	Sacred, horned container from which fluids were drunk or poured. See 'libation
sas efcharisto	'Thank you very much' (modern Greek)
sentina	Scum
Sesostris I	Second pharaoh of twelfth dynasty of Egypt, 1971–1926 BC
Seti	Seti I, Pharaoh of Egypt, 1294–1279 BC
Seven Entrances	Theseus had to battle the monsters at the Seven Entrances to the Underworld
Sherden	Race of Sea People depicted wearing two-horned helmets
shield wall	A wall of locked shields to block enemy attack
sistrum	Bronze rattle used by women in procession of goddess Isis

skata	Shit
skata alogo	Horse shit
skiff	Small sailing vessel
skyla	Bitch
slave rower	Ancient warships were powered by slaves (a twenty-slave rower = ten/side)
spelt	Native wheat
stadia/stadion	183 metres (600 feet)
stele	Ancient stone or wooden slab on which inscriptions have been carved
sun year	One year (12 months)
talents	one talent = 26– 36 kilograms
Tartarus	Entrance to Hades
taverna	Greek café serving food and wine
Thanatos	Guardian of Tartarus (entrance to Hades)
Thira	Present day Santorini
Thracians	Barbaric race of warriors from N Greece
Thutmose	Thutmose I, Pharoah of Egypt, 1506–1493 BC
Tjekker	Race of Sea People from northern Mediterranean
triantaconter	Main ship used by Mycenaeans in Trojan war. Fifteen rowers per side.
trierarch	Wealthy citizen of Athens responsible for maintaining the naval force
trireme	Ancient warship, three banks of rowers per side
Troia	Homer's Troy, ancient Roman settlement of Ilium, Hisarlik, Anatolia (Turkey)
twenty slave rower	Small warship with ten slave rowers per side

Ugarit	Now Ras Shamra. Famous for 'Ugarit Letters' from Ammurapi (1215–1180BC)
vizier	Second in command of Egypt after the pharaoh
vlaka	Idiot
Weshesh	Race of Sea People from Libya
xaonon	Wooden cult image of a god. Part of Snake goddess xaonon found at Anemospilia
xiphos	Short stabbing and slashing sword popular in the late Bronze Age
Zahi	Site of the battle of Djahy
Zephyrus	Westerly wind god
zeugitai	Spartan upper class warriors

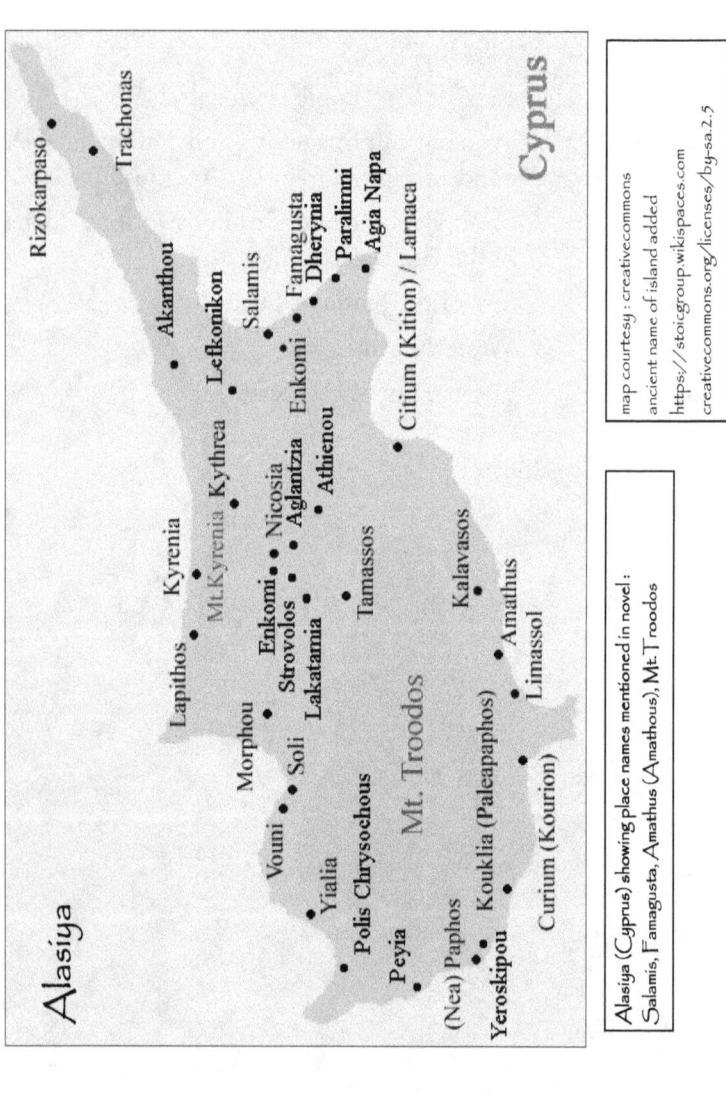

Alasiya

Cyprus

Rizokarpaso
Trachonas
Akanthou
Lefkonikon
Mt. Kyrenia Kythrea
Salamis
Famagusta
Enkomi Dherynia
Paralimni
Agia Napa
Kyrenia
Nicosia
Aglantzia
Athienou
Citium (Kition) / Larnaca
Lapithos
Enkomi
Strovolos
Lakatamia
Tamassos
Kalavasos
Morphou
Amathus
Soli
Limassol
Vouni
Mt. Troodos
Yialia
Polis Chrysochous
Kouklia (Paleapaphos)
Peyia
(Nea) Paphos
Yeroskipou
Curium (Kourion)

Alasiya (Cyprus) showing place names mentioned in novel :
Salamis, Famagusta, Amathus (Amathous), Mt.Troodos

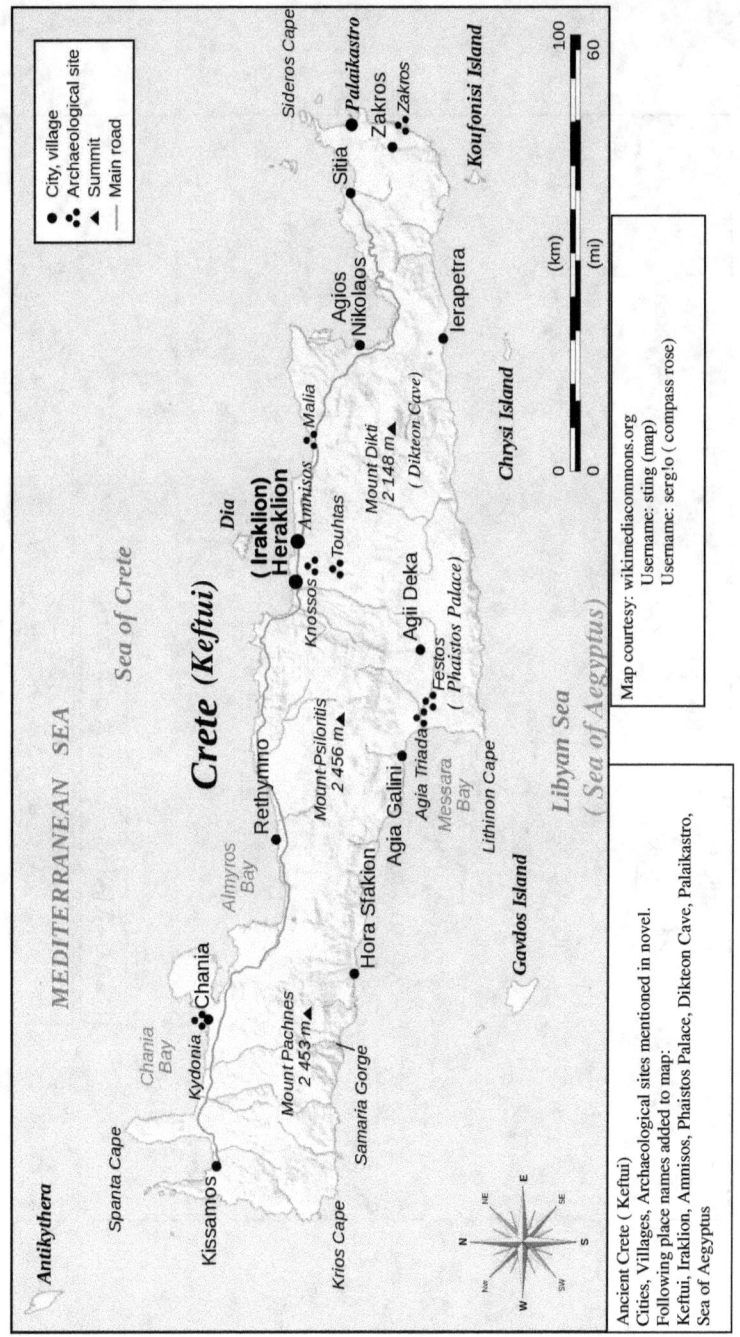

Map courtesy: wikimediacommons.org
Username: sting (map)
Username: serg!o (compass rose)

Ancient Crete (Keftui)
Cities, Villages, Archaeological sites mentioned in novel.
Following place names added to map:
Keftui, Iraklion, Amnisos, Phaistos Palace, Dikteon Cave, Palaikastro,
Sea of Aegyptus

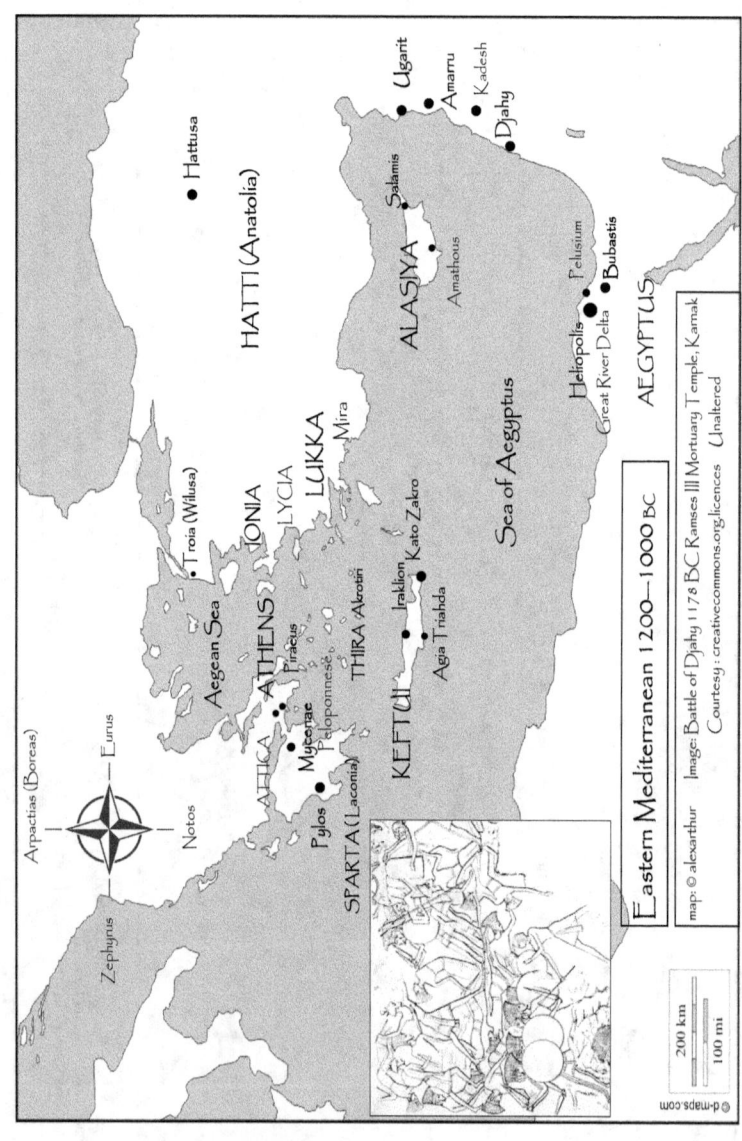

Apactias (Boreas)

Eurus

Notos

Zephyrus

Aegean Sea

Troia (Wilusa)

IONIA

LYCIA

LUKKA

Mira

HATTI (Anatolia)

Hattusa

Ugarit

Amarru

Kadesh

Djahy

Salamis

Amathous

ALASIYA

Heliopolis

Pelusium

Bubastis

Great River Delta

AEGYPTUS

Sea of Aegyptus

KEFTIU

Iraklion

Kato Zakro

Akrotiri

THIRA

Agia Triahda

ATTICA

ATHENS

Piraeus

Mycenae

Peloponnese

Pylos

SPARTA (Laconia)

Eastern Mediterranean 1200—1000 BC

map: © alexarthur   Image: Battle of Djahy 1178 BC Ramses III Mortuary Temple, Karnak

Courtesy : creativecommons.org/licences   Unaltered

200 km

100 mi

© d-maps.com

About the Author

Alex Arthur was raised on the Darling Downs, Queensland. During his youth, he spent many years cataloguing and researching Aboriginal artifacts along the Condamine River, near his family's cattle property at Chinchilla on the western Darling Downs. He graduated from University of Queensland (Gatton) as an agricultural adviser and was employed as a beef cattle husbandry officer at the Queensland Department of Primary Industries.

In later years, he visited Greece, Santorini and Crete and fell in love with the ancient history of the Mediterranean. He visited many Bronze Age settlements, including Mycenae, Tiryns and Knossos.

Nearing retirement age, he commenced studying at University of New England, Armidale. In 2014, he graduated with a BA majoring in archaeology, paleoanthropology and ancient history. He now lectures in ancient history at University of Third Age, Toowoomba and is continuing his research into the Bronze Age Aegean while studying for a Master of History degree.

Alex Arthur

www.ingramcontent.com/pod-product-compliance
Lightning Source LLC
Chambersburg PA
CBHW051532260626
47170CB00003B/899